THE WITCHWOOD KNOT

VICTORIAN FAERIE TALES

BOOK ONE

OLIVIA ATWATER

STARWATCH
PRESS

CONTENT WARNING

Dear Readers,

I would like you to know that *The Witchwood Knot* includes mild, non-graphic sexual harassment of both a female employee and a child. Though these instances are unlikely to trouble the average reader, those with a specific history of sexual harassment might find them distressing. Please be kind to yourselves.

CHAPTER 1

*T*he hundred eyes of Witchwood Manor loomed above, grinning through torrential rain.

Winnie had secured a ride up to the house from a charitable farmer in the village—but his charity had run out at the wrought-iron fence line of the property, such that she now dragged both her skirts and her travel trunk through the mud. Thunder rumbled ominously overhead, and she found herself quietly cursing the sky for its insolence.

On a clear and sunny day, Witchwood Manor might have been beautiful. The countryside mansion sprawled so broadly in either direction that several of its famous stained glass windows disappeared entirely behind the Witchwood's tall oak trees. Pointed gables pierced the cloudy sky, reaching for arrogant heights, while elegant white columns rooted themselves in the earth below like skeletal fingers. Though it had long been the style to build such splendid manors from stone, Lord Longfell had chosen to build the impressive Gothic house from the English white oak trees which had once stood in its place. Despite this eccentricity, he had clearly spared

1

little expense in the manor's construction; even in the gloom, it was a wonder to behold.

Winnie's breath came short and laboured as she hauled her trunk up the stairs to the door. Cold, miserable rain dripped down her neck, pasting white-blonde strands of hair to her skin. Half of the pins that had once held her bun in place were missing; her coal grey frock lay soaked and limp against her skin, nearly as heavy as the trunk she pulled behind her. The silver chatelaine at her waist jingled sullenly with each step, knocking together the tools which dangled upon its chains.

Winnie drew herself up before the door, brushing excess water fruitlessly from her shoulders. A chill had already started setting into her limbs though, and she hadn't the patience to compose herself any further. She raised one white-gloved hand to pound at the heavy oak door.

Thud. Thud thud.

Winnie waited for nearly a minute with no reply, before knocking once again.

Thud-thud-thud.

Again, there was no response. Winnie's teeth chattered, and she let out a soft growl of frustration. Surely, someone was at home; she had seen distant threads of smoke rising from the house's chimneys on her way up to the manor. "Hello!" she yelled over the storm. "Would someone please let me inside? I daresay this is terrible hospitality!"

Winnie leaned her full weight into another series of hard raps at the door. This time, she continued knocking without pause—until finally, the heavy wooden door creaked open all at once.

Winnie's fervent knocking nearly overbalanced her as the door gave way to air. She caught herself against the doorframe just in time, though rough splinters dug through the fabric of her glove to bite into the skin beneath.

Someone else reached out to steady her smartly, with a hand against her shoulder.

"Goodness," drawled the man who'd caught her, "let us not be inhospitable." His voice was dark and low, with a hint of dangerous humour.

Winnie glanced up at him through her sopping mess of hair.

He was a tall man of short black hair and ghastly pale complexion. His eyes were narrow and naturally suspicious, tinted the colour of dark red wine. The crimson jacket he wore offered him the air of a servant—but there was something insubordinate about his posture which immediately warmed Winnie's opinion towards him.

Winnie straightened her shoulders—and then, very delicately, she reached up to remove his hand from her shoulder.

"Finally," she said. "I was beginning to think that the house was empty, after all."

The man at the door looked down at her with one raised eyebrow. There was an odd depth to his reddish eyes which seemed to draw in all of the light surrounding them. "And who is it that comes calling at Witchwood Manor?" he asked.

Winnie plucked absently at the slivers which still jabbed into her lefthand glove. Distantly, she noted that several red pinpricks of blood had now stained the white fabric. The doorframe *had* bitten her, she decided abruptly—rather like a surly old hound. "My name is Winifred Hall," she said. "I have come to fill the governess position. The dowager invited me here. And yourself, sir?"

"I am the butler here, Miss Hall," the man replied smoothly. "You may call me Mr Quincy." There was still an air of dark amusement about him as he spoke—as though he'd made a private jest of their entire conversation.

Winnie squinted at him dubiously, trying to decide whether she was the butt of whatever joke he'd told himself. "Are there no footmen on hand to answer the door?" she asked.

Mr Quincy offered her a sharp smile. His teeth flashed far too white and feral in the darkness of the house. "You will soon find that Witchwood Manor has great trouble keeping servants," he told her. "If you are indeed the new governess, then I suppose we shall discover your mettle in short order." He stepped back from the door in order to admit her.

Winnie eyed him, considering her options. "I don't suppose that you might help me with my trunk, Mr Quincy?" she asked. "I am awfully tired, and I seem to have hurt my hand."

The butler glanced idly at the trunk next to her feet. He'd clasped his arms behind his back now, and the gesture lent him a faintly arrogant posture. "You are correct," he said.

Winnie blinked. "Pardon?" she asked slowly, replaying the conversation in her mind. "Correct about... what?"

Mr Quincy's feral smile now turned bland. "You are correct in not supposing," he said. "I will not step outside with you." But his reddish eyes flickered to the blood on Winnie's hand, and he inclined his head in an odd gesture of deference. "If you bring your things inside, however, I will handle them for you from there."

Winnie thought this was awfully contrary of the butler—but she didn't see the point in pressing him further. She hauled her trunk through the door one-handed, letting it thud to the ground on the wooden floor inside. The cloister which acted as Witchwood Manor's entryway was panelled in the same beautiful oak that made up the house's bones. Carved leaves wound their way around the mouldings, writhing oddly in the flickering light of the candelabra next to the door. A small recess in the wall concealed a reliquary shrine with its own stained glass window, but the picture in the glass was neither saint nor family crest—rather, it had the appearance of a black and green knot twisting in upon itself.

"I believe you will find Cook in the kitchen at this hour," Mr Quincy told Winnie conversationally. "Ask her for some tea to warm yourself up—but don't let her go at your splinters unless you want to lose more blood." He leaned down to pick up the travel trunk with surprising ease, balancing it upon one slender shoulder.

Winnie nodded at him with a bit more gratitude, rubbing at her injured hand. "I'll do just that, Mr Quincy," she said. "My thanks for the assistance." She turned her head to search for an obvious way into the servants' passageways, and saw that there was a green baize door nestled just beneath the stairs.

"Oh... I wouldn't thank me if I were you, Winifred Hall," Mr Quincy said. The dark humour had seeped back into his tone.

Winnie frowned. "And why is that—"

But by the time she turned her head again, the butler had entirely vanished.

THE STAIRCASE which led down into the servants' passageways was dark and narrow. No candles currently burned there, and Winnie soon decided to pull off her walking boots rather than attempting the tiny stairs with her slick rubber heels. Exposed copper piping ran along the walls beside her like a geometric spider's web. She couldn't help but imagine the walls reaching out to snag her like a foolish wandering fly—but the only thing which assaulted her was a stray drop of water leaking from the ceiling.

Despite the labyrinthine nature of the servants' passageways, the kitchen was relatively simple to find; as Winnie turned a corner in the darkness, she discovered a glimmer of candlelight near the end of the hall, where a door had been left open.

Winnie paused just outside of the doorway, looking into the room. A weak, greyish light filtered down from a tiny window near the kitchen ceiling, barely enough to illuminate the cramped quarters within. Tallow candles flickered on counters at each corner of the room, pushing back the stormy gloom. The scent of beef and cooking fat suffused the air with a surprisingly pleasant aroma, which nearly warmed Winnie's bones all on its own.

A short woman in a black frock and a white apron toiled over a coal range near the window, stirring a large stew pot with a tall wooden spoon. Though there were only a few threads of silver in her chestnut hair, her posture was stooped and tired, and her hands shook visibly on the spoon.

"Cook?" Winnie asked politely.

The woman turned her head to look at Winnie. Her skin was somehow even more sickly and sallow than Mr Quincy's had been. Black circles had taken up residence beneath her bloodshot brown eyes. "That's me," said the woman, in a clipped and weary tone. "But who're you?"

Winnie swept her eyes over the woman's bent posture, taking in each detail of her obvious misery. "I'm Winifred Hall," she replied. "I'm the new governess."

Cook turned back to her stew pot, and the slump in her shoulders deepened once again. "You should leave," she told Winnie simply. "This place is unwholesome."

Winnie settled herself at the long wooden table at the centre of the room, wiping the water from her eyes. Like everything else in this house, it was made of oak—the same wood that currently itched beneath her skin. The idea made her strangely uncomfortable. "I certainly won't be walking back out into that storm within the next hour," Winnie replied. "But I would be obliged for a hot cup of tea, and perhaps for something with which to dry off."

Cook glanced at Winnie again, wrinkling her nose. Winnie had a fair guess at what she saw there. It was the same thing people always saw: a prim and proper spinster in her twenties, both lovely and suspiciously unmarried. "Fine," she said. "But only because you're dripping on my floor." She tilted her head towards the hotplate. "You'll have to stir the pot while I'm gone."

Winnie sighed and pushed to her feet. "Everyone here is just so welcoming," she murmured. "At least you're straight to the point."

Winnie took Cook's place at the stove, stirring slowly at the pot while the woman disappeared down the hallway. Eventually, Cook returned with a stack of towels, which she left upon the table. She then put a kettle on the hotplate next to the pot and took the spoon back from Winnie. "You don't seem troubled by the state of things at Witchwood Manor," Cook observed brusquely. "Most new people who show up here have the good sense to look uncomfortable about it."

Winnie sat back down in a chair, pulling the remaining pins out from her hair one by one. Wet blonde strands uncoiled from her head like serpents. "I've seen far worse," she said simply. "I spent some time in the workhouses."

Cook stopped stirring abruptly, once again. Most people, Winnie knew, would not have admitted to such a shameful thing so openly. But Cook must have decided to err on the side of politeness, for all that she said next was: "A pretty thing like you?"

The last pin came free of Winnie's hair, and she shook it out around her shoulders. "How do you think I *survived* the workhouses?" she asked wryly. "People often have a soft spot for pretty things." Winnie dabbed at her hair with a towel. "This place is a drain on the spirit in other ways though, isn't it? The farmer who brought me here told me that the house is cursed."

This time, Cook did not respond. Instead, Winnie's words dropped to the floor like lead weights, holding down the silence between them.

Winnie considered herself to be a sensible, straightforward sort of woman. She barrelled on regardless. "Is Witchwood Manor truly cursed?" she asked.

Cook let out an odd sound—something between a low growl and an exasperated hiss. Her lip curled with faint derision. "You should leave, Miss Hall," she said again.

Winnie narrowed her eyes at the other woman's back, considering that response. "I have made up my mind to stay," she replied, with cold steel in her tone. "I decided that well before I ever left London. I would be grateful for any help which you can offer me to make the best of my position here."

The kettle began to whistle—a high, keening noise, growing louder by the second. Cook jerked her chin towards it, and Winnie rose to take it off the heat.

Cook weighed the woman in front of her. Whatever her

prejudices, she must have set them aside in a moment of Christian charity—for finally, she spoke again. "I cannot help you in the way you want," Cook said simply. "It's beyond me, Miss Hall. But if you keep your eyes open, I'd wager you'll find something to assist you."

She gestured towards a cabinet. "Tea's in there."

Winnie rummaged in the cabinet, searching through the drawers and coming up with a tin full of tea leaves. She took a teapot from one of the shelves on the wall and measured out a generous dose of tea. As she did, she cast her eyes around the kitchen, searching for the clues which Cook had clearly implied that she might find.

Finally, Winnie's eyes fell upon the doorway through which she'd just entered. Above it, someone had nailed an iron horseshoe—old and red, with flakes of bloody rust.

"Hm," murmured Winnie. "As I thought."

"Indeed," rasped Cook. She stared down at her wooden spoon.

Winnie left the tea to steep as she continued blotting the rain from her skin and clothes. "There are faeries, then, at Witchwood Manor," she mused aloud. "But you cannot speak of them, can you? I find that most intriguing."

"Lord Longfell doesn't believe in faeries," Cook informed her curtly. "You'd best not mention that theory around him once he arrives, Miss Hall."

Winnie blinked with surprise. "Doesn't believe in faeries?" she repeated. "But that's nonsensical. I understand they're rare these days—but everyone knows *someone* who has met a faerie."

"Lord Longfell says the Lord Sorcier drove all the faeries out of England," Cook murmured. She lifted a spoonful of stew broth to her lips—then scowled, and reached for another dash of rosemary. "He won't hear otherwise, so don't you try arguing the matter with him."

Winnie draped one of the towels around her shoulders like a shawl, turning this idea over in her mind. "And what of Mr Quincy?" she asked. "Does *he* believe in faeries?"

Cook released the wooden spoon. It thudded against the pot with a hollow sound.

"Is something the matter?" Winnie asked curiously.

"Where did you hear that name?" Cook asked sharply. Her shoulders had now gone visibly tense.

Winnie knitted her brow. "Mr Quincy is the one who let me in the door," she said. "He *is* the butler here, isn't he?"

Cook turned to look at Winnie directly; her fingers curled tightly into her palms at her sides. "Witchwood Manor has not had a butler for weeks now," she said. "Not since Mr Williams fled the manor in the middle of the night."

Winnie closed her eyes and let out a long sigh. "Oh dear," she said. "It seems a faerie has just stolen all of my unmentionables."

CHAPTER 2

*W*itchwood Manor was indeed supremely understaffed, with only a cook, a gardener, a gamekeeper, and a maid-of-all-work—the last of whom refused to work at night or sleep upon the grounds. Thankfully, Lord Longfell rarely visited the estate, and so the servants upkept only the most important areas of the house, leaving the rest of the place carefully packed away while they waited upon the dowager's needs.

The maid in question, Miss Margaret Chambers, eventually came down to the kitchens to retrieve the dowager's supper, at which point Cook instructed her to lead Winnie to her bedroom.

Margaret was young and gangly, with the last flush of youth still on her cheeks. Though she was obviously harried by the volume of her work, she responded to Winnie's inquiries with carefully guarded cheer as they mounted the narrow servants' stairs. "I've just turned nineteen years of age," the maid told Winnie. "The dowager pays me nicely for my trouble—I'm one of the only people willin' to see to the house these days. She said if I worked hard enough, she'd make me housekeeper—a housekeeper, at nineteen!—but then I'd have to sleep here, an' I'm still not sure I'd dare it."

As they left the underground passages and came back out into the main house, a subtle tightness in Winnie's chest began to ease. Margaret took her up the grand, curving staircase just beyond the cloister, balancing a silver dinner tray while Winnie carried a candle for the both of them. The storm still howled outside, casting strange, skittering lights through the stained glass windows and across the wooden floors; where the wind blew through the rafters of the house, it evoked such a dreadful moan that Winnie found herself wondering just how sturdy the walls truly were.

"And why don't you dare to sleep here?" Winnie asked Margaret absently—as though that awful moaning wasn't more than reason enough.

Margaret glanced back at her from the top of the staircase. Shadows clung to her rounded apple cheeks in the candlelight. "I only slept here once," she said. "I tried to resign, after that... but the dowager begged me to stay, an' my family needs the money somethin' awful."

Winnie pursed her lips, raising her sodden skirts carefully with the hand that did not hold the candle. The main stairs were broader, at least, than those on the servants' staircase... but some niggling instinct told her that this was precisely the sort of house which might hide nasty trick stairs. "You slept here once," Winnie repeated slowly. "That does not... *precisely* answer my question, does it? But you cannot speak of what you've seen here, just like Cook."

Margaret fell silent, staring back at Winnie in the gloom. The maid fidgeted uncomfortably, pressing her lips together.

After a few seconds of this, Winnie nodded at her in acknowledgement.

"I understand," said Winnie simply.

Margaret turned back down the hall, now mildly subdued. "Everyone in the village thinks I'm mad to stay," she said.

"We all do what we must," Winnie observed quietly. "Especially for those we love."

Margaret's cheer returned somewhat at that statement, and she smiled back at Winnie hesitantly, over one shoulder. "Do you have family, Miss Hall?" she asked.

Winnie nodded. "My family is quite large," she said, "but I am closest with two of my sisters in particular. I believe they might have come here with me, if they could—but they have enough concerns, themselves."

Margaret came to a stop just outside of an ornately carved wooden door on the second floor. The leaves and branches that Winnie had seen below continued here, winding themselves around a twisted wrought iron door handle.

Winnie stared at the door handle for a long moment.

Margaret's smile weakened a bit. "Lots of iron in this house," she said. "Least there's that." She glanced up at Winnie from underneath her eyelashes. "I can get you a horseshoe if you want. The lord wouldn't like it—he thinks it's all nonsense—but he won't be goin' in your bedroom anyway once he gets here, will he?"

Winnie shot the maid a look of cool assessment. People often made assumptions about Winnie's *availability,* based solely on her lovely features. Governesses also had a reputation, for some reason, for being wanton women, no matter how carefully they acted or how muted they dressed.

But Margaret's expression held no trace of innuendo, and

Winnie finally decided that the girl was simply cheerfully oblivious.

"I need no horseshoe for my door, Miss Margaret," Winnie assured her. "I have my own ways of staying safe. But I do appreciate the offer."

Winnie closed one hand reluctantly around the iron door handle to open it. A nauseous shudder crawled its way along her skin as she touched it, even through the fabric of her glove—but she did her best not to show the revulsion on her face. Still, she released the handle instantly as soon as the heavy door creaked inwards.

"Do you require the candle?" Winnie asked Margaret, as she stared into the darkened bedroom.

"You keep it," Margaret assured her. "I know the house by now."

Winnie inclined her head. "If you would be so kind then, Miss Margaret... do let the dowager know that I am here. I will join her as soon as I've composed myself."

Margaret nodded back. "You'll find her in the attic," she said. At Winnie's arched eyebrow, the maid added: "She likes the height. I can't say as it makes much sense, but when the dowager gets somethin' in her head, there's not many as can tell her no."

"Interesting," Winnie murmured. "That is... a new quirk of hers, to be certain. I suppose that I will meet her in the attic, then."

Margaret hefted the silver tray once more and headed for the stairs, leaving Winnie alone in the doorway of her new bedroom.

Winnie had to admit that the quarters she'd been given were more than generous. Most governesses would have been thrilled to have a private room at all—but the dowager had clearly made certain that Winnie was kept in comfort, with a large four-poster bed, a feather down mattress, and even her very own writing desk. A circular stained glass window on the western side of the room cast the light of pale white daisies across the floor. A door to the left led into what Winnie supposed to be an adjacent classroom.

Much to Winnie's surprise, she found that her travel trunk had been left inside her bedroom, just next to the door. Though she had left the trunk locked, its brass latch was now undone. Someone had opened the trunk—and what's more, they wanted Winnie to *know* that they had done so.

Winnie glanced warily between the trunk and the twisted iron door handle. "Now *that* is troubling," she muttered darkly. Clearly, Mr Quincy *also* wanted Winnie to know that trifles such as iron door handles would be no real defence against him or his kin.

Nevertheless, she set her candle down on a side table and opened the trunk to check its contents. All of her clothing was still there, Winnie noted—neatly folded, just as she'd left it. But one thing was indeed now missing: Within a black silk handkerchief, in place of the tiny vial of bay berry perfume which Winnie's sister Clarimonde had given her, there was now a folded up bit of parchment.

Winnie unfolded the parchment to reveal a note, written in a long and spidery hand. It said:

> Miss Winifred Hall,
> For my service, I have taken as payment your lovely perfume. I believe that it will suit the lady of this house.

Do let me know if you require anything else.

The note was signed with the initials: AQ.

Winnie crumpled the note in her palm with a soft noise of fury.

The perfume which Mr Quincy had taken was important —Clarimonde had mixed it specifically in order to protect Winnie from dangerous magic. Though Winnie had dabbed some of the perfume at her neck and wrists that morning, the rain had already washed it all away. She had planned, in fact, to reapply the bay berry scent once she'd dried herself off.

Had Mr Quincy recognised the perfume's magic? Surely, he had. His choice of payment could not possibly be a coincidence.

"Well played, Mr Quincy," Winnie muttered tightly. "But now that I know what you are, you will find me a far more difficult target."

Winnie slipped a hand through the side slit in her frock to access the pocket she'd tied above her petticoat. She rummaged for a moment before extracting a tiny white cat's skull, barely the size of her palm. Winnie's other sister, Bellamira, had *insisted* that she bring the skull with her, despite her protests. The skull had once belonged to the mouser at Mrs Dun's orphanage—a deeply spoiled black shorthair who'd loved the girls there with a literal undying affection.

"Bellamira was right," Winnie sighed at the skull. "I *do* require your help, Oliver. I hope you don't mind terribly."

A single tiny pinprick of ghostly yellow light flared within one of the skull's eye sockets in reply.

Winnie smiled affectionately. "You're far too good to us,

Ollie," she said. She kissed the skull very gently and turned to place it on the mantle of the small fireplace opposite from the bed. "I just need you to watch my room," she told the cat. "I hear that there are faeries about, and they seem to have found a way around all of the iron here."

The yellow light within the skull flickered and curled, rather like a cat's broad yawn.

"If Mr Quincy should happen by," Winnie added, "I hope you'll give him a significant fright."

If cats could laugh, Winnie expected that she might have heard a breathy snigger.

Winnie settled onto the edge of her bed, peeling off her gloves to examine the splinters in her left hand. That the doorframe had afflicted her with splinters was a curious thing, since the wood there had seemed smooth to the touch. But there were indeed several long slivers of white oak stuck beneath the skin of her palm and fingers. Winnie did her best to pick them loose with her nails—but a few tiny splinters remained, despite her best efforts.

Finally, Winnie sighed and abandoned the attempt. She rose from the bed to dig into her trunk, pulling out her nice gown and shaking it loose before her. The high-collared green muslin was a bit worn, and a bit damp at the edges—but it was the perfect gown for a severe countryside governess with no desire to seem wanton.

"I suppose that I will leave the room in your care, Oliver," Winnie said to the skull. "It's well past time I greeted my employer."

～

By the time Winnie had redressed herself in dry clothing, her strength was badly flagging—but somehow, she still managed to climb her way up the creaky wooden stairs to the dowager's attic room.

Winnie stopped in front of the door at the top of the stairs, shivering against the cold. The wind was harshest here at the top of the manor, where it rattled the floorboards with every breath. Thunder cracked like fireworks when it struck, and the roof seemed like a terribly flimsy shield against it.

Though it had been years since Winnie's last in-person conversation with the dowager, she rapped only once at the door before entering, feeling confident of her reception.

Someone had done a passable job of converting the attic— once a servants' quarters—into a bedroom fit for a lady of the dowager's stature. Half of the broad, vaulted room had been given over to the lady's bed and dresser, while the half closest to the triangular oak and ivy stained glass window had been converted into a sitting room. The dowager herself sat in a tall-backed chair before a round oak table, picking absently at the rolls and stew which had been set before her. A second place was made up at the table across from her, with another covered tray of food.

Lady Longfell had aged badly since the last time that Winnie had seen her. The dowager's once-brown hair was now pure white, and noticeably brittle where it brushed the middle of her back. Her faded blue eyes were watery rather than alert, and her shoulders were thin and fragile-looking beneath her blue linen wrapper.

Though the attic had a stove left over from the days in which it had housed servants, it was still noticeably colder than the rest of the house. Surely, living there could not have been good for the dowager's health.

The lady looked up as Winnie entered the attic—and all at once, a great tension drained from her posture, replaced with palpable relief.

"Miss Winifred," the dowager sighed, in a faintly cracking voice. "Oh, there you are—every bit as lovely as the day I met you. Lovelier, in fact, if my eyes do not deceive me."

Winnie closed the door behind her, padding over to the small table on slippered feet. "You are too kind, Lady Longfell," she said. "The storm has made a mess of me." Winnie settled herself into the other chair at the table. "I assume that this supper is for me," she added. "Thank goodness. It has been an awfully long day."

Lady Longfell smiled tremulously at Winnie. "I asked Margaret to fetch you something when she said you had arrived," she explained. "Please—you must eat before we discuss anything else. You have come so far, just to help a silly old woman."

Winnie set aside the tray's cover. The bowl of stew beneath it still steamed against the cold air in the attic, and her stomach rumbled faintly with hunger. Most of the stew that could be had in London was thin, with tiny shreds of meat—but this meal was more meat than liquid, plentiful with beef and mutton, and Winnie couldn't help the surge of hungry greed which overcame her at the sight.

Supper before business, Winnie decided, as she dug into the meal. Though she did her best to display a semblance of polite manners, she soon discovered that such manners barely mattered. The dowager was watching Winnie with the same sort of hunger which Winnie had directed at the stew. The older woman was clearly desperate to discuss the matter which had brought them together in the first place.

Winnie finished her supper with slightly more haste than

she might otherwise have done. As she pulled out a handkerchief to dab at her mouth, Lady Longfell cleared her throat delicately.

"Would you care for something more substantial?" the lady asked tremulously. "I eat more lightly these days, but Cook always keeps something extra on hand. I could ask Margaret to fetch us some coffee—"

"If I put off this conversation any longer, I believe that you might eat *me*," Winnie observed dryly, settling back into her chair. "Let us get on with it, Lady Longfell."

The dowager let out a slow breath, straightening the collar of her night gown against the chill. "I am just so grateful you have come," she admitted in a small voice. "I was not certain that you would."

Winnie inclined her head in acknowledgement. "You were kinder than many to me, Lady Longfell," she said. "I believe I owe my own lessons with a governess to your good charity, in fact. But that is not why I have come. I have an interest in the history and circumstances of this manor for reasons of my own. And, of course... I was promised payment."

Lady Longfell twisted her fingers nervously in her lap, bunching up the fabric of her wrapper between them. Mention of *payment* was impolite in the extreme... but they both knew that Winnie was not really well-bred company. "You will be paid," the dowager assured Winnie. "I still have many resources to my name, despite appearances to the contrary. It's just that no money in the world can pay most servants to stay here. They all leave the manor eventually, one way or another."

"I do not require money, Lady Longfell," Winnie responded softly. "It is information that I want. But let us first speak of the work you wish to set for me."

Lady Longfell looked up at her sharply. "I have hired you on as a governess," she said. "I thought you understood—"

"But I am not a governess, Your Ladyship," Winnie said carefully. Despite her best efforts, she found herself reaching for another roll as she spoke. "I am terrible with children. I was under the impression you had different work for me—work which perhaps Lord Longfell would not understand."

The dowager smiled tightly. "You are here to protect my grandson, Robert," she told Winnie. "He need not like you, Miss Winifred—nor even learn a thing from you. I only ask that you keep him safe until he is able to leave for Eton in September. Robert and his father will be here very soon—perhaps tomorrow, if the weather calms."

Winnie frowned. "You want me to protect your grandson from... whatever is happening here in Witchwood Manor," she clarified. "But the servants cannot speak of it. Can you?" She stole a single, ladylike nibble from the roll in her hand.

If Lady Longfell found fault with Winnie's manners, then she kindly overlooked it. Instead, the dowager rubbed her withered hands together—partially for heat and partially from anxiety, Winnie thought. As she did, Winnie saw that there was a bulky ring upon her left thumb—a twisted knot of white oak and dull grey iron.

"I can speak of the curse," rasped the dowager, "but I fear I do not know the whole of it." She swallowed, with great difficulty. "There has always been something wrong with Witchwood Manor, ever since Lord Longfell had it built. At first, it was less noticeable—little noises in the dead of night, and whispers in the halls. But then... the servants started leaving. Some disappeared entirely. I woke at night to awful, screaming faces in the walls..."

The dowager shuddered and fell silent, now worrying directly at the ring on her finger.

Winnie took another, larger nibble of her roll. "You are aware that there are faeries here?" she asked.

Lady Longfell nodded dully. "I have seen the iron which the servants hang above the doorways," she said. "But the faeries here avoid me, Miss Winifred. When my son first left for London, he gave me this ring and told me never to take it off. It protects me, I believe, from the terrible things which haunt the others here."

Winnie pursed her lips, now eyeing the ring more openly. Iron was bane to faeries, and... *unkind*, at least, to human magicians. The idea of a magical iron ring seemed like a paradox. But just for now, she decided to accept the possibility. "Is Lord Longfell a magician, then?" Winnie asked. "He has no reputation for magic of which I am aware." In fact, the man had little reputation at all, except with regard to his impressive lumber exports and his eccentric country manor.

"I never thought so before," Lady Longfell murmured, shifting the knotted ring back and forth across her fragile thumb. "But perhaps he has acquired a secret talent for magic. If so, he has not shared the truth with me."

Winnie traced the room slowly with her eyes, as though she might discover screaming faces in the walls which she had not seen earlier. "Are there, perhaps, no faces in the attic walls?" she asked. "Is that why you are up here?"

The dowager reached for the glass of wine in front of her with shaking fingers. "I still see them sometimes," she admitted. "Even up here. But..." She trailed off uncertainly, before warning: "You will think me mad."

Winnie laughed pleasantly. "You are living in a house with

faeries, Lady Longfell," she said. "To be *sane* would be unnatural."

The old woman nodded uncertainly—but she lowered her voice when she next spoke, all the same. "It is the earth beneath us, Miss Winifred," she said quietly. "The earth, and the trees which surround this house. They have such hate for me—I can *feel* it. If I could climb up to the roof, by God, then I would do it, just to gain an extra inch between us."

Winnie thought again of the splinters in her left hand, which by all rights should not have been there. "This house was built from Witchwood oaks," she observed. "If the trees despise you, Lady Longfell, then surely the walls and the doors and the tables do, as well."

The dowager's hand now shook so badly that she had to put down her glass. As she fumbled the motion, a few drops of blood red wine spilled across the table, and Winnie found herself remembering the faint sense of scorn in Mr Quincy's wine-red eyes.

"The house despises *all* of us," said Lady Longfell hoarsely. "It will be the death of me, I know it. All I ask is that you save my grandson, Miss Winifred. I know that you can do it. Your magic—"

Winnie set down the remnants of her roll sharply. "Speak more softly of that subject, Lady Longfell," she warned the other woman. "You have not been to London recently. The new Lord Sorcier has staunch opinions on most forms of magic. The lower classes do not have sufficient character to practise magic at all, he says. We are all black magicians, in his mind."

The dowager blinked at Winnie very slowly. The idea had shocked her visibly. "But… surely he could not take issue with *you*, Miss Winifred—" she started.

"He could," Winnie interrupted her bluntly. "He very well might do. Especially since I have taken issue with *him*." She reached into the pocket which she had left tied beneath her gown, drawing out a small black box. "I will ask you only once, Lady Longfell—and you must be certain of your answer. Are you *sure* that you wish for me to perform this task? I will do it, if you ask. But you understand now that you have employed a black magician, and that is surely bad enough. Where *faeries* are involved, as well... the price might be unthinkably high."

Lady Longfell crossed her arms over her chest, curling in upon herself. "I am committed," she said, in a deceptively strong voice. "I am already dying, Miss Winifred. If there is some terrible price to be paid... then let me be the one to pay it."

Winnie had not known this particular detail... but it did not terribly surprise her, on reflection. The woman across the table from her was frail and waning, compared to the one from her memories, and there was a weary certainty in her voice as she made the declaration. Winnie decided to acknowledge the fact without further comment. "Then let us start by asking questions," she said.

She opened up the wooden box in front of her, slipping free a battered deck of playing cards. As she started shuffling the cards, Lady Longfell looked on with open fascination.

"It has been ages since I saw you do this," the dowager murmured. "What question will you ask the cards, Miss Winifred?"

"I will ask about your grandson, Robert, and his future," Winnie replied. "But I will need you to describe him for me. Be as honest as you can be, Lady Longfell. What sort of boy is he?"

The dowager hesitated. "Robert is... unruly," she admitted, with a hint of apology. "I have not seen him in some time—but I hear he is a monster to his tutors back in London. He has always been an angel to me personally... but I suppose that is to be expected."

Winnie nodded to herself. "He is selfish, with a streak of cunning," she said firmly. "I was the same, I think, when I was young."

The dowager blinked. "You were so well-behaved, though, when I visited," she said. "You climbed into my lap and read to me from your primers."

Winnie smiled very pleasantly at her. "My point precisely," she replied. "Well then—we shall say that Robert is the Knave of Hearts."

With this decided, Winnie started laying out the cards by threes, withdrawing cards from each cluster as their relevance suggested. This work took quite some time—but the dowager kept her silence obediently. Cards soon cluttered up the table, so that Winnie was forced to shove her bowl aside and move the candles—and even stack one card atop a roll. Overhead, the sky continued rumbling, and the rafters shook.

Finally, Winnie looked over the cards before her, taking in their meaning.

"So many prisons," she murmured.

Lady Longfell frowned, craning her head to search the cards for some hint of the statement that Winnie had made. "I don't understand," she said.

Winnie glanced up at her. "Look," she commanded, gesturing towards a set of three cards. "The Knave of Hearts is penned in by two sevens. And here, the Queen of Spades—she is a widow, just like you. She has been trapped by the other two sevens. The Knave of Spades, an ill-bred and mischievous man, is trapped by tens." She knitted her brow. "All of you are tied together. Perhaps you trap each other?"

The dowager made a worried noise, near the back of her throat. "This house is a prison," she said. "Perhaps that is the meaning. You must make sure that Robert leaves again, Miss Winifred."

Winnie nodded. "I will do my best," she promised. "Thankfully, I am here in this reading as well... but I am not trapped." She tapped one finger on the card atop the roll. "I have always been the Knave of Diamonds—a liar, through and through. I have the Ten of Diamonds soon ahead of me—a journey which the Nine of Diamonds says will be exhausting."

Winnie looked over the entire series of cards again, and drew in a hiss of irritation. "We are three Knaves, all together," she bit out. "What a mess. We cannot help but trouble one another. Quarrels and false friendships lie ahead."

Lady Longfell now plucked at her wrapper with agitation. "This is all so very ephemeral," she said. "Can you not ask the cards how best to help my grandson?"

Winnie raised one pale eyebrow at her. "The more exact I make my readings, the less accurate they will become, Your Ladyship," she said. "The future is a river with many trickling branches. I must start by gauging where the general current leads." She pointed at the sevens. "Four of these means intrigue with a servant. I think the Knave of Spades must then be Mr Quincy. That feels correct to me; he is central to your grandson's future. What do you know of Mr Quincy, Lady Longfell?"

The dowager shook her head. "I do not know the name," she admitted. "Who is he, Miss Winifred?"

Winnie thought back to the man who'd opened Witchwood Manor's front door. "Mr Quincy said he was the butler here," she observed. "If he was a faerie, then he cannot lie... but I do not know what that could mean. You did not hire him, and so he cannot be *your* butler."

Lady Longfell cracked a weary smile. "My memory is not yet so far gone that I would forget an extra butler," she assured Winnie.

"Two tens," Winnie murmured to herself, still staring at the table. "Someone here might change their role. That does make sense; most faeries only play at being servants in the first place. Perhaps tomorrow, Mr Quincy will decide to be the gamekeeper."

She scanned the cards a few more times, ruminating on their meaning. Eventually, however, Winnie began to scoop them back up one by one, tucking them back into their deck.

"Is that all?" Lady Longfell asked, bewildered.

"Not at all," Winnie told her. "It is a start. I know, at least, that I must find out more about the extra butler."

This, at least, seemed to mollify the dowager's anxiety a bit. "You said that you required information, Miss Winifred," she said. "Whatever you are seeking, I will do my best to offer it."

Winnie slipped the box back into her pocket—along with the extra roll. She pushed up from her chair with a prim smile. "I have already learned some answers which I sought," she told the dowager. "I will have more questions for you at a later date."

Lady Longfell nodded slowly, though this reply had clearly baffled her. As Winnie headed for the door, however, she said: "Sweet dreams, Miss Winifred."

I do not think that likely, Winnie mused internally.

But she kept the statement to herself as she closed the attic door behind her.

~

Margaret had taken the time to light Winnie's fireplace, at least, before she left for the night. The heat took time to sink into the air, however, and Winnie shivered as she sat before the fireplace, digging the last of Witchwood Manor's tiny splinters from beneath her skin. The brutal exercise smeared blood across her hands—but Winnie persevered, suspecting greatly that the pain was worth the task. She tossed each splinter into the fireplace in turn, watching as the flames consumed them.

Only once Winnie was absolutely certain that she had torn free every splinter did she wipe her hands and crawl beneath the covers of her bed, waiting for the down feathers to trap her body heat and warm her further.

Eventually, she must have drifted off—for sometime in the dead of night, she woke abruptly to a still and silent room. The storm, she realised, had now passed.

Dimly, Winnie became aware of twisted whorls within the ivy carvings on her walls which had not been there previously. Though the embers of her fireplace were not bright enough to illuminate their detail, she knew in her heart that they were faces.

Even as Winnie perceived those whorls, she heard a rising susurrus of whispers from the hallway. The breathy voices which had made them were dark, and unmistakably unfriendly.

Winnie shook her head and buried herself beneath the covers once again. "No," she declared tiredly. "Absolutely not. I haven't the energy to be investigating apparitions tonight. I'll walk your ghostly halls tomorrow night, I promise."

The whispers, of course, did not reply. But later in the

evening, Winnie heard a high yowl and a muffled *crash* in the hallway outside of her room, even from beneath her pillow. Incredulous male swearing soon followed.

Perhaps five minutes later, a heavy feline weight settled itself atop Winnie's feet, with a deeply satisfied purr.

Winnie smiled and went back to sleep.

innie awoke to the sound of someone fiddling with her fireplace.

Margaret had stepped in quietly to sweep the ashes from the hearth and start a fresh new fire with some sturdy logs. Though Winnie had seen at least one coal-fired stove since her arrival, the fireplaces in her bedchamber and the common rooms still burned wood—likely taken from the Witchwood oaks nearby. The maid was clearly trying not to wake up Winnie as she worked, which Winnie thought was awfully kind of her—but old instincts always seemed to flare when people approached her while she was sleeping, such that she was now woefully and irreversibly alert.

The feline weight at Winnie's feet had gone, but she knew that Oliver was likely prowling around, on guard for enemies (or treats). Though the tom cat could no longer *eat* anything, he still seemed to appreciate the chance to sniff at a bit of fish or a bowl of cream when such was provided.

Winnie had pulled the covers over her head while sleeping, in order to block out the whispers—but now, she poked her nose out with a soft yawn. "Good morning, Miss Margaret," she said primly. "I take it that the faces in the walls are gone?"

Margaret squeaked and nearly fumbled her small broom. She glanced sharply at Winnie over her shoulder, with a pinched and wary look upon her soft features. "The... the walls seem normal, Miss Hall," she said tremulously.

Though Winnie was loath to leave her nice warm bed, she wriggled up to a seated position and started combing through the tangles in her hair with her fingers. "The whispering is fairly harmless, as far as faerie tricks are concerned," Winnie said absently, "but I will admit, the faces in the walls are somewhat harrowing. I wonder if the faces signify, or if they're simply further frightening illusion."

Margaret stared at her. "Tricks?" she repeated dimly.

Winnie smiled at her slyly. "Mr Quincy was prowling outside of my door last night," she said. "He has been putting on illusory performances for the servants here at night, in order to frighten them off. He has a flair for the dramatic—I will readily admit it. But he slipped up and revealed himself last night, and now the curtain is pulled back."

On some level, Winnie couldn't help but admire the faerie. If he was indeed the primary instigator of all of Witchwood Manor's troubles, he had made a sterling job of them with only dreadful hints and bits of cobweb magic. He was, in short, a one-man terror.

Margaret now looked stunned and faintly nauseous, as though Winnie had struck her over the head. "D'you mean to say that... that Witchwood Manor isn't even dangerous?" the maid demanded. "We've all been scared for nothin'?"

Winnie shook her head. "This place *is* dangerous in some way," she assured the other woman. "I am certain of it. But I suspect that most of you were frightened off too quickly to meet its true dangers." She pulled the blankets around her shoulders like a cape, now seriously considering that idea. "Mr Quincy has all of the answers that I seek, I am sure of it. But how will I force him to *tell* me those answers?"

"Are you... askin' *me?*" Margaret interjected tremulously.

Winnie blinked. "What?" she asked. "Oh, no. My apologies. I didn't mean to draw you into all of this, Miss Margaret. I'm simply speaking to myself aloud." She peeled the blankets carefully from her shoulders, daring the chill morning air only reluctantly in order to fetch her housecoat. "I'll need to corner him somehow. But Mr Quincy knows this house much better than I do, I would hazard. I'll spend today looking through the manor and getting a sense for it—"

"After you meet the young master, you mean t'say?" Margaret asked carefully. Her tone was wary now, as though she were addressing a wild animal and not the lovely woman she had met the night before.

Winnie stumbled over one of her walking boots with a soft curse. "Yes?" she said—though the word sounded more like a question than she might have preferred. "I mean... yes, of course. I'll meet with the young master. If he should arrive today, that is." A hint of crossness slipped into the words, despite Winnie's best efforts. Really, it was ridiculous, the idea of handing her a child to mind. She'd barely enjoyed the company of children when she *was* a child.

"Lord Longfell's footman arrived ahead of him a few minutes ago, along with some of their things," Margaret informed her. "He said His Lordship will be here well before noon."

Winnie pressed her lips together, mentally revising her schedule for the day. In fact, she realised, she barely had enough time to eat and make herself presentable. She glanced warily at Margaret.

"Have you ever met him?" Winnie asked. "The young master, I mean to say."

Margaret shook her head. "Lord Longfell only visits every so often," she said. "An' he's never brought his son before."

Winnie narrowed her eyes. "Curious," she muttered. "Why go to such expense to build a house you never live in?" Perhaps, she thought, the faeries were an unexpected menace. The servants had all warned her that Lord Longfell did not believe in faeries... but Winnie had begun to think that this was not true either.

She sighed and straightened her shoulders. "There is a long day ahead of me, I think," she said more loudly. "Would you mind telling me, Miss Margaret, how we take our breakfast here in Witchwood Manor?"

GIVEN that the dowager took most of her meals in her room, this meant that there was little structure to breakfast for the rest of the household. Winnie stopped by the kitchen to procure some cold eggs and sausage; there were a handful of half-stale bread rolls from the evening before as well, which she purloined without hesitation.

"You're well-rested," Cook observed suspiciously, as Winnie nibbled at a sausage. The other woman's eyes were still sunken with exhaustion as she sat down at the table to eat her own breakfast.

"For now," Winnie replied. She studied Cook consideringly. "But you have been awake all night. It cannot only be the whispers, can it?"

Cook, of course, did not respond. She speared a forkful of eggs instead, with a bleak hint of violence.

"I am going to look through the house today," Winnie continued blithely. "Are there any rooms I should avoid?"

Cook sighed and rubbed at her eyes. "We've shut up several rooms," she said. "That doesn't mean they're empty. If you see a room with Holland covers, I wouldn't wander through it." She paused, then added: "Stay away from the conservatory, especially."

Winnie nodded dutifully. Eventually, she would inspect the conservatory, of course—but it seemed most reasonable to learn the safer areas of Witchwood Manor first, in order to establish some familiar ground.

Footsteps sounded on the stairs—and soon enough, Margaret peeked her head into the kitchen. "They're here!" she said breathlessly. "Lord Longfell's valet is puttin' up a fuss. He says he wants to hand the young lord over to the butler— but I keep tellin' him we haven't got one!"

"I'll need to take charge of the boy, I expect," Winnie sighed. She stood up from the table, abandoning her plate with one last longing look. "What is his name? The valet, I mean to say."

Margaret shot her a grateful look. "It's Mr Turner, I think," she said. "I barely got a word in edgeways, but I heard someone use his name."

Winnie brushed out her green muslin gown and put on her most severe expression. "I will handle them both," she assured the maid.

As Winnie made her way back above-stairs, she discovered travel trunks of every size littering the house; luggage was still stacked within the cloister, such that she had to step around it. An unfamiliar man lingered near the front door, looking terribly put upon by the child standing next to him.

The man in question was tall and handsome; his long black hair was pulled back neatly from his face, displaying his shapely cheekbones to best effect. His dress had something of the city about it, despite his recent journey—his dark waistcoat was too-neatly pressed, and his calves were left on display in somewhat impractical stockings.

The brown-haired boy next to him was also dressed quite well, but with less overall dignity to his manner. He wore tailored breeches and a waistcoat, except in miniature, with a long jacket overtop them. Though his clothing was adult, his expression was decidedly childish—the sour twist of his mouth made it clear how little he wished to be there.

"Mr Turner?" Winnie asked, as she stepped around a leather trunk.

The man in the doorway responded to his name by turning to look at her. He quickly took in her gown and her general comportment, as though calculating how much respect he ought to offer her. Quietly, Winnie thought that he *should* have paid a great deal of respect to the wicked silver pocket knife visible upon her chatelaine—but men rarely did notice the important details. Regardless, he settled on a neutral sort of politeness. "That would be me," he replied. "And who am I addressing?"

"My name is Winifred Hall," she told him. "I am the governess. I will take charge of the young man from here."

Mr Turner adjusted his expression with an inch more civility at Winnie's stated position. As a governess, Winnie was neither servant nor quite Family—but either way, she was not a safe target for his current poor humour in the same way that a maid like Margaret might be. Nevertheless, the valet nudged the boy towards Winnie with impatience, obviously eager to be rid of him.

"Miss Hall," he said, "this is Lord Longfell's only son, Master Robert. I leave him in your capable care."

Winnie glanced at the boy, who had yet to speak a word. "You look weary, Master Robert," she said. "I believe your room is ready, if you wish to rest before supper."

Robert's surly expression deepened at this suggestion. "I would rather stay at the lodge with Father," he said. His voice was high and slightly nasal; this alone would not have been unpleasant—but every word he spoke seemed to come with a hint of a sneer, which set Winnie's teeth decidedly on edge.

Winnie redirected her attention to the valet. "At the lodge?" she repeated questioningly.

Mr Turner had already begun to turn for the door. At this latest interruption, he paused with a grimace, with his hand at the doorframe. "Lord Longfell has settled himself into the gamekeeper's old residence," he explained. "Master Robert is to stay here at Witchwood Manor, where you can look after him."

"I see," said Winnie. Those two words carried an entire world of meaning, which it might have been imprudent to speak aloud. What Winnie saw, in fact, was that the lord of the manor knew better than to sleep beneath its roof. Despite this fact, Lord Longfell did *not* seem terribly concerned about leaving his son to deal with Witchwood Manor's curse.

Mr Turner did not understand any of these things from Winnie's two word response. Rather, he took her reply as a dismissal, and as a chance to escape the conversation entirely. He straightened his jacket, nodded once at Winnie, and then whirled back outside—presumably angling to join Lord Longfell at the lodge in question.

Robert stared up at Winnie. Winnie stared back at Robert.

In this moment of extended silence, it swiftly became clear that neither of them wished to remain in the other's presence.

"I'll show you to your room, Master Robert," Winnie said finally. "Perhaps you could do with some tea to help settle you." The words sounded awkward, even to her own ears.

"I don't require a nursery maid," Robert said flatly. His expression was downright hostile, now that the valet had gone.

"How fortunate," Winnie replied smartly. "I happen to be a governess, and not a nursery maid. In fact—one might say that it is incumbent upon me to teach you the difference between the two, among other things." Though Winnie had no desire to be a governess in the first place, she never had been able to ignore an opportunity for acerbic commentary.

Robert narrowed his eyes darkly, crossing his arms over his chest. "I have real tutors, back in London," he said. "They teach me maths and Greek and history. What are *you* going to teach me? Embroidery?"

"Oho," said Winnie. "What a quick study you are, Master Robert. You have already learned to insult the servants." She clasped her hands behind her back and leaned in towards him. "Since you have so kindly asked—I think that I *will* teach you embroidery. We will make it your first lesson."

Robert recoiled with such abject horror that Winnie briefly felt the need to apologise to embroidery on his behalf. "You can't do that!" he hissed. "I'll tell my father!"

"Will you?" Winnie asked him archly. "It sounds as though you'd need to *find* your father first."

This observation, Winnie realised belatedly, was perhaps a bit too cutting. She was far too used to dealing with adults, who endured such slings and arrows with relative stoicism—

or who did, at least, deserve them roundly. Though Robert had opened their verbal sparring match with as much cruelty as his inexperience could muster, he now fell conspicuously silent, staring down at the floor with a trembling in his jaw.

Robert had—like so many upper-class children—been shoved into a corner like a piece of unused furniture. Had his father been able, Winnie was certain that he would have thrown a sheet over the boy until he was considered old enough to be interesting. In this respect, Robert was rather like the closed-up rooms in Witchwood Manor.

It was not, however, within Winnie's nature to retreat from those who had declared themselves her enemy. Despite her sudden unease, the thought of apology was so very foreign that it did not even occur to her. Instead, she offered mercy by pretending they had fully resolved their conversation. "Upstairs, Master Robert," she said. "Follow me."

Robert followed wearily as Winnie led him to the bedroom a few doors down from her own. Though larger than her own room, it was still quite plain for a young lord-to-be, with only a small bed and a few pieces of utilitarian furniture. Robert's nostrils flared with distaste as he stood in the doorway surveying it. The final insult, of course, was the stained glass window wrought with cheerful yellow daffodils. Daffodils were a child's flower—a fact which marked the room as more of a nursery than a bedroom.

Thankfully, Margaret had started up a fire in the hearth in anticipation of Robert's arrival; this lured him inside, despite his abject loathing for his new surroundings, and he soon stood warming his hands before the flames.

"I'll go request some tea," Winnie told him.

This time, Robert did not reply. After his ill-fated attempts to sting Winnie with conversation, he seemed intent now on remaining sullenly silent.

Perhaps that is for the best, Winnie thought, as she closed the bedroom door behind herself and headed below-stairs.

There was already hot water on the boil when she reached the kitchen, since Cook was making tea for herself. As such, Winnie decided to simply take a pot of tea back with her, along with the last few cold sausages. But by the time she made her way back upstairs with both, a niggling feeling of unease had begun to tickle at the back of her mind.

When she saw that the door to Robert's bedroom was standing open, she let loose a very unladylike word.

"Of course," Winnie muttered to herself. "I'd probably have done the same." She left the tray on a side table in the empty bedroom and stormed back out, searching the hallway for clues to the young master's whereabouts.

Winnie's wish to explore the manor was soon granted in a backhanded sort of way, as she threw open doors one by one in search of her lost charge—though she hadn't the time to investigate any of the rooms in detail.

Her search led her down to the ground floor, currently empty of servants. Even during the daytime, Witchwood Manor seemed as quiet as a graveyard—littered with abandoned travel trunks like awkward headstones. Lord Longfell's city servants had clearly decided that, in the absence of a butler or a resident footman, they might simply leave the luggage where it lay and wait for someone else to handle it.

Winnie was *relatively* certain that Robert was not hiding in one of the travel trunks. If he was, she thought, he well deserved to stay there for a good long while. As such, she passed the luggage by—spiralling slowly outwards from the centre of the manor, from empty room to empty room. The first door she attempted, just off the main hall, was locked. Across from it, she found the dining room, which had very few potential hiding places for a determined young boy. To the east, there was an ante room still kept in relative order, though the drawing room beyond it looked as though it hadn't seen a servant's broom in ages.

Frustration built within Winnie with each new door she opened, along with keen embarrassment. Perhaps Lady Longfell did not expect her to be a proper governess—but Winnie *had* promised to watch over Robert while he was at Witchwood Manor, and she could hardly accomplish that goal without him present to be watched. Briefly, she considered letting Robert navigate his own fate. Perhaps the dangers of Witchwood Manor would snatch him up; perhaps they would not. Either way, wasn't it natural for faeries to abduct naughty children who refused to listen to adults?

But Winnie required the excuse of her employment as a governess in order to investigate the manor. If Robert disappeared, then that employment would be over.

Winnie sighed heavily and returned to her fruitless search. Just as she was beginning to despair that she had been outwitted by a twelve-year-old boy, however, she heard the scrabble of small shoes on wooden floorboards, just behind her. She turned just in time to catch a flash of Robert's half-sized jacket tails disappearing around a corner.

"Hide and seek in a faerie-cursed house was *not* on my schedule for today," Winnie groused beneath her breath. Nevertheless, she hiked up one side of her skirt and followed after the young master, keeping her steps as light and stealthy as possible.

As Winnie headed up the northern hallway, her slippers began to collect dark smudges of dust. The early afternoon light which filtered through the windows was barely adequate to light her way—but while her eyes struggled to adjust, she caught the unmistakable creak of a door opening, just ahead of her.

She picked up speed, intent on catching the boy before he could outpace her. A thread of sickly light announced the door that she was looking for at the very end of the hallway, still partially ajar. Winnie shoved her way beyond it...

...and found herself in the exact room which she had hoped to avoid.

Witchwood Manor's conservatory was a relatively small, octagonal room, all draped in ghostly white hangings. Abandoned planters lingered in the corners, crawling with the dry remnants of dead flowers. Two bare orange trees clawed for the ceiling, as though attempting to escape their torment. The room had only one wall of which to speak—across from that wall, dusty stained glass windows stretched from floor to ceiling, straining any genuine sustenance from the feeble sunlight. Sharp images of multi-coloured roses crowded the stained glass, choking out all suggestion of the world beyond the house—and for the first time since her arrival, Winnie found herself truly thinking of the place as a prison, just as her cards had portrayed it.

Cook had warned Winnie that there was something dangerous about the conservatory, though the woman seemed unable to elaborate upon it. Winnie believed her, of course... but if Robert had come here, then she had little choice but to follow him inside.

Winnie slowed her gait warily as she entered, eyeing the white-draped furniture around her. Each lump was an ominous mystery waiting to be unveiled—all easily large enough to hide an unruly child beneath them, had said boy been of a mind. The slightest draft within the manor set them rippling here and there, as though they were all phantoms, gently breathing. The Holland covers in the conservatory should have been dusty and relatively undisturbed... but Winnie's sharp gaze caught upon one sheet near the far window which had no dust at all, covering something which she guessed to be a pianoforte. She walked towards it as silently as she could manage, measuring each slippered step with care.

Winnie narrowed her eyes at the sheet. The unimpressive light of the conservatory still outlined a faint silhouette beneath it—roughly the size and shape of an irritating young boy hiding beneath a piano bench.

"This has all been so *thoroughly* unnecessary, Master Robert—" Winnie began.

But as she tore the sheet away, she found herself perplexed.

Beneath the white drape was indeed a pianoforte—old and dignified, stained such a deep brown colour as to be nearly black. Its ivory keys had clearly seen significant use; some of them had tiny grooves where ghostly fingers had once touched them.

But now that Winnie had unveiled the piano, there was no boy beneath the bench.

The scent of Clarimonde's bay berry perfume tickled at her nostrils, sweet and taunting.

"How far the governess has wandered," Mr Quincy said from behind her.

Winnie heaved a heavy sigh, pressing a hand to the back of the piano in front of her. "Another illusion," she observed. "Well done, Mr Quincy. I thought you were all sound and fury

43

and no subtlety... but in truth, you have an artist's flair for details. I wonder just how detailed you can be."

Mr Quincy circled Winnie slowly, out of the corner of her eye. There was an obviously predatory nature to his movements now that his identity had been called into question. The butler had cast off the mild disguise which he'd employed upon their first meeting. His wine-red eyes were brighter and more unnerving than Winnie last recalled them; his cheekbones were inhumanly stark, and his figure far too slim. Most startling of all was a long rat's tail which trailed out from beneath his jacket, careless as you please.

"I would not wonder," Mr Quincy told her. "It is likely bad for your health, Miss Winifred Hall."

He emphasised the name with a peculiar, threatening air... and Winnie realised then that Mr Quincy believed it to be her *true* name.

Every magician knew well that names had a deep and terrible power. Any creature with a hint of magic could make dreadful use of a person's full and honest name.

Truly, Winnie thought to herself, this world was made for liars. The name 'Winifred Hall' was something which she had created specifically for this position, with the assistance of the dowager's endorsement. Only Winnie's old mentor knew her true name, which was likely too strange to use in human company.

Nevertheless, Mr Quincy's crimson eyes watched her with great expectation, and Winnie decided it was best to let him think that he had cornered her.

"I find that I dislike the way in which you speak my name, Mr Quincy," Winnie told him slowly, injecting a hint of wariness into her voice. "Have I done something to offend you?"

Mr Quincy's circling steps continued, angling for the

other side of the pianoforte. He entered Winnie's line of sight directly now, fixing her with a hard stare. His rat's tail twitched behind him furiously. "You know very well what you have done," he responded in an icy tone. The butler's hand, which rested now upon the pianoforte, was marred by several ugly-looking gashes—roughly in the shape of Oliver's claws.

Winnie couldn't help it. She burst out into high, mirthful laughter.

Mr Quincy raised his eyebrows with cold fury. Ominous whispers hissed to life within the conservatory, as though to punctuate his dark mood. Strange, sinister growls accompanied them, crawling along the stained glass roses like angry, writhing insects.

Had Winnie been anyone else, she might have found this appropriately terrifying—but since she knew these sounds to be an illusion, she couldn't help perceiving them instead as a kind of childish tantrum, all too similar to Robert's earlier posturing. *This* revelation only made her laugh even harder, clutching at the pianoforte for support as she imagined Mr Quincy as a child half his size, scowling up at her with a sullen faerie pout.

"Am I humorous to you, Miss Hall?" the butler hissed, leaning across the piano towards her. "I could remedy that shortly, if you wish." His rat's tail thrashed again, with obvious, growing violence.

Winnie wiped at her eyes, struggling to catch her breath. "Well, I… it's just…" She gestured helplessly towards his tail. "I had no idea. Oliver always was a champion mouser. He must have found you irresistible indeed."

Mr Quincy's jaw tightened. His crimson eyes flashed. "How pleased I am to be of entertainment," he said. But since the illusion had so obviously failed to move her, he seemed content to let the magic slowly fade. The ominous whispers died, trickling back into an icy silence.

Winnie sucked in a few deep, steadying breaths, reaching up to push back the strands of hair which had come loose from her bun. "I might feel sorry for you if you hadn't been skulking around outside my room in the middle of the night," she told him bluntly. "You *must* admit how very untoward that is, Mr Quincy."

At this, the butler rounded the piano. In the space of a single, sudden breath, he was there before her—tall and looming and foreboding. His dark figure made a smudge against the dirty stained glass roses as he leaned over Winnie, curling his lip into a sneer.

"You have come here with some cunning tricks, Miss Hall," he drawled, with quiet menace. "But they will not save you. And if you continue with this false bravado... I do believe that it may be your end."

Winnie looked up at Mr Quincy, studying his features closely. His face was even narrower than she recalled, and his chin a hint more pointed. There was a striking magnetism to him, though, which could not be denied—as though the darkest corners of the manor were drawn to the edges of his figure, offering an outline to his gaunt and ghostly form.

"Bravado?" Winnie asked softly. "I fear you're incorrect, Mr Quincy. I have not put on any false bravado." She offered a regretful smile. "All of my worst fears take the form of human beings, you see. As soon as I realised you were a faerie, I lost my fear entirely. Unwise as that may be, it's simply how I feel —I cannot change my own mind for your benefit."

The darkness in Mr Quincy's gaze did not falter... but somehow, Winnie thought that she detected a subtle shift in his appreciation of the situation. For once, she had uttered a

46

truth aloud, unprompted; perhaps he had detected its veracity.

Mr Quincy tilted his head at her, now lowering his voice. His red eyes burned strangely in the gloom of the conservatory. "Nevertheless," he murmured, "what you do not fear will deign to eat you up, Miss Hall. I have your magical perfume. Your churlish cat cannot be everywhere. And now, you cannot even ask for help."

This last suggestion baffled Winnie. "Can I not?" she asked.

Mr Quincy's lips curved up into a ghost of a smile. "Do try," he told her. "You will find you cannot speak of me to others. Nor can you discuss the nature of the curse on Witchwood Manor."

Winnie pursed her lips thoughtfully. *I was perfectly able to speak of Mr Quincy to Margaret earlier this morning,* she thought. But slowly, a suspicion came upon her, and she let out a soft 'ah'.

"You have used my name to bind me," Winnie guessed. "Just as you have bound every other servant in this household. How many names have you collected, Mr Quincy?"

The butler smiled tauntingly. He leaned in closer, such that his breath brushed Winnie's ear. The scent of bay berry was warmer than she remembered, as it wafted off his skin. Beneath it, she could swear there was a hint of copper-tasting blood.

"I have collected one *more* name since this morning," Mr Quincy whispered to her.

Winnie froze.

"You *have* seen Master Robert, then," she observed carefully. Suddenly, she did not dare to move, despite the faerie's close proximity.

"Oh, I have," Mr Quincy told her pleasantly. Now that he had discovered an advantage over Winnie, he was suddenly all smiles. "Ask me where he is, Miss Hall."

Winnie clenched her fingers into her palms. She had little choice but to play along. "Where has Robert gone, Mr Quincy?" she asked, with forced obedience.

The faerie laughed and drew back once again. "Somewhere very dangerous," he assured her. "Give me a truthful answer to one question of my own, and I will tell you more."

Winnie drew in a long and forceful breath, reminding herself to practice patience. Mr Quincy *wanted* her to be afraid. Perhaps, if she conjured up an illusion of that fear, he'd offer her more answers. It was a little lie, all things considered.

Winnie slipped a quavering note into her voice. "What do you want to know?" she asked.

Mr Quincy narrowed his red eyes. "Tell me of another trick you've brought with you to Witchwood Manor," he said. "One I do not know of yet."

Winnie pressed her lips together, thinking quickly. "I have a very sharp knife upon my chatelaine," she said, "and I am practised in its use."

Mr Quincy scoffed. "I saw your knife yesterday, when I opened the door for you," he said. "Tell me something *useful*, Miss Hall—or else I shall take my leave."

Winnie cursed internally. Mr Quincy was still too clever by half. She had only two useful answers left to give—and of course, she did not wish to give them. But that was in the nature of a deal, after all.

Winnie debated for a long and painful moment, before deciding that her cartomancy was the worthier secret of the two which she had left. Instead, she offered up the other one.

"I have brought lies with me, Mr Quincy," she responded reluctantly. "I have told you several crucial lies already—and to my knowledge, you've believed them."

The butler weighed this answer strongly. Faeries could not lie—though neither were they bound to tell the truth, exactly. That other creatures might tell outright falsehoods rarely occurred to them, as a result.

But Winnie had reminded Mr Quincy of this oversight now... and surely, he would be on guard against it in the future.

"*Take me to the gamekeeper's lodge,*" Robert's voice demanded suddenly. His small silhouette appeared beneath a white sheet across from Winnie with its hands on its hips, addressing Mr Quincy with the boy's trademark sneer. The drape rippled like a faceless funeral shroud—as though Robert's ghost had moved it.

Mr Quincy turned his head towards the illusory voice with a smile. "And who is it that asks me?" he addressed the shadow, pressing a hand to his chest.

"*I am the next Lord Longfell, you dolt,*" Robert's illusion declared with contempt. The likeness was so perfect that Winnie couldn't help but cringe.

"Of course, my lord," Mr Quincy said, with an obsequious bow. "But please, what is your *full* name? I find myself at quite the disadvantage."

"*I am the Honourable Mr Robert Murray,*" the young boy's voice said with impatience, "*and I demand you show me to the gamekeeper's lodge.*" The shape beneath the white drape pointed its finger at Mr Quincy.

"I fear that I cannot go with you," Mr Quincy replied, with gravest apology in his tone and a sinister amusement in his dark red eyes. "But I will give you the directions that you seek, since you have so kindly offered me your name. You will find the gamekeeper's lodge to the east of Witchwood Manor, down a trail which leads into the woods."

Winnie groaned aloud. Already, the foolish boy had made her job a hundred times more difficult, handing out his name so casually—and for such a *pittance*, too.

The shadow disappeared. The white drape slowly fluttered into stillness. When it had settled entirely, Mr Quincy turned to look at Winnie with his hands spread at his sides. "There," he told her. "To the best of my knowledge, the Honourable Mr Robert Murray has gone to the gamekeeper's lodge. I trust that answer is sufficient to your question."

Winnie pressed her lips together. "You told me he was somewhere very *dangerous*, Mr Quincy," she observed.

The butler straightened and stepped aside with a mocking smile. "I always tell the truth, Miss Hall," he said. "There is a monster in the Witchwood. I count it very dangerous, myself."

Winnie nearly bolted for the exit of the room, all at once—but she forced herself to linger, painfully aware that further information would be far more valuable than speed. "What sort of monster is it?" she asked, with a rising edge to her voice.

Mr Quincy shook his head. "You have had your question," he told her. "I'll be of no more use to you today, Miss Hall—you may rely upon it."

Winnie whirled with a curse, and started sprinting for the front door of Witchwood Manor.

CHAPTER 4

"Children," Winnie grumbled to herself. "I *despise* children."

A chill gust of wind bit at her skin, and she rubbed at her arms with a grimace. Dead wood and sodden, rotting leaves crunched beneath her slippers—likely ruined by the mud—as she tromped through the Witchwood in search of the Honourable Mr Robert Murray.

The Witchwood had an ominous quality to it, befitting its name. The silence which surrounded Winnie here was visceral—so heavy that each footfall made her flinch with awareness of the sound. It was a graveyard's silence—the silence of the dead, who slept and dreamt beneath the earth. Each tall and twisted misbegotten tree was like a gravestone, hinting at what tangled in its roots. And all along, there was a tickling feeling at the back of Winnie's neck which suggested she was being watched... though perhaps, she thought, that was simply her imagination making Mr Quincy's words about a monster feel more solid.

Winnie had discovered the trail to the gamekeeper's lodge

without much trouble—but after only five minutes of walking, the Witchwood had swallowed it up with twisted old roots and half-skeletal branches. Without a clear path to guide her, she had been forced to mark the trees with her silver knife as she went, carving slashes in crude x shapes at her eye-level in order to avoid getting lost. Robert, she thought, had probably done no such thing. The boy was probably wandering the Witchwood even now, with little sense of where he was going.

A different governess might have called out for her charge —but Winnie greatly suspected that this would only warn Robert of her approach and give him the chance to hide. Besides which, she thought, yelling loudly was an excellent way to call monstrous attention to oneself while wandering alone in the woods. Her best option, she thought, was to find the lodge. Either Robert had already made his way safely there—in which case, she would simply collect him and be on her way—or else he was lost, in which case she might be able to enlist the aid of the gamekeeper in order to find him.

Where does one put a lodge in these woods? Winnie pondered, as she stepped across a fallen tree. *Close to water, I presume. Hauling water through this underbrush would be tiring.*

Winnie paused and held her breath, listening in the silence. Nearby, she thought she heard the trickle of a river. The sound came from downhill, which only made sense. She marked an x upon the tree before her, and started carefully downwards.

The thick branches and choked underbrush gave way to a steep incline nearly all at once, as Winnie came out onto a riverbank. Her foot came down onto thin air—and she had only long enough to think *I really should have expected that,* before gravity handled the rest.

Winnie skidded down the riverbank in a heap of skirts, clawing for purchase in the mud which surrounded her. Exposed tree roots bruised at her shins and tore at the skin of her hands like grasping fingers. For just a moment, she worried that she might slam headfirst into the swiftly flowing creek just ahead—but she managed to arrest her momentum just before the toe of her right slipper could dip into the icy water.

Winnie sat up slowly, trying to calm her rabbit-like heartbeat as she took stock of her condition. Several cuts and scratches bled sluggishly on her palms. As she raised her sodden skirts to check beneath them, she was unsurprised to discover that her knees were smeared with blood as well. Most problematic, however, was the painful twinge in her right ankle which told her that she had done something unmentionable to it during her initial fall.

Winnie stared down at her ankle as though it had offended her. "You had better not be broken," she said aloud—as though she could browbeat her own bones into submission, if only she used a stern enough tone.

Presently, however, she became aware that someone was laughing. The sound trickled down from above, barely muffled into someone's hand.

If that is a faerie, Winnie thought crossly, *I will have several pointed words for them.*

Winnie leaned her head back to glance upwards. There— sitting in a tree looking down at her—was the Honourable Mr Robert Murray, sniggering at her misfortune with obvious glee. The twelve-year-old boy had climbed his way up into one of the tall oak trees which leaned over the edge of the riverbank. His adult-looking clothing was now spattered in places with mud. His shoes, Winnie thought, were in such a hopeless state that they would likely be discarded along with her slippers.

Not a faerie, then.

"I despise children," Winnie muttered again, beneath her breath.

She pushed herself gingerly back to her feet, careful to lean most of her weight onto her left foot. Now that Robert knew she had seen him, he ceased trying to hide his amusement at all; nasty peals of laughter jabbed at Winnie as she smoothed down her wet skirts and dabbed at the gashes on her hands with soft hisses of pain.

"You have little cause to laugh, Robert Murray!" Winnie snapped. "I will be coming after you shortly. Indeed, I will drag you down from that tree and carry you back like a sack of potatoes, if I must."

The laughter continued, unabated. "I didn't know governesses climbed trees!" Robert gasped. "Are you part lizard? Will I find you on the ceiling tomorrow, doing your embroidery?"

Winnie clenched her jaw. Her current lack of dignity did not bother her terribly—she had borne far worse injuries with far more stoicism, in her time. But Robert's cruel, needling laughter stoked a fury in her stomach which made her want to rub his face into the mud. Pain and misfortune, Winnie thought, were not meant to be inherently amusing.

"What on earth is going on out here?" a voice demanded from the riverbank. It was a man's voice, deep and cultured and commanding.

Robert's laughter stopped abruptly.

Winnie shifted her gaze and saw that a tall brown-haired gentleman had approached the edge of the drop which she herself had overlooked. Compared to either Winnie or

Robert, he was the very picture of composure; his old grey shooting jacket was worn but unstained, while his knee-high Hessian boots looked freshly shined. Though his cheekbones and his jaw held harder angles than those in Robert's face, there was an unmistakable resemblance there which suggested to Winnie that she was looking at Lord Longfell.

Robert's father stared up at his son, utterly aghast. "I ordered you to stay at the manor, Robert," he said, with growing fury in his tone. "Instead, I find you climbing trees outside the lodge? What is this flagrant disobedience?"

Robert shrank back within the branches of his tree. His face had paled so badly that even Winnie could see it from where she currently stood. His taunting wit was gone. Instead, his mouth worked soundlessly as he searched for excuses which he knew would fall upon deaf ears.

Winnie did not pity him. As a rule, she reserved her minimal supply of pity first for herself, and then for her sisters. On rare occasions, she deigned to offer the leftovers of her pity to perfect strangers—but since she was currently muddy and bleeding, she had little left to spare.

She started up the hill of the riverbank, hobbling as she went.

"You have my deepest apologies for this, Lord Longfell," Winnie said, by way of introduction. "I left Robert in his room in order to fetch some tea. By the time I returned, he was gone."

Lord Longfell dropped his eyes to Winnie. A swift series of emotions played out across his face as he did. Surprise was chief among them; until she spoke, he had overlooked her presence entirely. Soon, however, his dark eyes lingered on Winnie's hair and face and figure, and a familiar hint of appreciation slipped into his expression—as though she were a pheasant of particularly handsome plumage.

His fury evaporated into the chill air which surrounded them, replaced by faint horror and gentlemanly concern. "Good God," he said. "You're injured. Please, let me help you."

He knelt to offer his hand to Winnie, over the edge of the escarpment. Having few options, Winnie accepted it, clasping his arm with her other hand in order to scramble up the hill. Lord Longfell steadied her with his palm at her waist—unnecessarily, Winnie thought, as she had already regained her balance. When he failed to move away, she remedied the matter herself by sidestepping past him.

"My son owes all apologies in this matter, madam," Lord Longfell said, as he took in Winnie's injuries and the state of her gown. "And he *will* apologise." His voice hardened briefly again on the words, before it dropped into a more soothing register. "But what a strange and silly introduction this is. I have yet to have the pleasure of your name."

Again, Lord Longfell stepped towards Winnie, gingerly taking her hand in his. His skin was hot against the cold that had bitten its way deep into her bones—but Winnie found no comfort in it.

"I am Robert's governess, Miss Winifred Hall," she replied stiffly. Winnie inclined her head appropriately, even as she slipped her hand neatly free, leaving a smear of blood behind on Lord Longfell's palm. "It seems that I have offered a poor impression of my capabilities already, on my very first day." She settled her hands behind her back, determined to make any further attempts at handholding very awkward indeed.

At this revelation, Lord Longfell glanced her over again with obvious astonishment. "Robert's governess?" he repeated.

Winnie knitted her brow. "The dowager assured me that she had informed you—"

"Oh—certainly, she did inform me," Lord Longfell interrupted her. "But knowing my mother, I had pictured... well. Someone far older and more dour." A faint laugh escaped him. "But a lovely young governess! Now I have seen everything."

This, Lord Longfell must have thought to be a compliment. But Winnie set her jaw and clasped her wrists more tightly behind herself. All thoughts of angry, clawing branches and silent tree-like gravestones had fled her mind; instead, she found herself keenly focussed on the man in front of her, counting the steps which she had managed to put between them. There were not nearly *enough* of those steps for Winnie's peace of mind. Despite Lord Longfell's affability, a subtle, well-honed instinct warned of danger at the back of her mind—a reminder of other powerful men whom she had met before. Winnie reached for her chatelaine, searching for the silver knife she kept there... but several of the chatelaine's chains had snapped during her fall, and the knife was missing.

Her throat closed up at the discovery.

Some of Winnie's distress must have shown upon her face —for Lord Longfell paused, affecting concern once more. "I have been a boor," he said. "There will be ample time for introductions later. I should get you indoors, Miss Hall. The lodge is closer than the manor. There is a fire there—and I am certain we can find you something dry to wear." He moved as though to take Winnie by the arm—but she flinched back quickly, shaking her head.

"I have lost some of my things," Winnie said. Her voice came out pinched and faint, in a way that she did not like. "I should collect them now, or else I will never find them again."

Lord Longfell smiled ruefully. "Well," he said. "That much

can be remedied." He glanced up at his son, who still watched silently from his tree. "Robert," he said, in a deceptively calm tone, "you will come down from there now and retrieve Miss Hall's things from the creek. When you are done, you will come to the lodge and apologise profusely for everything which you have put this poor woman through. And then—so help me God—you will obey her dutifully for the rest of your time here."

Robert swallowed visibly. Slowly, however, he began to climb his way down, branch by branch, until he had dropped to the ground with a wet and heavy thud. He cast one last worried glance at his father, before sliding his way carefully down the escarpment to head for the creek.

Winnie—who had tracked Lord Longfell's words with perfect precision—now spoke an observation aloud. "I did not say that I would come with you to the lodge, Your Lordship," she rasped.

Lord Longfell blinked. "You cannot mean to walk all the way back to Witchwood Manor in your current state?" he asked incredulously. "I could not possibly allow it—not in good conscience, I mean to say."

Normally, Winnie would have had a polite but incisive response ready to hand—but an old, familiar veil of fear had clouded all her thoughts. She sucked in a deep, shuddering breath and straightened her posture, forcing cold steel back into her spine. "Am I weeping, Your Lordship?" she asked him. Suddenly, her voice was calm and sensible again.

Lord Longfell frowned. "You are not, of course," he said slowly.

"Then I cannot be in *too* much distress, now can I?" Winnie asked him. She forced a pleasant smile across her lips, shoving down the nausea which had threatened to overtake her. "I will endure a little hardship now, in order to return to my own room and wear my own dry clothing. That is my preference. Besides which... the dowager expressed to me that she would like to see her grandson when he arrives. It would break my heart to deny her such a small request, given her waning condition."

Lord Longfell considered Winnie for a long moment, searching her face. Winnie did her best to project only earnest, heartfelt sentiment, despite her blatant lie. The dowager had made no such request of her—but it was certainly plausible that Lady Longfell *might* have requested such a thing, if she had thought to do so.

Robert's shoes scrabbled against the mud behind Winnie, interrupting the exchange. The boy shuffled forward—now nearly as muddy as Winnie—with several silver trinkets dangling from his fist. He stopped in front of Winnie, offering them out to her in silence. He had managed to collect her scissors, her thimble, and her pencil... as well as her wicked silver knife.

Winnie took back her accoutrements. The chains which normally would have attached them to her chatelaine had broken, and so she tucked them into one of her pockets. The knife, she kept curled tightly in her palm; its heavy, reassuring weight made the ground beneath her feet feel just a bit more solid.

Lord Longfell observed the knife with polite surprise. "That is... quite a weapon, Miss Hall," he said.

The smile which Winnie offered him was slightly sharper this time. "A weapon?" she asked. "Goodness, no. It's just that one never knows when one might require a knife." She bowed her head to him again. "Thank you very much for your assistance, Lord Longfell. I will strive not to trouble you again."

Lord Longfell ignored the implied dismissal—or else entirely failed to notice it. He fell into step on her opposite side, offering out his arm. "I will see you back to the manor, Miss Hall," he told her. "The woods here can be dangerous."

Winnie tried to weigh her options rationally. The silence of the Witchwood leaned in upon her from every side, heavy and oppressive—and she reminded herself that there was still a monster somewhere in these woods. Further company was likely prudent.

Winnie accepted his arm reluctantly.

"Come, Robert," Lord Longfell ordered his son, without so much as turning his head.

Winnie did her best not to betray her hobble, as Lord Longfell led them back to Witchwood Manor. But by the time they made it to the cloister, she was leaning very heavily upon him—a fact which clearly pleased him far more than she would have liked.

IF WINNIE WAS HOPING that Lord Longfell's aversion to the manor would convince him to leave her there, then she was disabused of this notion in very short order. Her overly solicitous employer remained, ordering Robert up to his room and instructing Cook to see to Winnie's injuries. Winnie finally had to elude him with the blunt observation that she required some time alone in order to wash the mud from her skin and hair.

She did, in fact, spend some time in front of her basin, wiping off the worst of it. But once Winnie had made herself marginally presentable, she pulled on her threadbare frock, dropped another kiss upon Oliver's tiny skull, and hobbled barefoot through the doors which led first into the classroom and then to Robert's bedroom.

The boy in question had thrown himself miserably onto his bed, staring up at the ceiling with such existential consternation that one would think the world had ended. And perhaps it had, in a way, as far as he was concerned. Mud still caked his clothing from his brief excursion to the creek, when he had retrieved Winnie's things.

"We are going up to greet your grandmother," Winnie informed him. "You will need to change your clothing."

Robert did not look at her. "My grandmother doesn't know we're going to see her," he addressed the ceiling, "does she?"

Winnie scrutinised him more closely. His face was curiously void of emotion as he spoke. The words were an observation, she decided, rather than an accusation. "And what would give you that impression?" she asked.

Robert rubbed one muddy, sock-covered foot against his ankle, scratching at it idly. "You don't like my father," he said. "You're avoiding him."

Winnie leaned against the doorframe, crossing her arms. "Interesting that you should notice that, while he refuses to do so," she said.

This brought a faint scowl to Robert's lips. "You spoke nicely to him," he said. "You lied to him. Why should he have noticed?"

"Oh, do be realistic, Robert," Winnie said briskly. "We are both liars when we see the need. Your father has power over both of us in different ways. I will not speak back to him any more than you would do. You are his son, and yet you fear him—do not demand more courage from *me* than you dare to show yourself."

This time, Robert did not venture a response.

"You have five minutes to put on something clean," Winnie told him.

She left the bedroom, and closed the door behind her.

If nothing else, Lord Longfell's ongoing presence ensured that Robert appeared five minutes later in the hallway, without a single smudge of mud upon his face or clothing. Unfortunately, Lord Longfell *did* insist on escorting Winnie up to the attic room, observing that her ankle must be troubling her. He lingered just outside of the dowager's room until Winnie spared him a smile and a thank you.

"Do take care with that injury," Lord Longfell told her. "I will check in tomorrow, to make sure that you are healing properly."

Winnie's pleasant expression turned brittle, despite her best efforts. But Lord Longfell did not seem to notice. "Do not overly trouble yourself on my behalf, Your Lordship," she said. "You have already been far too kind."

Lord Longfell smiled back at her, and raised her gloved hand to his lips. "What charming nonsense," he said. "Any decent man should do so little for a woman in distress."

Though Winnie's fingers crawled with discomfort, she forced herself to pull her hand back slowly, so as not to insult the man. She curtsied as best she could on one bad ankle, before knocking at the attic door and heading inside.

Margaret had set up afternoon tea at the dowager's small table. An intricate porcelain tea set took up most of the room there, along with several little plates of sandwiches and scones. Though the dowager had roused herself, it was immediately clear to Winnie that doing so had been an effort; the old woman was still wearing the same blue linen wrapper which she had worn the evening before.

Still, the dowager turned a brilliant smile upon the three people in the doorway. "Miss Winifred!" she said. "This is a pleasant surprise. If you had warned me, I would have had Robert's favourite treats prepared." The lines on her weathered face crinkled into a deeper smile as she looked past Winnie at the boy who had accompanied her. "Robert," she said, "my heart. I will be sure to have your lavender biscuits on hand tomorrow. You *do* still enjoy those, I hope?"

Much to Winnie's surprise, Robert perked up with a gleam of interest in his eyes. "I will have whatever you are having, Grandmama," he said, with overly officious politeness. But Winnie saw him lick his lips in expectation, and she greatly suspected that he was already imagining a plate of lavender biscuits on the table in front of them.

Lord Longfell raised his eyebrows at his mother. "I was under the impression that *you* had requested Robert for afternoon tea, Mother," he said.

The dowager tilted her head with momentary confusion—but Winnie shot her a severe look, nodding minutely, and the older woman laughed uncomfortably. "Oh dear," she said. "I do remember that now. My memory is going, my darling, you must forgive me. If I forget again, Miss Winifred, you must be sure to ask for lavender biscuits tomorrow, on my behalf." She gestured towards two extra seats at the table. "Do join me, please."

Again, Lord Longfell took Winnie's arm without preamble, in order to help her to the table. The dowager's frown returned as she saw Winnie's difficulty; her eyes glanced down to the bare stockings on Winnie's feet where her slippers should have been. "Are you quite well, Miss Winifred?" she asked.

Winnie settled into the chair which Lord Longfell had pulled out for her. "I fear I turned an ankle on the stairs, Lady Longfell," she lied smoothly. "I understand now why you said you find this house contrary."

Lord Longfell shot Winnie a strange look, with his hand still on the back of her chair. Surely, Winnie thought, he had been about to remark on their *charming* first meeting. But Winnie had no wish to delve into such stories at the moment. She had far more important things to discuss with Lady Longfell, and she suspected that the morning's escapades— and Robert's contributions to them—might easily take up the entire afternoon tea.

Despite his original intentions, Lord Longfell cleared his throat. "I feel responsible, somehow," he said. "I oversaw the house's construction, after all. We could have done with wider stairs."

Robert pulled out his own chair and climbed into it, with a wary glance at Winnie and his father. "You don't seem well, Grandmama," he said. "Hasn't someone called a physician?"

The observation was unforgivably blunt—but Lady Longfell laughed and reached out to pat Robert's hand. "I am as well as I can be," she said. "I am so glad to see you, Robert. It has been too long by far." She looked back at her son. "Will I see you for supper, darling?"

Lord Longfell shifted on his feet, releasing the back of Winnie's chair. "I am staying at the lodge," he said. "I could join you now, for afternoon tea—"

The dowager tsked at him. "Afternoon tea is a ladies' affair," she said. "I make an exception for Robert, since he is still young. But I have juicy gossip for Miss Winifred which will not wait. If you truly love me, darling, then you will have to abandon your pheasants for a second time—perhaps at breakfast tomorrow."

Lord Longfell chuckled—though Winnie thought that there was little actual humour in the sound. "As you wish, Mother," he said. "I see no point in arguing the matter. We both know you will always have your way." He bowed to the entire table then and took a step back, with one last meaningful look at Robert. "Behave," he said. For the first time since they'd entered the attic room, his voice took on a frightful edge which made Winnie tense in her chair.

Robert gave a very tiny nod.

Lord Longfell departed with a strong, decisive stride, closing the door behind him with a *snap*.

A few seconds later, the dowager turned her gaze upon Winnie. "And why did I invite you both for afternoon tea?" she asked.

Winnie offered the woman a cold, flat look. Rather than respond directly, she said: "I have thought of my first payment, Lady Longfell. I would like you to remind your son that I am here as a personal favour to you, and not out of any financial desperation. Imply that I have family who might still take umbrage if he were to make himself overly familiar with me, spinster or not."

Lady Longfell let out a long, slow breath. "I see," she said. There was no surprise in her tone, Winnie noted, nor any hint of insult. Instead, she merely sounded tired. "I will do exactly that, Miss Winifred," she continued. "And... you have my apologies. Had I been more clear-headed, I would have realised this could be a problem and warned you properly ahead of time."

"What *are* we talking about?" Robert interrupted crossly.

Again, his mien shifted from that of a small adult to an impatient child; he believed that they were talking over his head on purpose.

"Your father has forgotten his decorum with Miss Winifred," Lady Longfell said quietly. "It is a problem which he first picked up at school, in fact. I hope you will not learn that nasty habit when you take your lessons there, Robert."

"I do not wish to go to school," Robert said promptly. The very word made his mouth twist with distaste.

"Well, you will *have* to go to school, my heart," the dowager told him gently.

Winnie reached for a scone as they talked—and then, on second thought, she took another for her pocket.

"What can Eton teach me that my tutors cannot?" Robert wheedled. "I *do* have the best tutors, don't I?" Winnie recognised the sense of a carefully planned argument in his tone. Robert had clearly prepared himself for battle before coming here.

"You cannot be a recluse, Robert," Lady Longfell said. "You must make friends with others of your station. You will be at a grave disadvantage if you do not."

"I don't want to leave home!" Robert said. His voice was more openly plaintive now. "I like my bedroom, and my things—"

"This is not open for discussion," Lady Longfell said in a steely tone. "You must leave for school in September, Robert. And you will."

Winnie finished swallowing the last bite of the scone in front of her and cleared her throat. "He *may*," she corrected. "But only if he keeps this with him at all times." So saying, she produced a white handkerchief from her pocket and placed it on the table between them.

Lady Longfell glanced at the handkerchief, perplexed. Slowly, she reached out to unfold it. Inside was a bright green sprig of mistletoe.

"I took this from a tree within the Witchwood," Winnie said. "Mistletoe is fond of children. It will protect him from the faeries here."

"From the *what?*" Robert scoffed.

The dowager levelled a severe look at her grandson. "You will take this mistletoe and do as Miss Winifred says," she told him gravely. "I do not wish to see you come to harm, Robert."

Robert shook his head incredulously, glancing between them. "You're both being foolish women," he said authoritatively—and though he seemed to *think* that the words were his own, Winnie guessed that they belonged to his father. "There are no faeries left in England."

"No, Master Robert," Winnie contradicted him. "There are very *few* faeries left in England. But there is a faerie here at Witchwood Manor—the first that I have seen in years. And he already has your name. Do you remember him? You met him in the manor, only a few hours ago."

Robert opened his mouth to offer further scathing scepticism… but this time, no sound came out. He blinked quickly, reaching up to touch his throat in obvious confusion.

"You cannot speak of him," Winnie explained to Robert patiently. "You will find it very difficult to speak of *any* of the strange happenings here at Witchwood Manor, I expect. Not that your father would listen, even if you could speak. He has some reason to deny that there are faeries here. Perhaps he is too frightened to believe it. But… he knows. On some level, he does. That is why he will not sleep here."

The dowager paled visibly. "The faeries have Robert's name?" she whispered, with obvious horror.

Winnie sighed. "I was going to warn Master Robert earlier, over tea," she said. "He sneaked away before I could elaborate upon the matter. Mr Quincy must stalk this house quite avidly, for he took immediate advantage. It shouldn't be a deadly mistake—so far as I can tell, no other faeries heard the name, and Mr Quincy's magic will not kill him. But it certainly does complicate my work."

Winnie plucked the handkerchief from Lady Longfell's fingers and offered it to Robert directly. "I will not force you to accept this, Mr Robert Murray," she said. "But neither will I take responsibility if you decline your own protection out of pride. That is why I am offering this to you now—so that your grandmother will know that I have done my best to honour the spirit of our bargain."

Robert tried again to speak. A few wordless croaks trickled from his throat—but little else. With every passing second, his expression grew more frightened and alarmed.

Finally, he snatched the handkerchief from Winnie with a wheezing gasp, and clutched it to his chest.

"Excellent," said Winnie—though some part of her had hoped that Robert would decline, so that she might safely wash her hands of him. "Now—while we are being conversational—I traded Mr Quincy for some information earlier. There is a monster in the Witchwood, Master Robert. Do not wander there again without me by your side."

When Robert failed to respond, Winnie arched an eyebrow at him. "You could simply nod if you understand me, Master Robert," she said.

Robert nodded very slowly, as his fingers turned white upon the handkerchief.

"And do not speak again to Mr Quincy," Winnie continued. "Or indeed to *any* stranger here. Faeries use your words against you. The safest course of action for a person unfamiliar with them is to speak nothing at all. I will handle any conversation for the both of us, until you have learned better."

The dowager glanced sharply at Winnie. "Until *he* has learned better?" she repeated.

Winnie considered her own words seriously. Finally, she nodded. "Until I have *taught* him better," she corrected herself. "I am his governess, after all. And it seems that Mr Robert is in need of otherworldly lessons."

"If you trip me down the stairs, Master Robert, I will retract all of my promises to your grandmother," Winnie warned the boy.

Robert had offered to help Winnie down the stairs from the attic—mostly due to the dowager's not-so-subtle prompting. Though noticeably shorter than Winnie, he was still tall enough, in his gangly sort of way, to let her lean one arm upon his shoulder.

"I won't let you fall," Robert said flatly. "I'm not *foolish*, Miss Hall."

Winnie arched an eyebrow at him as they struggled down another of the precariously narrow stairs. *It's Miss Hall now, is it?* she thought. She nearly spoke the words aloud; but she knew that saying them would instantly reverse whatever tiny victories she had won over the boy. She focussed instead on the staircase before them.

"It defies me," she said finally, "just how it is that the dowager gets up and down these stairs. But I suppose that she does not leave her room very much at all."

"Suppose we'll find out when we go to service," Robert

muttered. "She used to drag me to church every Sunday, when she was back in London. I tried crying off sick once, and she just said the Lord would cure me of what ailed me."

Winnie couldn't help responding this time. "I shall have to inform the dowager that the Lord has failed," she replied dryly.

Robert rolled his eyes. "You're so bloody pert," he said. "How do I scare you off like Father does?"

All hint of humour fled Winnie's manner abruptly. There was an extended moment of silence, rather than the shocked correction of language which Robert might have been expecting. Eventually, however, the boy spoke again. "How did you learn all of those things about—about—" His tongue tied itself in knots again, and he scowled darkly.

"Faeries?" Winnie finished for him. Her eyes flickered around them, searching for signs of eavesdropping. But Lord Longfell was absent, and she had begun to suspect that Mr Quincy mostly avoided the dowager's room, given Lady Longfell's previous comments about the ring on her finger. "I had a faerie tutor, Master Robert. One could not call her lessons very disciplined—but I still learned much from her, regardless."

Robert eyed her sceptically. "You just walked into... you know, over *there*... and asked for a tutor, then?" he scoffed.

"Hardly," Winnie replied. "I called upon her long ago in my hour of need, and offered her something which she greatly desired." She wobbled briefly on the next stair, and steadied herself more heavily on Robert's shoulder. "She took a lock of my hair with her when she departed. From then on, she visited me in my dreams—or perhaps I visited *her*. She deigned to teach me things, when she was of a mind. That is how it mostly goes with faeries."

Finally, they reached the bottom of the stairs, and Robert made as though to leave—but Winnie caught him by the shoulder.

"Your lessons start now," she told him. "We have been unprepared at every turn so far. You have much catching up to do." Winnie jerked her chin down the hallway. "I believe there is a classroom we can use."

Robert grimaced—but to his credit, did not protest. Despite his contrary nature, Winnie suspected that he had honed a certain instinct for survival. He turned down the hall with her until they had come to the classroom.

Poor Robert's disgust was not entirely misplaced. The classroom, once a nursery, had clearly been built and furnished for a far younger boy—a consequence, perhaps, of the dowager's fading faculties. Though there was now a desk inside, outdated toys still cluttered the area at every turn. Faded but meticulously painted red and white toy soldiers stood at attention on a shelf against one wall, next to a bulky kaleidoscope. A tiny, handsomely carved hobby horse had been tucked into the far corner of the room; had Robert desired for some reason to make use of it, he probably would have broken it.

Winnie settled herself uncomfortably onto the edge of a child-sized stool, while Robert walked to the shelf to inspect the toy soldiers with a wrinkle in his nose.

"The first thing which you must know about faeries," Winnie said, "is that they do not think as we do. They live in a world which largely obeys their whims—and even when they visit us in England, their magic makes them very powerful."

Robert plucked a little red soldier from the shelf, turning it over in his palm. "And what does that have to do with their thinking?" he asked.

Winnie studied his awkwardly upright form from behind, thinking to herself of powerful people and their foibles. "Perhaps faeries are not all that different from certain human beings I have known," she admitted. "What I mean to say is this: Because they are so powerful, they do not fully appreciate the consequences of their actions. In fact, they rarely appreciate that human beings are of consequence at all. They are callous, and they like the world to follow certain rules which only ever make much sense to them. When those rules are broken, they become quite fearsome."

Robert replaced the soldier on the shelf, with a last dismissive look at it. "Was your tutor fearsome?" he asked.

"Oh, she was *terrifying*," Winnie said. Her voice took on a dreamy tone. "London cowered from her, for a time. She had at least a dozen titles—but the workhouse masters called her the Hollow Lady. They put up iron horseshoes in their offices, out of fear that she might creep inside and drag them away forever."

Robert frowned and turned to look at her. "You don't sound very terrified," he pointed out.

Winnie smiled with fond memory. "I was not the object of her wickedness," she said. "I learned eventually that she would never harm a child. Other faeries might well do—but not the Hollow Lady." She heaved a wistful sigh. "I wanted to be just like her."

"I can believe *that* part," Robert said flatly.

Winnie blinked. "Well, that hardly matters to the two of us, just now," she said. "All that you need understand is that faeries follow very strict, nonsensical rules. If you can learn a particular faerie's rules, then you will know much better how to handle them. If you can bind them into promises—then that is even better."

Robert crossed his arms and leaned against the shelf, absorbing this information with more seriousness than Winnie had anticipated. Then—to her surprise—he asked: "Can you give me some examples?"

Though it had not been her original intention, Winnie spent the next few hours spinning faerie tales for her young charge. These *specific* faerie tales, of course, had the benefit of being true. She related the tale of Saint Ardent, the faerie who stole an entire abbey and crowned himself a miracle-worker, and the tale of Bluebeard, who married and devoured several human wives.

And then—because she was feeling in a charitable mood— Winnie told the Honourable Mr Robert Murray a different faerie tale entirely.

This is how it went.

CHAPTER 5

*O*nce upon a time, a little girl ran away into the wild English woods. While she was climbing trees, she came upon a cruel and noble faerie called Lord Hollowvale, who declared that he would be her father from that moment onwards.

Though the little girl had no parents, she did not like the idea of going away with a faerie. Unfortunately, faeries are much more powerful than little girls are, and Lord Hollowvale had decided to be a stern father indeed. As he tried to force his newest English daughter to come with him, however, the little girl's cousin found them both and stabbed the faerie in the leg with her iron embroidery scissors.

Like all faeries, Lord Hollowvale feared iron most of all—and so he departed with only half of the little girl, leaving her other half behind in England to grow up there.

The half of the little girl which Lord Hollowvale took with him was the more emotional half by far—for all of the little girl's patience had been stranded in England. This did not suit

Lord Hollowvale, who hoped to turn his English daughter into a perfectly well-behaved child. From studying the English nobility, he had determined that children best learned patience through fear—and so, he gave his daughter to the most terrifying faerie that he knew, and asked that she be educated.

Lady Mourningwood—a hard faerie woman with eyes like coal and a voice like a deep, dark well—became the little girl's tutor. Thenceforth, the little girl took her lessons in the Mourningwood, where dead things lurked within the streams and black trees whispered terrible things.

Lady Mourningwood began the little girl's lessons by teaching her embroidery. The faerie gave the little girl a ball of thread-like regrets and a needle made of silver, and showed her how to stitch a pattern.

"But beware," Lady Mourningwood said. "If you should prick your finger, do not let your blood touch the earth—for there are things sleeping beneath it which crave human blood, and they might well wake."

Lady Mourningwood left the little girl to practise her embroidery as night fell and whispers rose and trees groaned. But though Lord Hollowvale's daughter did her best, she had no patience and too much fear inside her, and the needle pricked her thumb a hundred times. Eventually, a drop of her blood fell to the loamy earth, and something stirred within. The earth began to breathe, thrumming like an awful heart-beat, and the little girl knew that if she did not do something, it would swallow her whole.

That might have been the end of this sad tale—but the little girl was made of sterner stuff than any faerie might have guessed. As the dead earth shifted beneath her feet, she sang a lullaby to soothe it back to sleep. She sang the whole night through, until the strange stars in the sky winked out and light returned to the Mourningwood, and her messy embroidery was complete.

Lady Mourningwood was not satisfied with the little girl's embroidery, of course. The regrets were crooked, the faerie declared—and she ordered the little girl to unpick all of the progress she had made in order to start again.

The little girl was forced to practise every night, until her regrets were neat and even. At first, she pricked her finger far too often, and was forced to sing the earth to sleep until her voice was barely a whisper. Eventually, however, she became quite good at stitching, whereupon Lady Mourningwood immediately decided that Lord Hollowvale's daughter should learn the pianoforte.

The faerie brought the little girl to a pianoforte which had grown from one of the black trees in the Mourningwood, set with keys which had been carved from human ivory. Lord Hollowvale's daughter was told that she might be allowed to leave once she composed a tune which moved Lady Mourningwood to smile.

Sadly, while the little girl had taken some piano lessons back in England, nothing in the Mourningwood inspired very much happiness, and she found the composition difficult indeed. Though she played through the night until her fingers ached, each attempt at sprightly music seemed even less cheerful and more lacklustre than the previous one.

After several days of playing without end, the little girl's music attracted a shadow from the forest, who settled at the other side of the piano to listen. At her next pause, it said: "What awful racket. You sang so sweetly for so many evenings, but this music is unpleasant."

The little girl could not help but weep. "I do not *want* to play the pianoforte," she said, "but Lady Mourningwood has said that I must compose something to make her smile, or else I will never be allowed to leave."

The shadow shook its head at her. "You will never make Lady Mourningwood smile with that cacophony," it said, "for she delights in requiems and funeral marches. Play instead the most miserable tune that you can, and she will surely let you leave."

The shadow left again, and the little girl did as it had told her. She thought of her cousin, whom she dearly missed, and of wild English woods which she would never see again—and she played a requiem for all that she had lost.

When Lady Mourningwood heard the song, the faerie smiled for the first time in a hundred years, and declared that the little girl was surely the most accomplished piano player in all of faerie. She returned the girl to Hollowvale, where her faerie father put her on display and crowed about her talents.

As years passed in faerie and in England, Lord Hollowvale's daughter learned everything she could from her new family, until she became a lovely young woman with a wild, wicked heart. She nursed a terrible hatred for her father and for Lady Mourningwood—until the day that her other half arrived in faerie with a familiar pair of iron scissors.

On that day, Lord Hollowvale's daughter stabbed him through the heart with iron and stole his place in faerie. The new Lady Hollowvale swore to Lady Mourningwood that someday, she would prick her old faerie tutor a thousand thousand times with a silver needle and force her to play the pianoforte until she found a tune to make Lady Hollowvale smile.

To this day, Lady Mourningwood hides within her realm

in faerie, wary of her old charge. But while Lady Hollowvale waits for her tutor to emerge, she vents her hatred upon all of those in England who are cruel to children.

CHAPTER 6

*W*innie might have instructed Robert to sleep in her room that night, if not for Oliver—who still despised boys, even after death. Instead, she pried a silver locket from her chatelaine and tucked the mistletoe inside it, hanging the chain around Robert's neck.

"Do not take this off, whatever you do," she told him. "Do you understand me, Master Robert? I have just told you several stories about all of the disasters which befall people who cannot obey a simple rule."

"I understand," Robert assured her. And Winnie believed that he *did* understand, given the way that he clutched the locket in his hand.

She left him in his bedroom and hobbled back through the class room to her own bed.

Winnie expected that she might dream wistfully of Hollowvale that evening. Instead, she dreamt of nothing at all —until she woke abruptly to a knocking at her bedroom door.

Winnie startled awake, glancing around her darkened room. Twisted wooden faces looked out from the walls once again, staring at her in silent, screaming judgement. There were no whispers this time, however, and Winnie wondered if Mr Quincy had decided to avoid her hallway now, as well as the dowager's attic. But then—if it was not Mr Quincy knocking at her door, who *was* it?

Winnie slipped out of bed, placing her weight gingerly upon her injured foot... but to her surprise, there was no pain there. She glanced down in puzzled astonishment, and saw that the unpleasant bruise on her ankle had disappeared.

The person at her bedroom door knocked more firmly now, and Winnie hurried to pull on her threadbare frock before she answered it; the faces in the walls followed her with accusatory wooden eyes as she moved. Though she flinched instinctively as she placed her hand upon the door handle, the nausea which she had come to associate with it failed to materialise—the handle was no longer made of iron, but of tarnished silver.

Winnie stared at it, increasingly perplexed, as another knock sounded. But finally, she pushed the door open. Standing on the other side, in the darkness of the hallway, was a short, familiar-looking woman with chestnut hair.

"Ah," said Cook. "So the Witchwood Knot *has* caught you." The other woman was wearing her own housecoat—a sturdy, dark green paisley thing which barely covered her knees. In her right hand, she carried a brass candlestick with a single, guttering white candle which highlighted the blackened circles beneath her eyes.

"The Witchwood Knot?" Winnie asked breathlessly. "I've never heard of anything like that before." She glanced down the darkened hall curiously, searching for other people—but Cook seemed to be alone. The hallway yawned behind her, just a bit too long for itself; though Winnie should have been able to see the stairs from where they were, the walls stretched onwards into blackness. A warm breeze tickled past her shoulder in the stillness, before shifting back the other way again—as though the house were breathing.

"That's what the faeries call it," Cook replied. "We're on the other side of the manor now—the one where Mr Quincy is the butler. This place catches hold of us when we sleep, I think. The longer that you stay here, the more you'll dream of it."

Winnie returned her gaze to Cook, suddenly feeling sharper than before. *We are in faerie!* she thought, with rising excitement. But she calmed her expression forcibly, smoothing the creases along her forehead and relaxing the twitch of her lips. "You can speak of Mr Quincy now," Winnie observed to Cook. "Because we are dreaming?"

Cook nodded listlessly. "I've been at Witchwood Manor for so long now, I barely rest at all," she sighed. "But... perhaps we ought to check on Master Robert? I wonder if the Knot has caught him, too."

Winnie nodded quickly, sweeping down the hall towards Robert's bedroom. She knocked several times upon the door. "Robert?" she called out. "Are you awake? Or... well. Are you dreaming along with us?"

The door creaked open warily to reveal Robert. He looked somewhat smaller than usual, with his shoulders hunched and trembling and his hand clutched desperately around Winnie's silver locket. All bravado had utterly fled him as he looked up at her.

"There are faces in the walls," he whispered, in a terrified tone. "What are they, Miss Hall?"

Winnie blinked. *Oh,* she thought. *A normal child would find that frightening, wouldn't they?* For once, she found herself speaking to the boy in a soothing voice. "I haven't the first idea what has caused those faces, Master Robert," she said. "But they have been here for many years now, and they have yet to harm anyone. Isn't that right, Cook?"

Cook padded over slowly, pulling her housecoat closer about herself. "I don't like 'em," she declared fervently. "But no —they haven't ever hurt me."

This observation did not fully reassure Robert. He inched subtly closer to Winnie as the conversation continued, as though her extra height would protect him. A sudden hiss at Winnie's feet made him stumble back with wide eyes, however, and Winnie glanced down.

A ragged, short-haired black cat with one good eye rubbed against her legs, glaring evilly at the boy next to them. Oliver let out another low, dangerous noise which promised extreme harm to any human appendages which might enter striking range of his claws.

Winnie couldn't help it—she broke out into a soppy, adoring smile. "Oh, *Ollie!*" she gushed. "Look at you, my little bit of fuzz! You haven't changed a bit!" She reached down to scoop up the tomcat, cradling him in her arms as she had done when he was alive. Oliver's low growls instantly died, replaced by a deep, rolling purr.

Robert stared at the cat with horror. "That thing is *yours?*" he asked Winnie. "It's a menace!"

Winnie cooed at the cat, who now looked eminently contented with himself. "Oh, Ollie is just prickly around men," she said. "The local boys used to throw stones at him, before we took him in. He's not growling because he *hates* you, Master Robert. He's simply afraid of you."

Robert stared warily at the pleased-looking cat in Winnie's arms. "So... he *won't* attack me?" he asked.

"Of course he'll attack you," Winnie replied promptly, as she touched her nose to Oliver's. "He's learned that he needs to frighten off boys *before* they pick up stones, in order to survive. That isn't the sort of instinct one unlearns in a hurry... even if one *is* technically deceased."

Robert had clearly decided that *this* revelation was a step too far for him. He shook his head and took another careful step back from Winnie. "How do we get rid of the faces?" he asked. His eyes flickered along the hallway, where more wooden eyes stared and more agonised mouths yawned wide.

"They'll disappear when we wake up again," Winnie told him. There was a hint of question in the statement, as she worked her way through the implications of everything she'd heard so far. She glanced at Cook. "That is why the faces only ever show up at night, isn't it? Because they are *always* here, on the other side of Witchwood Manor."

Cook nodded in tired agreement. "I've spent years now gathering all manner of answers which I cannot speak to anyone," she said. "But you seem to know your way around this other world, Miss Hall. Do you believe you might be able to help us?"

Winnie smiled wryly, still holding Oliver close to her chest. "I will not presume to predict my success," she said. "I am here because I must be here. I will try to help because I have no choice. But I am what you have—so please, tell me everything you know."

Cook seemed reasonably mollified by this response. She gestured at the hallway behind her. "Come," she said. "I'll tell you what I can, and show you the rest. There are dangerous paths in the Knot... but I know the safer parts by now."

Robert shivered. "We're going *wandering* out there?" he asked fearfully.

Winnie set Oliver back down, with one last scratch behind his ears. She straightened and turned to look at her young charge. "At some point, Master Robert," she said, "one must gather information. We are now in faerie, where one must walk a wild path. This world devours those who are too bold —but those who hide and refuse to take risks are also taken unaware by danger."

She paused, as Oliver twined himself around her legs once again. "I would do the wandering *for* us, but I worry to leave you here alone, even with your mistletoe. Stay close to me, and silent—but watch everything around us carefully. You may spot something crucial which I do not."

Robert glanced one more time behind him at the faces in the walls. He nodded slowly, though he looked increasingly worried and uncertain.

Winnie swept her arm before them, with a slight bow to Cook. "Please lead the way," she said.

AT FIRST, the Witchwood Knot was very similar in form to Witchwood Manor—with the immediately obvious exception that the house's beautiful English oak was all blackened, and the iron accents were instead made of tarnished silver. Oh, some of the hallways still seemed a bit too long, and the shadows were deeper than they ought to be... but as far as realms in faerie went, Winnie had seen stranger.

"I grew up in the village," Cook told Winnie, as they walked. "We all knew there were faeries in the Witchwood, and we rightly feared them. We did our best to only take the trees we needed most—and even then, we left out offerings to stave off otherworldly ire."

Winnie pursed her lips. "And did those offerings help?" she asked.

Cook shrugged uncomfortably. "Sometimes yes," she said. "And sometimes no. We always knew when we'd crossed the creatures in the woods. People vanished in the night, never to be seen again."

Oliver nudged at Winnie's leg again, and she stumbled. She was still so pleased to see him that she couldn't bring herself to scold him, though.

"Didn't you put up iron horseshoes?" Robert asked, in a superior sort of tone. After only one day of studying faerie tales with Winnie, he had already decided himself an expert on the subject.

"Oh yes, most certainly," said Cook. Her voice trailed back towards them from beyond her bobbing candle. "It never helped at all. You see how it is at Witchwood Manor. Iron everywhere—and yet, somehow, the faeries manage."

"I've yet to solve that mystery," Winnie murmured, somewhat crossly. "Mr Quincy was so pleased to throw it in my face, my first day here."

"Ah, Mr Quincy," Cook sighed. "What a frightening little puzzle he is. I met him as a young girl, you know. Back then, we called him the red man." She slowed significantly as they came to the stairs, so that Robert and Winnie could use her candlelight on the way down. The house's warm breath tugged the candle's flame back and forth, making it waver in the darkness.

"My father was the village baker," Cook continued, as they descended. "A man who feared both God and faeries in equal measure. We left out something for the Witchwood creatures every evening, hoping they'd remember and pass over our house whenever they were angered. I stayed up late one night to watch... and there was Mr Quincy in his dark red jacket, eating scones. He caught me—but I offered him another scone, and we had a pleasant conversation."

Winnie chuckled softly. "Mr Quincy *can* be bribed, then," she observed. "Perhaps I should have brought baked goods instead of magical perfume."

"The time for bribes has passed, I fear," Cook told her darkly. "When the old Lord Longfell passed, the current lord came back from school. He coveted the lumber in the Witchwood—he knew the Navy would pay well for it. He ordered us to cut down swaths of forest. It was tantamount to war."

Robert bristled. "The Witchwood is in England, not in faerie!" he said. "It belongs to *us*. The faeries have their own entire world!"

"Oh, maybe that's so, Master Robert," Cook said. "But that hardly changes what came next, now does it?" She was clearly too exhausted to bother censoring herself in front of him. "I still saw Mr Quincy at night, sometimes. He warned me—he said that his lady was cruel, and she'd not hesitate to punish us. I told the village, and we all refused Lord Longfell. But His Lordship started throwing people off the land for disobedience. One family lost everything, and the rest of us fell into line."

The main stairs led down to a familiar-looking foyer. At the bottom, they passed a large, silver-backed mirror—but as Winnie looked closer at it, she realised that Cook's flickering candle had no twin within the glass. She slowed her steps, studying the reflection more intently.

The foyer in the mirror was devoid of people. Its oak panelling was lighter in colour—and most importantly, she saw, there were no faces in the walls.

"That is Witchwood Manor," Winnie said. "Beyond the mirror."

Cook turned back, retracing her steps. She settled next to Winnie, staring through the glass. "The Witchwood Knot is connected to the manor," she said. "Mr Quincy must find his way across somehow. I had suspected he could do it—the kitchen is always missing sweets—but I never knew for certain until you told me you had met him at the door."

Winnie waved a hand in front of the mirror experimentally. But there was no version of her on the other side to wave back at her. The room on the other side was like a painting, frozen in time.

"The Witchwood Knot could not *always* have been here," Winnie murmured thoughtfully, "or else it would have looked much different. Witchwood Manor was only built a few years ago."

"That's right," said Cook. "His Lordship knew the faeries would interfere with his lumber. He called in several magicians to handle 'em. Most of *them* disappeared, too. But finally, he found a magician who... *did* something. We built Witchwood Manor on his say-so, I think, though none of us ever met him. After we cut down all the trees to build this place, the faeries stole near twenty people in one night, just as Mr Quincy warned me." She gestured at the mirror. "But this was the result. Now all of the faeries are *here*, and Lord Longfell sells the Witchwood lumber as he pleases."

Winnie rubbed at her forehead. "What a mess," she sighed. "The faeries must be *furious*. No wonder Lord Longfell doesn't wish to sleep here."

"Good riddance," Robert muttered. "At least they can't steal people now."

"I don't entirely disagree," Cook admitted. "Their lady is a nasty one. Even Mr Quincy fears her some, I think. But now it's all gone even *worse*, it feels like. If the faeries find their way outside the Witchwood Knot, I doubt the village will survive it."

"There is no way into the rest of faerie from the Witchwood Knot, then?" Winnie asked her. The realisation made her stomach drop with disappointment. "What lies outside the cloister door, then?"

Cook shrugged. "I'll show you, if you like," she said.

There were candles burning in the cloister—ghostly blue lights which announced themselves long before Cook led them into the room. The carved vines within the woodwork twitched at the edge of Winnie's vision, like a warning... but every time she turned to look at them directly, they were still.

The reliquary shrine had changed, however. The stained glass window there no longer showed its black and green knot. Instead, there was a single, burning red eye which sent a subtle shudder down Winnie's spine. It seemed distantly familiar, for some reason... but try as she might, she could not put her finger on where it was that she had seen it. Robert lingered curiously at the shrine, tilting his head at the window—but there was no recognition in his eyes as he looked at it.

"Here," said Cook, from the cloister entrance. "Look."

She tugged open the heavy door which normally might have led outside. Behind it, Winnie saw, there was only a dull grey wall blocking the way.

"Iron!" Winnie said, with a hint of exasperation. "Again with iron! There should be no iron here in faerie. It simply doesn't work that way!"

Oliver offered a ragged meow of agreement, near her feet.

Cook shook her head. "And yet, here it is," she said. "I

suppose if a magician wanted to trap faeries, then iron would be proper."

"Iron *loathes* magicians," Winnie corrected her. "It simply won't cooperate with magic. Whoever this mysterious magician was, he's nothing like the rest."

"I know very little about magic," Cook said apologetically, as she shoved the cloister door closed again. "I've asked Mr Quincy several times now what he knows about the Knot, but he never deigns to answer."

Winnie blinked. "I thought you never saw Mr Quincy in Witchwood Manor," she said.

"Never," Cook replied smartly. "But I play cards with him every evening in the Witchwood Knot." She smiled ruefully. "We are trapped here together, in a way, though we are enemies. It helps to pass the time."

Winnie sharpened her attention on Cook. "And... where is it that the two of you play cards?" she asked.

"In the conservatory, of course," said Cook. "It is his favourite room."

THE CONSERVATORY in the Witchwood Knot was far larger than the one in Witchwood Manor. In fact, it was nearly as big as the foyer. The tall stained glass windows which ought to have looked outside stretched further than the real conservatory's windows, as though the roses had overgrown their place.

Several small, round tables littered the area, lit by the same unearthly blue candles which Winnie had seen in the cloister. Faeries of every shape and size crowded the tables, playing strange parlour games and murmuring to one another. Most of them were slender, bark-skinned dryads and watery-looking naiads—but there were also a few shadowy brownies and shaggy-haired satyrs.

The dead orange saplings which Winnie had seen before were nowhere to be found; rather, the room sported a veritable forest of wild, vibrant trees. Every tree branch sagged visibly with the weight of colourful, poisonous strychnine fruit. The faeries here clearly thought nothing of the danger—for several of them sucked pulp from the orange fruit's seeds as they gamed, as though it were a delicious dessert.

Despite the press of bodies, Winnie picked out Mr Quincy with surprising ease. The butler was seated alone at a table next to the white-draped pianoforte. He'd set his feet upon the table, leaning back in his chair with a terminally bored expression on his pale, narrow features as he cracked the outside of a pale orange strychnine fruit. His rat's tail dangled over the chair's arm, swinging lazily just above the floor.

Faeries glanced at their small group as they wove their way between the tables—but Oliver patrolled before Winnie, warning off the creatures with angry hisses. Though he was a small cat, the faeries jerked back from him with wary expressions, suggesting that they had kenned more of his true nature than the average human would.

Mr Quincy straightened abruptly as he saw their group approach. At first, he nodded at Cook... but then, his reddish eyes fixed upon Oliver, and his jaw twitched. Winnie scooped the cat up in her arms as they approached, calming him against her chest—but this barely made a dent in Mr Quincy's rigid posture.

"Must you bring that creature with you, even *here?*" he demanded.

Winnie arched an eyebrow at him. "That is hardly any way to speak of Robert, Mr Quincy," she replied.

Robert let out an angry huff and opened his mouth to speak—but Winnie interrupted him.

"That was a *joke*, Master Robert," she told him. "And you should be especially silent while we are *here*, entirely surrounded by faeries."

Mr Quincy narrowed his eyes at their group, digging his long fingers into the strychnine fruit in his hand. "Let him speak," he suggested. "I want to hear what the boy has to say."

"Of course you do," said Winnie. "Last time he spoke to you, you learned his name. And now, I'm sure you would like nothing better than to catch him in some breach of faerie protocol. But Master Robert is too clever to be caught off-guard a *second* time." *Please do be cleverer than that, Master Robert,* Winnie thought at the boy silently.

Mr Quincy turned his attention to Winnie more fully, forcing a polite smile onto his lips. "How relieved I am to see you safe and sound, Miss Winifred Hall," he said, as though their previous exchange had never happened. "And here I thought for certain that the monster of the Witchwood had caught you."

Winnie pulled out a chair for Robert, while Cook settled herself in another. "I never met any monsters in the Witchwood," she said. "In fact, I begin to wonder if you might have lied to me... but faeries cannot lie." She studied him intently, trying to make sense of the smooth expression on his features.

Faeries cannot lie, Winnie thought. *But neither can they pass by iron horseshoes. Are you indeed a faerie, Mr Quincy? Or are you something else entirely?*

Mr Quincy leaned back in his chair again, affecting mild

disinterest—though his eyes remained fixed upon Oliver, in Winnie's arms. "But you walked into the cloister with a monster," said the butler. "You looked afraid, I thought. As well you should have been."

Winnie's lips parted in surprise. "You mean Lord Longfell?" she asked. "*He's* your monster in the Witchwood? You said that he was dangerous."

"Oh, he is *very* dangerous," Mr Quincy said. "I would hazard every creature at this table knows as much."

"That is my *father* you are speaking of—" Robert burst out.

Cook threw a hand across the boy's mouth before Winnie could reach him. The rest of whatever he'd intended to say was muffled against her palm.

"He's goading you on purpose, Robert," Winnie said flatly. "Don't give him what he wants." She considered asking more about Lord Longfell... but Mr Quincy's red eyes were glittering with malice, and she knew that if she did, the faerie's responses might well set off Robert once again.

Mr Quincy pried one pulp-covered seed from the strychnine fruit he was holding, offering it out to Robert with mocking generosity. "Would you like a bit of dessert, Mr Robert Murray?" he asked.

Winnie let out a soft sound of exasperation. "Offering poisoned sweets to a child is awfully... on the nose, isn't it?" she asked the butler.

Mr Quincy pressed one hand to his chest. "Is this poisonous to humans?" he asked. "How terrible. But why would you assume that I knew such a thing, Miss Hall?"

Robert turned a silent, withering glare upon the faerie— but Mr Quincy ignored him entirely now, leaning back in his chair and popping the strychnine seed between his lips.

"Cards tonight, Mr Quincy?" Cook asked wearily, even as she kept her hand at Robert's mouth.

Mr Quincy licked his fingers clean and crossed his arms in front of his chest. "What else are we to do with ourselves, Sarah Baker?" he asked acidly. "You will not leave the manor, I take it."

Cook shook her head. "Of course not," she replied. "My answer is the same as ever. My fate is tied to yours, and to the dowager's, and to this cursed house. That is the choice I've made. We might as well play cards." Robert had now fallen silent, and she eased her hand carefully from his mouth. The boy glowered at Mr Quincy in silence now—but he did not speak again.

Mr Quincy glanced at Winnie. "We have four people at the table," he said. "We could play... Whist?"

"Yes, Whist," Cook agreed. "That is played in pairs. But who would play on *your* side, Mr Quincy?"

"True," said Mr Quincy slowly. There was a subtle calculation in his tone, however, and Winnie greatly suspected that he had planned his next words well before their arrival. "Then I will play the other game with Miss Hall. She is new, after all."

Winnie arched an eyebrow at him. "The other game?" she asked.

"Écarté," Cook explained. "It is one of the first games that I ever taught him. We play it often, since it only has two players."

"Perhaps we could make a wager of it, Miss Hall," the butler offered. "I have more questions for you. I am sure that you have some for me. We could play for full and truthful answers, of the sort that we exchanged earlier today."

"I wouldn't," Cook warned Winnie. "That is *exactly* how he won Margaret's name from her."

Mr Quincy waved a hand. "But I already *have* Miss Hall's name," he said. "What other question could concern her quite so terribly?"

Oh, there is something dangerous which he hopes to ask me, Winnie thought grimly. *And he is very certain he can win the answer.*

Mr Quincy was wrong, of course—though there was no reasonable way for him to know it. Winnie was a cartomancer. She had never lost at cards before unless she chose to do so.

He wouldn't *start* with his most dangerous question, though, she decided. They both had smaller questions which they wanted answers to. That, Winnie thought, could work in her favour.

"I am open to your wager, Mr Quincy," Winnie told him. "But I have conditions. We will use my card deck—"

Mr Quincy shook his head. "We will use *my* deck," he cut in. "I do not play with human cards. But you may be the dealer. I think that should be fair, Miss Hall?"

Winnie pursed her lips, pretending to consider. Given her own abilities, she was not *truly* worried about Mr Quincy's deck... but it seemed prudent to pretend some hesitation. "As you wish," she said finally. "But we will ask our questions *before* the game. That way, we can both be sure our questions are of equal weight."

Winnie's latest stipulation drew a faint frown from Mr Quincy—but he smoothed it over quickly. "That is... reasonable," he said.

Robert glanced between the two of them in silent fascination, as though he were witnessing a duel. In some respects, Winnie thought, perhaps he was.

"What question will you ask?" Winnie inquired mildly.

Mr Quincy offered her a pleasant smile, entirely at odds with the malevolence in his crimson eyes. "I would like to know why it is that the dowager recommended you for the position of governess, Miss Hall," he said.

Winnie bit down on the inside of her cheek, trying not to let her face twitch. Mr Quincy probably thought the question small and innocent—a good way to set her at ease. But the answer was more telling than he knew.

"Then for myself," Winnie said slowly, "I would like to know why it is that you are trying to chase people away from Witchwood Manor—myself included."

Mr Quincy narrowed his eyes at her. "Do you truly consider that an answer of *equal* worth, Miss Hall?" he asked.

"I do," she replied smoothly. "But you are free to decline the game, Mr Quincy." Winnie scratched absently at Oliver's ears, and the cat let out a long, low purr.

The butler studied her for another long moment... but eventually, he set aside the rest of his strychnine fruit and plucked a set of cards from a pocket in his crimson jacket. The pocket should not have been large enough to hold the cards, Winnie noted—but that was a relatively common faerie trick.

"This is a traditional faerie deck," said Mr Quincy. "It is a fair deck—I have not marked or altered it. But you may inspect it if you like." He offered out the cards, and Winnie made a show of taking them in order to look through them. She could not help but notice that the cards were faintly perfumed with blood and bay berry, as Mr Quincy seemed to be. The scent made for an oddly potent mixture, though Clarimonde had certainly not intended her perfume for *him*.

It was indeed a normal faerie deck—the sort which Lady Hollowvale preferred. But Winnie pretended curiosity as though she'd never seen one before, laying out several cards before her on the table.

"These are strange pips," she commented, pointing to the squiggly, abstract symbols on the cards. "I cannot make them out. Do they represent anything in particular?"

Mr Quincy inclined his head. "This is the suit of Promises," he said, pointing to a jagged golden symbol. "This one is the suit of Memories—and here we have the twin suits of Fears and Desires." He indicated each one in turn, gesturing at a curved golden symbol, an arrow-like silver symbol, and one last silver shape which reminded Winnie of an outstretched hand.

Robert was listening very intently now, and Winnie could not help but feel a stab of approval. He was keeping his mouth closed and his eyes open, just as she had instructed him to do.

"Odd choices," Winnie mused aloud, as she returned her attention to the cards on the table.

"Not at all," said Mr Quincy. "They are the currency which faeries normally wager. At one time, the entire deck would be the winner's earnings, too."

Winnie smiled quietly down at the remaining cards in her palm. Divination was even simpler in faerie, where magic was eager to play games. On top of which, Mr Quincy had given her his very own deck, which he had played with several times. She could hardly have asked for a more perfect opportunity to read his cards.

She concentrated on the next card in the deck. *Tell me one of your owner's secrets,* she encouraged it.

Winnie turned another card face-up before her. The card in question had no pip. In fact, it was a pure black card with a single red eye at the centre—the spitting image of the stained glass window in the reliquary shrine of the Witchwood Knot.

Robert straightened minutely in his chair, and Winnie knew that he had remembered the shrine as well.

Now I know where I have seen that eye before, Winnie thought. She had noticed it before in Lady Hollowvale's faerie deck. It was an extra card which most games set aside.

"This card does not belong to any of the suits you've named," Winnie observed to the butler. "What is it?"

Mr Quincy's eyes flickered down to the card. His lip curled into a grimace. "That is... the Eye," he said. "Sometimes called the *Fomórach*. It is an extra card. This game is played without it."

Winnie ran her fingers lightly over the card. A fresh shiver went down her spine as she touched it. The card was trying to answer her request. Winnie let herself tune out for a moment... and listened to what it was saying.

She became aware of the earth beneath their feet, cold and dark and deep. Something dead was buried there... and yet, somehow, it dreamed.

Winnie drew in a sharp breath, jerking her fingers back from the card. "What does *fomórach* mean?" she asked. "Is it a person or a thing?"

Mr Quincy snatched up the card abruptly, as though the sight of it offended him. "That is a question, Miss Hall," he said shortly. "You could play for the answer, if you would like, instead of asking your *other* question."

Winnie chewed at her lip. Mr Quincy was going to let her win the first game on purpose, she was *certain* of it. He needed to lure her in so that he could ask his ultimate question. Was the *Fomórach* more important than the reason he kept trying to convince the manor's residents to leave?

"Perhaps I will play for that answer next," Winnie conceded. "But I maintain my original question. I would like to know why you are so keen to drive us all away from Witchwood Manor."

"As you like." Mr Quincy gathered up the rest of the cards, handing them over to Winnie. He set the *Fomórach* aside at the edge of the table, as far away from himself as he could manage.

Winnie went through the remainder of the deck, removing everything below the 7s. She shuffled thoroughly, and even offered out the deck to Mr Quincy in order to let him cut the cards. Finally, she held out the deck to Robert.

"Take the top card, Mr Robert, if you please," she said. "It will be our trump suit."

Robert pulled the top card carefully, with a wary glance at Mr Quincy. He laid it out near the centre of the table, face-up, and Winnie saw that it had a golden squiggle at one corner— though rather than a number, it showed a snarling, rampant chimaera.

"The Beast of Promises," Mr Quincy observed. "Then Promises will be high."

Winnie set the card aside and dealt them both their hands. She had a sense for Mr Quincy's cards—he had a dubious hand, unlikely to win him the round. But when she proposed that they both discard, he refused and made himself vulnerable, confirming her suspicions that he intended to lose.

Winnie won three of the first five tricks. The next two rounds got her to five points, at which point Mr Quincy inclined his head at her. "Your win," he said.

"It is a relatively simple game," Winnie replied, allowing

her confidence to show upon her face. She ran her fingers through Oliver's short black hair, eliciting another purr from him. "I have earned an answer then, Mr Quincy—full and true, I believe you said?"

The butler grimaced visibly—and though he'd let her win on purpose, Winnie knew that he did not relish what he'd given up. "It is my aim to empty Witchwood Manor," he said. "The dowager is old and feeble. If all of her servants leave, then she cannot possibly fend for herself. She would be forced to leave as well... and her absence would unravel the Witchwood Knot."

Cook tightened her hands in her lap. "What has the dowager to do with the Witchwood Knot?" she asked. "She is no magician. She was not even here while the manor was being built."

"I have already answered more than fairly," Mr Quincy told them in a clipped voice. "We can play another round. Perhaps Miss Hall would like to ask your question next, Sarah Baker."

"No," said Winnie. "I would like to know about the *Fomórach*." Mr Quincy was too keen to avoid that subject, she thought, and the cards had insisted that it was one of his secrets.

Mr Quincy kept his expression carefully still. "As you wish," he said. "I maintain my previous question. Why did the dowager recommend you for your current position, Miss Hall?"

"Win the game, and I shall tell you," Winnie promised him.

This time, Winnie asked Cook to pull the top card, revealing Memories as the trump suit. She played the next few rounds straight, waiting to see whether Mr Quincy would throw another game on purpose. But he did not—and so, reluctantly, she let him win.

I want to know the question that he is leading up to, Winnie thought. *Even if I do not ultimately answer it.*

"Well, Miss Hall?" Mr Quincy asked. "Your answer?"

Winnie sighed and leaned back in her chair, with one hand on Oliver's back. "The dowager has known me for years," she said. "Though I spent time in London's workhouses, a disaster there convinced several important people to take a sudden interest in me. I was moved to a private orphanage to which the dowager contributed funds—a house run by a woman named Mrs Dun." She had to force herself to speak the next words, knowing that they would whittle away at her advantages over the butler yet again. "I was, in some respects, a ward of the old Lord Sorcier—a better man by far than the current Lord Sorcier can claim. And that is how Lady Longfell knows that I am a magician."

"You're *what?*" Robert demanded abruptly. The outburst startled Oliver in Winnie's lap, and the cat dug his claws into her thighs, hissing in Robert's general direction.

Winnie clenched her teeth together, holding Oliver carefully in place while she reached down to gently extract his claws from her housecoat. "A magician, Mr Robert," she repeated. "And it is best to *listen* when a magician gives you warnings. I could always simply steal your voice, you know." That was a lie, of course. Winnie did not specialise in any such magic. But Robert didn't need to know that—and indeed, the boy soon shut his mouth again with a snap.

Cook let out a shaky breath. "The dowager has finally called for proper help, then," she said.

"No," said Winnie. "Hardly *proper* help." She glanced at Mr Quincy, who had gone silent. There was a thoughtful expression on his narrow face which Winnie did not like. He was not angry. He was *absorbing*. He was planning. And none of that boded particularly well for them. "That is the problem with the magicians whom Lord Longfell first employed, I'd wager," Winnie continued grimly. "They were all proper gentlemen, who studied very proper magic. But magic alone is not enough to win against a faerie. Such creatures only *play* at being proper."

"Oh, I am *far* from proper," Mr Quincy agreed, with a slow, unnerving smile. His red eyes fixed upon Winnie, pinning her breathlessly against her chair. "You bought that magical perfume from elsewhere," he mused softly. "You would not be so angered by its absence if you could easily make more. Your evil cat serves you out of loyalty, and not because you command him. The old Lord Sorcier was faerie-touched... but he can't have given you *that* magic. What is *your* magic then, Miss Hall? What terribly improper spells have caught your fancy?"

Winnie dug her fingers into Oliver's fur. "More questions," she said. "You must hope that your luck holds at Écarté, Mr Quincy. I will not answer you for free."

Mr Quincy spread his hands helplessly. "Another time, perhaps," he said. A smirk crossed his lips. "We will be here when you sleep again, Miss Hall... unless, of course, you decide to let us out."

Winnie opened her mouth to reply—

—but even as she did, she became aware of distant, whistling birds and tepid sunlight shining against her closed eyelids.

She woke in her bed, unusually weary from a poor night's sleep, with the image of Mr Quincy waving her goodbye still clearly imprinted on her mind.

CHAPTER 7

Though Winnie had awoken earlier than usual, she had little desire to join the breakfast which Lady Longfell had promised to attend with her son. As such, she spent the early hours of the morning working on a letter instead, while nibbling at one of her purloined scones.

Clarimonde,

the letter began,

I have safely arrived at Witchwood Manor. To be clear, 'safety' may be relative here—but I did not overturn on the road, and the farmer who brought me up the hill on his cart did not let his ornery horse kill me (though the beast certainly gave it his very best effort).

You will be pleased to know that there are faeries here, as we suspected. The faerie who met me at the door, Mr Quincy, is even more ornery than the horse. So far, he has not killed me either; whether he intends to give it his best effort is as yet unclear.

Mr Quincy claims to be the butler at Witchwood Manor, but the mortals who live here insist that Witchwood Manor has no butler. I suspect that he is working for Someone Else. Mr Quincy has many peculiarities to him—even more so than the average faerie, I mean, which makes him very peculiar indeed. In fact, I write to ask whether you have ever met a faerie who could stand the touch of iron? Moreover: Have you ever heard of something called a fomórach?

Give Bellamira all my best, if you should see her.

All my love,
Winifred

Winnie did not mention that the perfume which Clarimonde had given her was missing. The ingredients had been expensive, and she knew that her sister did not have the money to spare in order to make more. *Perhaps if I am clever,* Winnie thought, *I can win the perfume back from Mr Quincy.*

She sealed the letter just as Margaret appeared to check

the fireplace in her room. The maid blinked as she saw that Winnie was already awake.

"Would you do me the favour of sending this for me today, from the village shop?" Winnie asked, offering over the letter. "It is a very important letter, but my ankle is still giving me trouble."

Margaret took it from her with a faint frown. "You want the letter sent from the village?" she asked. "But why?"

Winnie smiled at her wryly. "There are extra eyes at Witchwood Manor," she said. "If we had a butler, I am sure that he would find the mail to be of interest. I would prefer my correspondence to be a bit more private."

Margaret winced. "I see," she said. She tucked away the letter as she knelt before the fireplace with her bucket of ash. "I'll send it on as soon as I can, then."

Winnie fished out two shillings, holding them out in her palm. "You can keep the extra money if you manage it in the next few hours," she said.

Margaret considered that thoughtfully, before collecting the money from Winnie's outstretched hand. "I'm sure there's *something* urgent I ought to buy for the manor," she said, stashing the coins into a pocket of her apron. "I'll make the time."

Winnie made an effort to get Robert ready for breakfast and walked him down to the dining room, which had been opened up for the occasion. When she turned away to leave him there, however, Robert scowled.

"Are you not joining us?" he asked.

"I was not invited," Winnie replied smoothly. "It would be impolite for me to interject myself." She nudged Robert through the door, and headed back for the stairs before he could respond.

Winnie remained in the classroom until she could be certain that breakfast was wrapping up. Lord Longfell had indeed come by that morning—but thankfully, he did not linger as Robert joined her for his lessons.

"Today, we are discussing faerie etiquette," Winnie announced, as Robert entered the classroom. "Mr Quincy clearly intends to bait you into rudeness—in the way that faeries define rudeness, that is—and we shall not give him the opportunity."

"Father asked after you at breakfast," Robert observed, by way of reply. He crossed his arms and leaned against the wall. "He said I should invite you for next time."

Winnie arched one white-blonde eyebrow at him. "I will... keep that very generous offer in mind," she said. "Now: Do focus, Master Robert. We shall start with the basics. You must never insult a faerie directly. You may *imply* that they are foolish, for instance—but if you *call* them foolish, then they will have opportunity to punish you. This is why wise people call them the Fair Folk, even when they act with awful malice."

Robert studied Winnie for a long moment. There was a glint of slowly dawning cunning in his eyes which Winnie suspected did not bode well for either of them. "Father doesn't know you're a magician," he said. "Is that part of why you're avoiding him?"

Winnie reached up to pinch at the bridge of her nose. "You have forgotten your fears in the cold light of morning, Master Robert," she said. "But mark my words: The Witchwood Knot is far from done with us. I expect that we will both wake there again tonight. You would do well to pay attention."

"Never insult a you-know-what directly," Robert drawled back at her. "Call them fair, especially when they're being foul." A haughty expression came over his young features. "All of you are awfully certain that you know what's best for me—you and my father and my grandmama. But I didn't choose to come here, and I didn't choose to sleep in this miserable house. I'm tired of being told what to do all of the time." He straightened with a deep breath. "I'll help you keep your secrets, Miss Hall. But I want things in return."

A fresh snap of irritation uncurled in Winnie's chest. "I am *protecting* you, Master Robert," she replied tightly. "If you drive me away, then you will have no one to keep you safe from the faeries here."

"Well, perhaps I don't *require* protecting!" Robert retorted angrily. "What could they do to me, Miss Hall? Will they steal me away from here and take me somewhere I don't wish to go?" He narrowed his eyes at her. "If I had to choose, then I would rather be abducted than be forced to go to Eton—"

"Hush!" Winnie hissed at him urgently. She crossed the distance between them, lowering her voice. "You had better *hope* that Mr Quincy is not lurking anywhere nearby," she said. "Faeries take such statements very seriously, Master Robert."

Robert lifted his chin at her. "I meant every word," he assured her belligerently. "You don't even like me, Miss Hall. You're protecting me for reasons of your own. I don't mind that—but I'm not grateful, either. I'm not going to be quiet and let you run my life. The more you try to do it, the more I'll make you regret it."

Winnie stared down at him in helpless fury. This, she thought, was why she so despised children. They were all so stupid and so *certain* of themselves—so convinced that they already understood the consequences of their actions.

I cannot do this, Winnie thought dizzily. *I came here prepared to deal with faeries—not with spoiled, self-important boys.*

In fact, Winnie was just opening her mouth to declare her resignation when Robert cleared his throat to interrupt her.

"I would like to propose an alliance, Miss Hall," he told her.

Winnie snapped her mouth shut, blinking down at him.

"I will stay quiet about your magic," Robert told her. "In fact, I will be perfectly behaved, and I'll do everything you say. But in return..." He summoned up his courage with another breath. "I would like you to convince my father and my grandmama that I do not need to go to school. They don't listen to me—but they'll listen to *you*. Tell Father that I'm ahead of everyone else my age. Tell him I'm already bright enough to handle whatever he requires. I'll learn everything you have to teach me. I'll stay here with Grandmama and watch the manor. *Anything* but Eton."

It was the earnest desperation in Robert's face which gave Winnie pause. His eyes were wide, and a pleading thread had wormed its way into his voice. Gradually, the fury in her chest subsided, replaced by puzzled curiosity.

She nearly asked him why he was so terribly opposed to schooling... but it occurred to her a moment later that the answer didn't matter. Robert had offered her a fleeting, golden opportunity which she could not possibly ignore.

"I suspect that you have overestimated the extent to which your father will listen to me," Winnie said finally. "But I will earnestly try to convince both him and your grandmother that you do not require schooling. You have my word. Is that sufficient, Master Robert?"

Robert's jaw trembled as he stood before her. The proposition had taken much more of his daring than he wanted to let on—and Winnie's agreement had clearly surprised him. But finally, he nodded slowly. "That will... suffice," he said. "But I will hold you to it, Miss Hall."

"Excellent," said Winnie. She took a step back. "Then let us return to your lessons. We have quite a lot to cover."

JUST AS WINNIE HAD EXPECTED, they awoke that evening in the darkest hours to twisted faces in the walls. She had no intention of facing Mr Quincy again so soon, however—every answer she had torn from him so far had cost her dearly, and she still held hope that Clarimonde or Bellamira might be able to answer the questions that she had asked in her letter. When Cook came again to knock on her door, Winnie opened it with a careful glance down the darkened hallway.

"I will stay up here with Robert this evening," Winnie told the other woman. "You can imply to Mr Quincy that I am worried Master Robert will say something wrong. Do you believe that you can keep him distracted?"

Cook inclined her head. "I will play Beggar My Neighbour with him," she said. "He's always enjoyed that game."

Oliver, who was still curled up into a tight black circle at the end of Winnie's bed, gave an enormous yawn and thudded to the floor.

"Will you watch the hallway tonight, Oliver?" Winnie asked the cat. "I'm certain you can help keep Mr Quincy's curiosity at bay."

Oliver blinked his one good eye at Winnie and meowed. It was a high, sweet-sounding meow for such a large and ratty-looking cat. Winnie couldn't help but smile at him.

"I'll make sure you have a bowl of cream tomorrow," she promised him.

Winnie settled herself in Robert's room for the rest of the night, quietly continuing his lessons on faerie beneath the hollow eyes within the walls until the morning light awoke them both.

Winnie woke feeling less well-rested than ever, already steeling herself for breakfast with the Family... but as it turned out, she had entirely forgotten the day. Even as she hobbled down the stairs, she discovered that Robert and Lord Longfell had dressed themselves for church.

Robert was wearing a severe, adult-looking jacket and a slightly messy neck cloth—but his father's presence next to him made his childish flaws seem oddly charming, rather than disrespectful. Lord Longfell, for his part, was reminiscent of a sober country squire with an unusually expensive tailor. His windswept hair and morning coat suggested that he had been out riding, but the cut and colour of his dress was still appropriately subdued.

Lord Longfell straightened slightly as he saw Winnie. The smile that bloomed across his face sent a flicker of unease across her skin—though that expression soon took on a hint of puzzlement. "Miss Hall," he greeted her. "You are not dressed for Sunday service."

Winnie glanced down at her threadbare frock. "I have yet to wash my better gown," she said. "I doubt the Lord would mind a bit of mud, but the vicar might well do. Besides... my ankle is still healing."

Lord Longfell's eyes flickered to the toe of her foot, which currently peeked out from beneath her skirts. For want of slippers, Winnie had been forced to continue walking about the manor with only her stockings covering her feet. She curled her toes beneath the skirt and moved quickly to change the subject. "Where is the dowager, by the way?" she asked. "I have never known her to miss a good sermon. Nor have I ever known her to miss a bad one, now that I think on it further."

Lord Longfell's smile faltered. "My mother's health does not permit her to leave the manor these days," he said. "The vicar visits her once a week for homilies and tea, instead. She is still abed right now. Perhaps she would appreciate your company."

Winnie fought to keep the frown from her features. The dowager had claimed that she was dying... but somehow, the idea had not taken proper root in Winnie's mind until this moment. In London, Lady Longfell had been a tireless (and somewhat terrifying) social butterfly; that she had ceased to leave the manor entirely was a terrible omen indeed.

"I will check on her shortly," Winnie assured Lord Longfell. "I had something to discuss with her, regardless." She met Robert's eyes just past the lord's shoulder, inclining her head minutely. Though the dowager had been firm in her opinions on Eton, Winnie still believed that she would find the woman easier to convince than Lord Longfell, given their history together.

Robert's face took on a mollified expression. He drew himself up and spoke in a magnanimous tone. "I feel awfully responsible for your ankle, Miss Hall," he said. "I think more rest would be appropriate."

Lord Longfell glanced sharply at his son, searching for any hint of sarcasm in his manner. Finding none there, however, he bit back whatever warning he had been about to express.

"Perhaps I will join Lady Longfell for her homilies this week, if everyone involved will have me," Winnie said. "I would be obliged if you could pass on my interest to the vicar, Your Lordship." Winnie did not *really* have any desire to have tea with the local vicar—but pretending some amount of pious interest might blunt the gossip which was sure to follow her absence from the very first Sunday service after her arrival.

Lord Longfell inclined his head at her. "I will be sure to let him know, Miss Hall," he assured her. "We would not wish for anyone to call your faith into question."

Something about his tone and phrasing reignited Winnie's niggling unease. Surely, Lord Longfell was simply reassuring her... but was there something of a subtle threat beneath his generous air? One doubtful word from Winnie's employer to the vicar could set the entire village against her—a miserable circumstance for a governess with few other prospects and nowhere else to go.

It was maddening, Winnie thought, how difficult it was to read the man. A less paranoid woman might have taken him at his word and brushed the matter off... but Mr Quincy's warning about the monster in the Witchwood trickled back to the front of her mind. Though Mr Quincy was prone to cruel misdirection, Winnie found herself inclined to take this particular warning to heart.

There was only one appropriate response, regardless. Winnie smiled at Lord Longfell, willing a pretence at gratitude into her expression. "Thank you, Your Lordship," she said. "That sets my mind at ease."

"My mother is very fond of you, Miss Hall," Lord Longfell told her. "She would be wroth with me if I did not take special care of you. And I am sure we *both* know just how eagerly she metes out her displeasure."

Again, his choice of words jangled at Winnie's nerves. Were they slightly too bitter? Too sharp around the edges? She forced herself to maintain her smile. "I am very fond of her as well," Winnie assured him. "I suppose that I have always been indulgent of her moods—but I expect that she is harder with her own family than she is with others."

Winnie injected a healthy dose of sympathy into her tone, which Lord Longfell seemed only too pleased to absorb. "She is a monster," the lord said bluntly, "though I love her dearly." He flashed one more reassuring smile at Winnie and took his son firmly by the shoulder. "Let's not be late for service, Robert," he said.

Winnie waited until the two had disappeared through the cloister before turning back up the stairs. *Put Lord Longfell from your mind,* Winnie ordered herself sternly. *You have far more dangerous and immediate problems to worry about.*

Though she'd continued to claim injury, her ankle *was* feeling much better than before. Despite this, the narrow attic stairs pressed her hard enough to make it twinge with warning by the time she'd reached the dowager's bedroom.

Lady Longfell had yet to leave her bed. A tray of breakfast was set next to her on the bedside table—but so far as Winnie could tell, it had not been touched at all. Extra blankets had been piled atop the woman, and the fireplace was burning so feverishly high that Winnie loosened the top few buttons of her frock as she stepped inside. The dowager was drawn and pale, and her watery blue eyes were vaguely confused.

Margaret had lingered in the room after delivering breakfast; the maid sat in a chair near the bed, rubbing one of Lady Longfell's hands between her own. As Winnie entered, she glanced up sharply.

"Well now, here's Miss Hall," Margaret said with forced cheer. "I could go get her breakfast an' the two of you could eat together!"

The dowager pried her hand from Margaret's, curling it around the blanket at her shoulders. The bulky wood and iron ring she had been given looked far too large against her skeletal fingers. "I am not hungry," Lady Longfell declared with a rasp. "Miss Hall may have my breakfast; it should not go to waste. But I will speak with her alone, Margaret."

The maid bit at her lip uncertainly—but she had no authority to overrule the dowager, and so she rose to leave. "Will you please see that she eats *something?*" Margaret whispered to Winnie as she passed.

"I heard that, Miss Margaret!" the dowager barked. "I am old, not *deaf.*"

Margaret winced and scurried out the door.

Winnie frowned at the woman in the bed. The dowager's body was smaller than it should have been, and her arms were thin and brittle-looking, now that she had only a blanket to hide them. The sight of Lady Longfell in such terrible decline squeezed at Winnie's heart in a way that caught her by surprise. Though she had believed herself to be at a safe emotional remove from the dowager, the truth of the woman's illness now flooded the banks of her thoughts, tightening her throat with unexpected tears.

Winnie swallowed down the emotion with a deep breath. "You are in rare form today," she observed to the dowager. She paced over to take the chair which Margaret had so recently vacated, settling her skirts about her knees. "You do not look well."

Lady Longfell laughed hoarsely. "You dare much, now that you think me too infirm to scold you for your manners," she said. There was a faint scent of blood about her today, though Winnie could not make out any stains on her sleeping gown.

Winnie reached for the old woman's coffee and took a sip to ground her nerves. "Why make excuses for me, Lady Longfell?" she asked dryly. "I dared just as much before this. I am a heartless black magician, and I have you over a barrel, remember?"

Lady Longfell cracked a smile at the statement, and the snappish strain in her face gentled. "I needed your company today," she sighed. "You are like a lodestar, Miss Winifred. Margaret frets, and Cook will scold me... but you are simply *here*, and that is lovely."

Winnie studied the dowager over her cup. A memory forced itself to mind, unbidden: Winnie was bright and young, wearing a lovely new muslin which the dowager had gifted to her in a box which was just as lush and expensive as the clothing itself. There was a colourful ribbon in her hair, and silken slippers on her feet—all things which she had hungered for in her workhouse years, nearly as much as she hungered for food.

The dowager had smiled dotingly upon her, and asked if she would play the pianoforte. *What song should I play?* Winnie had asked her. *Whatever song it is that you love best,* the dowager had replied.

At that age, Winnie had already brutally crushed any instinctive need to please others, replacing such naïve little thoughts with calculated smiles and curtsies. But that day, a secret bit of girlish affection had escaped those stern chains, and Winnie had settled at the pianoforte with a longing to share some part of herself with the woman who had patted her so fondly on the head and showered her with indulgent gifts.

It should have occurred to her, perhaps, that the doleful faerie tune which Lady Hollowvale had taught to her in dreams was not the sort of thing which most ladies of good breeding would enjoy. But it was Winnie's favourite song, regardless, because she had worked so hard to learn its strange intricacies.

When Winnie had finished the unearthly requiem, all flushed with pleasure at her competence, she found that Lady Longfell had an odd, unreadable expression on her face, and her exuberance deflated.

"Did you... not like it?" Winnie asked her tremulously.

The dowager's expression softened, and she smiled at Winnie encouragingly. "I loved it," she assured her. "What a complicated piece. You are so talented, Miss Winifred. I doubt that any other girl your age could play something so devilishly difficult."

Winnie plucked at her new gown shyly. "It is a faerie tune," she confided in Lady Longfell, in a very soft voice. "I learned it in my dreams. You must not tell anyone, please—but it is a special song, and I wanted you to hear it."

Lady Longfell's smile broadened gently, so that her eyes crinkled at the edges. "I am duly honoured, Miss Winifred," she told her. "I will not tell a soul. But... does your guardian know that you have been dreaming of faerie tunes?"

Winnie nodded slightly. "It is why the Lord Sorcier has taken me in at all," she admitted. "He is keeping his eye on me, he said. But I am safe from faeries, Lady Longfell. I am not afraid of them, or of anything that they might teach me."

"Well, that does not surprise me, Miss Winifred," Lady Longfell said with a fond laugh. "For I have never known you to fear anything at all." She patted Winnie on the head again, as she was wont to do, and Winnie's traitorous heart warmed at the compliment.

"Thank you for playing your song for me, Miss Winifred," the dowager said solemnly. "I will treasure the memory forever."

It was the thought of that little pat on the head which

made tears prick at the edges of Winnie's eyes now, as she absorbed Lady Longfell's wasted form and trembling jaw.

"What are you thinking of, Miss Winifred?" the dowager asked, in her rasping voice. "I swear that I have never seen you look so sad."

Winnie blinked several times, trying to banish the vice that clenched at her heart. "I had not seen you for so many years," she said. "But already, I feel as though I'm going to miss you."

Lady Longfell smiled. It was a pale shadow of the smiles which she had once bestowed so often upon Winnie—but the same doting sentiment was there in her blue eyes. "I am so pleased to know that," she said. "Perhaps it is selfish of me, but I would like someone to miss me. I wonder often if my son will do. Perhaps young Robert will, at least a bit."

Winnie wiped at the stubborn tears which had gathered in her eyes. "I try never to miss people, as a rule," she said. "I do not see the point in it."

Lady Longfell was silent for a long moment. When she spoke, it was with halting thoughtfulness. "I always suspected that you were someone's child out of wedlock, Miss Winifred," she said. "You spoke so prettily, and you took your tea with manners. Your parents must have left you at the workhouse relatively late in life. I have never forgiven them for that, whoever they were."

Hearing the words spoken aloud sent a nauseating shock through Winnie's stomach, and she forced down another swallow of coffee. "I barely remember it," she lied. "Nor do I wish to speak of it. I do not have parents, Lady Longfell, and I never will. But I have had people who care for me, and that is more than some can say."

Winnie *did* remember, of course—though much of it was

hazy and uncertain. She had indeed lived in a lovely cottage with her mother, with several servants close at hand. She had taken tea with too much milk, and learned to sit up properly, and tried to be a proper lady.

Just why it was that she'd been forced to leave that little cottage, she didn't rightly know. In fact, no one had bothered to tell her. But one of the servants had dragged her to a London workhouse and checked her in without a surname... and she had never seen a ruffle or a ribbon in the years to follow, until the Hollow Lady had rescued her, and the Lord Sorcier had taken her in, and Lady Longfell had taken a liking to her and her pianoforte.

"I have not been a good woman, Miss Winifred," the dowager said wearily. "When I pass from this world, I will have much to answer for. But I like to think that I was good to *you*. I am proud of that much, and it comforts me. It was a selfish, egotistical impulse which first led me to dote upon you—but you should know that I did grow to love you, in my way. I loved everything about you. I loved your dimples, and your little curls, and even your strange, sad piano music. I never enjoyed requiems until I met you; but I learned to hear them differently after you played one for me with a smile."

Winnie had never heard the dowager speak with such open, visceral emotion in her voice, nor seen such honesty on the other woman's features. She wanted to deny the words— to tuck them down into her lockbox where they could not hurt her—but they rang with such awful truth that she could not bring herself to disbelieve them.

She knew then what she had suspected since first walking into the attic that morning.

"You are dying," Winnie said in a choked voice. "You are

dying right now—today, right in front of me. That is why you are saying all of this."

Lady Longfell chuckled weakly. "Drink my coffee, Miss Winifred," she said. "I would not like to see it go cold."

What was there to say to that? Winnie took another swallow. She kept drinking and drinking, until she had finished off the glass entirely. But the coffee sat in her stomach like a lead lump, and she knew that she was in danger of becoming a weepy mess, as any other young lady might become under the circumstances.

"Let us finish our business, as much as we are able to do," Lady Longfell said. She straightened against her pillow, injecting a last bit of firmness into her voice. "What help can I offer you, Miss Winifred, before I depart?"

Winnie clenched her jaw against the uncomfortable emotions which still roiled within her. "There are two things," she said, with only a hint of hoarseness in her voice. "I will start with the simpler request." She snatched a crumpet from the dowager's plate, worrying at it in order to settle her stomach. "Lord Longfell hired several magicians in order to combat the faeries in the Witchwood. The last magician advised him to build Witchwood Manor. Do you remember him at all? Could you tell me his name, Lady Longfell?"

The dowager frowned deeply. "I... did not know that my son was hiring magicians," she admitted. "But there was an awful parade of arrogant scholars, now that you explain it to me." She knitted her brow and tried to think. "There was a man who greatly unsettled me. I wish I could recall his name for you, but I only met him once."

Winnie pressed her lips together. "Do you remember what he looked like?" she asked. "What unsettled you about him?"

Lady Longfell closed her eyes. After a moment, she spoke

very slowly. "He was so pale and unhealthy," she murmured. "Like a corpse. But he was beautiful, all the same. I don't know how else to describe it. I could have stared at him for hours, and it would have made me sick to my stomach." She pressed a shaking hand over her eyes. "He smelled of blood. That is what I remember. I wanted nothing more to do with him."

Winnie's eyes widened fractionally at that. Somehow, the description reminded her of Mr Quincy... but no. She would not have described the butler as sickeningly beautiful in any sense. Still, she prodded at the dowager again. "Did he have reddish eyes?" she asked. "Were his manners surly and unpleasant?"

Lady Longfell opened her eyes again, still frowning. "His eyes... yes, perhaps they were red," she said—but her tone was doubtful now. "But his manners were unimpeachable. Too much so. Everything he did was cold and perfect. I had no rational reason to believe it... but I could swear he thought I was amusing."

Could that possibly describe Mr Quincy? Winnie wondered, with her heart in her throat. *But he has been here for ages now. And why would he trap himself within the Witchwood Knot? He is so clearly angry about his situation.*

"That is all I can remember," Lady Longfell said apologetically. "I had put him from my mind on purpose, I believe."

Winnie jerked her head into a nod. "That is... still helpful, Lady Longfell," she assured the woman. "I will make use of it, I am certain."

The dowager shivered and clutched the blanket more tightly around herself. "You said you had another request," she observed. "Do make it while you can, Miss Winifred."

Winnie had to suppress the urge to snap at her. *You are*

being overdramatic now, she wanted to say. But if there were ever a time to be overdramatic, Winnie supposed, it would be when one was dying.

"You must convince your son that Robert need not go to Eton," Winnie told her bluntly. "Today, it seems, since time is short."

The dowager let out a sharp gasp. "What?" she asked. "But that's nonsensical. Robert *must* go to school. His future will suffer if he does not. And it will take him away from this place, which is the greater need."

Winnie met her gaze flatly. "Master Robert is adamant on the matter," she said. "He has promised to do everything I ask, if it is sorted—and *nothing* that I ask, if it is not. I believe that he is just stubborn enough to keep his word."

Now, the dowager was noticeably distressed. "But... he must leave Witchwood Manor in September," she said. "He *must.*"

Winnie nodded. "Surely, Lord Longfell can bring Robert back to London," she said. "There are fine tutors there who can teach him everything he would have learned at Eton. But even if Robert stays at Witchwood Manor, I will teach him everything I can about the faeries here. Someday, Lady Longfell, he will inherit this problem regardless. Schooling will not teach him how to deal with it... but perhaps I can."

Lady Longfell drifted into silence, worrying at her bottom lip with her teeth. A hint of blood now welled up where she chewed—the skin was noticeably thinner than ever.

"You swore that you would pay a dreadful cost for this," Winnie told her. "If Eton is the payment, Lady Longfell, then I *assure* you that it is an excellent trade."

The dowager let out a soft groan at the reminder. The idea seemed to pain her nearly as much as her illness did. But to her credit, she swallowed down the observation. "I will... ask my son today," she said, with great reluctance. "I will tell him that it is my dying wish. He cannot possibly ignore that."

Winnie let out a slow breath. "Then I will do my best to tutor Robert," she said. "I cannot promise that he will prevail over the things in this manor... but he will have every possible tool at his disposal. That is all that anyone can hope for when it comes to faeries."

Lady Longfell sighed. "Imperfect options are so very infuriating," she said. "But I have learned to live with several of them in the last few years." She hunched beneath her blanket, looking weary once again. "Will you keep me company until my son returns, Miss Winifred? That is how I would like to spend my morning, most of all."

"I will, of course," Winnie assured her. "Your breakfast is far too delicious to pass up." She reached for another crumpet... but found herself pausing, with her fingers closed around it.

Winnie took in a breath.

"I... do not know if I am capable of loving anyone," she said quietly. "But if I *am* capable of love, Lady Longfell... then I fear that I have loved you far better than I ever intended to do."

The dowager offered her a misty smile. "I should have bought you some new ribbons when you came here," she said absently. "I will leave you some of my nicest gowns, Miss Winifred. Do promise that you will wear them."

"I will wear them," Winnie promised.

～

ROBERT and his father returned some hours later. Winnie suspected that Margaret must have warned Lord Longfell of the dowager's decline—for she heard several people's heavy steps upon the attic stairs, at a far quicker pace than was usual.

Barely had Lord Longfell set eyes upon his mother before his face went pale, and he ordered Winnie to fetch Margaret once again. Winnie left the dowager with one last reluctant squeeze of her withered hands.

She discovered Robert just outside the attic bedroom's door, peering inside with naked distress on his young features. Lord Longfell caught sight of him, and he gestured sharply at Winnie. "For God's sake—get him out of here!" he ordered.

Winnie startled at the edge in his voice. Somehow, in the dizzy chaos which followed, she found herself corralling Robert gently down the stairs.

Lord Longfell soon called for the vicar—and then, on afterthought, for a physician. It was clear from his manner that he did not expect a physician to solve what plagued his mother, but there was some hope that medicine might ease her passing.

Winnie sat for several hours with Robert in his bedroom, as the day stretched on. For once, there was no hint of haughtiness in his expression; rather, there was fear, and worry, and no small amount of misery. More than once, he asked if he might go upstairs to see his grandmama—but Lord Longfell would not hear of anyone but those most strictly necessary joining him at the dowager's bedside.

Instead, Winnie held Robert awkwardly against her side and encouraged him to eat a pilfered crumpet from Lady Longfell's breakfast. As the afternoon dragged on into evening, she told him more faerie tales—pleasant ones, instead of fearful ones—and promised him that soon they would go walking through the Witchwood so that he could climb the trees there.

"Could magic save my grandmama?" Robert rasped, as Winnie held him against her.

Winnie winced. "I do not know of any," she told him truthfully. "One of my sisters is a necromancer—you must not tell anyone about that, Master Robert—but even she cannot preserve a life when it is fading."

Robert stared at her blankly. "But... perhaps a *faerie* could save her?" he asked. "They can do all manner of impossible things, from what you've told me."

Winnie chewed at her lip. This was a dangerous line of questioning, and she knew it. "They cannot," she told him. "I swear this to you, Master Robert, on my life: Only Lady Longshadow has the power to conquer death, and she may do so only once a century. She has already given that gift quite recently. I could tell you the story if you wanted."

Robert's expression crumpled at the assurance. "But you could find her," he pleaded. "You could ask her, just this once—"

Winnie hugged him more tightly. "I would do it for you if I could," she promised him—and in that moment, it was true. "I promise that I would, Master Robert. But I cannot. All of the faeries in England have disappeared. All of the ways that I once would have travelled into faerie have closed. That is why I am here in the first place. I am searching for them, Master Robert—for the Hollow Lady, and for Mr Jubilee of Blackthorn, and for Lady Longshadow. But all that I have found so far is the Witchwood Knot."

Robert shivered against her, and his tears began to wet the

shoulder of her frock. "I'll ask Mr Quincy," he rasped. "I'll give him whatever he wants, if he can show you the way into faerie."

Winnie froze, with her heart in her throat. It wasn't just the dire words—and they *were* quite dire. Rather, it was the knowledge that some ruthless, mercenary part of her was considering how useful it would be to take Robert up on his offer. If there was indeed a way into faerie from the Witchwood Knot, she knew that Mr Quincy would accept the bargain in a heartbeat.

There was no reasonable way for Winnie to find Lady Longshadow before the dowager passed. Nor did she truly believe that the faerie could offer the gift of life again so soon. But she had told all of this to Robert, after all, and if he insisted on making his desperate bargain regardless, then surely Winnie could not be held responsible for the results—

I will not harm a child, Winnie thought to herself firmly. *No, not even an annoying one. What on earth would the Hollow Lady think of me then?*

"Do not ask Mr Quincy for *anything*, Master Robert," Winnie told the boy instead. "Listen to me: He will gladly bargain with you. He will let you offer him the world, and he will give you *nothing* in return. That is the sort of faerie that he is. Remember how he took advantage of you and tricked your name from you. Remember that he offered you a poisoned bit of fruit."

Winnie could tell that the words were not penetrating. She dug her fingers into Robert's shoulder and sucked in a breath. There was only one more way that she could think of to get through to him. "I am so ashamed of you right now, Master Robert," she said in a clipped voice.

Robert looked up at her sharply.

"Your grandmama has gone to such great lengths to keep you safe from Mr Quincy," Winnie told him. "She has spent the last days of her life on you. How dare you throw that all away so easily? She would be so upset to hear you speak this way."

Robert's eyes filled with fresh tears. "I... I don't know what else to do, Miss Hall," he choked out. "What else should I do?"

Winnie swallowed hard. "You should... do what you can to honour her wishes," she said. "That is what she wants from you, Master Robert. It is what she said to me today, when I was with her."

This was a lie, of course. The dowager had said that what she wanted most was to be missed. But it was... a truthful lie. Winnie was absolutely certain that it was what the dowager would have *wanted* her to tell Robert, in order to protect him.

Robert nodded mutely. He buried his face against Winnie's shoulder once again, too helpless to do anything else.

It was a very long night of very awful waiting. Had Winnie been left to her own devices, she was sure that she would have endured it all with relative stoicism. But something about keeping Robert company and seeing his childish reactions made it impossible for her to properly numb herself to the affair.

Yet somehow—impossibly—Winnie blinked and found herself within a darkened, ominous version of Robert's bedroom.

Twisted, screaming faces looked down upon her from the walls and ceiling, clashing with the stained glass window's cheerful daffodils. But though Winnie now suspected that she'd drifted off to sleep despite herself, Robert's smaller form was nowhere to be seen, suggesting that he might be still awake.

Winnie cursed her own weariness—but she had no idea how to wake herself from here. The best that she could do was stay right where she was and hope that Robert would soon join her.

A firm knock sounded at the door, and Winnie rose to answer it. "Master Robert has not joined me yet," she started, as she opened it. "I think that I should stay here until he does—"

But it was not Cook who stood on the other side of Robert's bedroom door this time. Rather, it was a wan but cheerful younger woman, with coal black hair piled into a messy bun atop her head. Her deep brown eyes had been carefully traced with makeup in order to make her appear older than she was, though nothing could obscure the adorable effect of her small, button-like nose. The black cat which currently purred in her arms was barely visible among the mess of sober black widow's weeds that drowned his form.

"Oh, good, I *have* found you!" Bellamira breathed excitedly. "Hullo there, Winnie. I've managed to die again, just in the nick of time!"

CHAPTER 8

*W*innie stared at Bellamira, utterly aghast. "What on *earth* are you doing here?" she demanded.

Bellamira beamed at her, unfazed. Oliver stretched dramatically in her arms, still purring with absolute feline contentment. "Clarimonde read me your letter," she said. "I was awfully worried about what it said, and I couldn't wait for the post to warn you, so I asked Hugh to help me die—just a little bit, obviously—and then I used your hair to project myself and find you in your dreams, just like Lady Hollowvale used to do!" She tilted her head quizzically at Winnie, barely pausing for breath between words. "What *is* this dream, by the by? It's awfully grim, even for you—"

Winnie hauled Bellamira into Robert's room, slamming the door unceremoniously behind her. Oliver yowled in protest as Bellamira's arms slipped and dropped him to the floor. "We are in some pocket realm of faerie!" Winnie hissed. "I'm not at all certain that you can get back again, Bellamira! And—what do you mean, you asked Hugh to help you *die?*"

Bellamira blinked. "Oh, it's not as terrible as it sounds!"

131

she assured Winnie hastily. "I die in worse ways all of the time, you *know* that. This is really *barely* dying by comparison. I asked Hugh to give me more of my medicine than usual, so that I would sleep on the very edge of death. My body is perfectly cosy right now, back in London!"

Winnie sputtered for a moment with incoherent rage. "And he *humoured* you?" she asked. "I swear, as soon as I have a chance, I'll march straight back to London and kill *him* just a little bit—"

Bellamira rolled her eyes. "I told him I would do it to myself if he didn't," she said. "That's the only way I can ever convince any of you to stop arguing with me, you know. He's the physician, of course, so the dosage is much safer when *he* does it. Now, Winnie, I did *not* mostly die just so that you could yell at me. I have some very important things to tell you, and the sooner that you listen, the sooner I can go back to my body."

Winnie shut her mouth with a soft, frustrated click of her teeth.

There was a reason Bellamira had gravitated so naturally to necromancy. As a child, she had caught almost every debilitating illness in the workhouses—and while she had somehow survived them all, her heart had paid a permanent price. Winnie had tried everything under the sun to convince Bellamira to live a restful life, so as not to aggravate her condition... but every time she turned around, it seemed, Bellamira had pushed the limits once again and had another awful attack.

Mr Hugh Wilder—another of the old Lord Sorcier's wards —was now a well-respected physician in London. Though he was old enough to seem more like a cousin than a brother,

Winnie normally expected far better from him than to indulge one of Bellamira's self-destructive whims.

"Good," Bellamira said breezily. "You've seen some sense, then." She brushed some of Oliver's fur off the front of her dramatic black gown. "As I was saying before you interrupted me—you asked Clarimonde about a *fomórach*."

Winnie stiffened, suddenly alert. "I did," she said. "You've heard the term?"

Bellamira nodded seriously. "That's why I'm here," she said. "You know I spent some time in Longshadow, with the sluagh. They told me stories that I never knew I'd need to share." Oliver dropped to the floor in front of her, rolling over to show his belly with a plaintive meow. Bellamira knelt down absently to rub there. "Oh, you're really here then, aren't you, Oliver?" she said, distracted. "What a good boy you are! I hope you've been making sure Winnie doesn't get *too* grumpy—"

"*Bellamira!*" Winnie interrupted shortly. "Finish what you were saying, for goodness' sake, so you can go back to your body!"

Bellamira blinked. "Oh, yes!" she said. "The *fomóraig*. They are something dead, or... no, they *cannot* die, is what the sluagh said. You could chop them up into little pieces, and they'd only pull themselves back together all over again."

Winnie grimaced. "You say that so cheerfully," she muttered.

"Well, it *is* a fascinating thing to dangle in front of a necromancer," Bellamira admitted. "But because the *fomóraig* cannot die, the faeries put them all to sleep forever. I'm afraid the stories are all fuzzy to me now—I wish that I could tell you how or why it happened. All I know is that the *fomóraig* sleep beneath the mounds in faerie, and everyone is very careful not to wake them up. I asked what would happen if they *did* wake up, and Lady Longshadow said that we would all regret it."

Winnie pressed her lips together. A horrible, sinking suspicion had now begun to form in her mind. "So the *fomóraiġ* are not faeries at all," she said slowly. "They are something else entirely. And they are not afraid of iron either, are they?"

Bellamira snapped her fingers. "They are not!" she said. "In fact, their magic feeds on blood and iron! That is part of why the faeries fear them, I expect—that magic must be miserably poisonous to them."

Winnie closed her eyes. "There was a *fomórach* here, Bellamira," she said quietly. "I think Lord Longfell made a bargain with it, whether he understood what it was or not. That is why the Witchwood Knot exists. That is why the faeries here are trapped." She opened her eyes again, feeling bleak. "And maybe that is why the faeries have all disappeared from England."

Bellamira sobered. "Oh," she said. "Oh my."

"I would use stronger language," Winnie offered hollowly.

Bellamira straightened again, despite Oliver's rolling, meowing protests at her feet. "But what on earth are we supposed to do with that?" she asked worriedly. "Even if we *could* find a way still open into faerie... do you really think a handful of black magicians is enough to handle something of that nature?"

Winnie looked away. "I haven't the first idea," she admitted softly. "But I owe a debt to the Hollow Lady, Bellamira. I must try to help her, even if I fail. And that means finding a way into faerie through the Witchwood Knot."

Bellamira nodded slowly. "Well... I would be *awfully*

embarrassed to die of a silly fainting spell when I could die annoying some undying evil instead," she offered, suddenly cheerful once again. "What a lovely idea that is, actually. Oh! Now that I think about it—do you think that is what all of the ghosts here are screaming about?"

Winnie blinked and glanced around them. "Ghosts?" she asked. "I don't see any ghosts—other than Oliver, of course."

Bellamira gestured expansively. "The faces in the walls?" she clarified. "Can you not see them?"

Winnie's mouth dropped open. "They're *ghosts?*" she asked. "I honestly had no idea!" She paused, frowning. "I didn't even know that faeries *could* leave ghosts."

Bellamira shook her head. "Faeries *can't* leave ghosts," she said. "These are all human—and they are *very* prickly indeed. Why, they're screaming so loudly for vengeance that I might be deaf when I wake up."

Winnie focussed on her sharply. "For vengeance?" she asked. "Do you know who it is that they are after, Bellamira?"

"Oh, they want vengeance against *everyone,*" Bellamira assured Winnie, as she straightened out her widow's weeds. "But they are screaming about a lord and a lady in particular. I would need to come here in person in order to calm them down and ask them better questions."

"You will *not,*" Winnie said flatly. But since she knew that such commandments meant relatively little to Bellamira, she added: "You will want to be as strong as possible by the time I find our passage into faerie."

Bellamira made a face at her. "You *will* be taking me with you," she warned. "If you try to leave me behind, then I will only come after you all by myself."

Winnie scowled at her. "Oh, *do* go home, Bellamira," she

said. "Hugh and Clarimonde will need to know about all of this when you wake up."

Bellamira smiled at her, entirely unfazed. "I will tell them that you send your love," she said. "Now... let us see if I can wiggle my way out of this knot..."

Clearly, Bellamira must have managed *something*—because in the very next instant, Winnie was alone in Robert's room with the ghosts of the Witchwood Knot.

~

WINNIE LINGERED in Robert's room for a while longer, pacing with unusual agitation. Oliver perched himself neatly on the edge of the bed, following her steps with a curious one-eyed gaze, as though trying to discern the purpose of the exercise.

There was no purpose, of course. There was only dread, and helpless frustration over all of the things which Winnie could not currently control. Somewhere out there in the real Witchwood Manor, the dowager was still dying—or perhaps she had already passed away—and Robert was sitting in his room, awake and alone. Winnie did not even know if Bellamira had made it safely back to her body in London, or whether Hugh had managed to wake her properly again.

And lingering beneath it all like a sinister mirage was the prospect of an ancient *fomórach*, awake and wandering England once again.

"Mr Quincy knows all about this, I am certain," Winnie muttered to Oliver tightly. "That smell of blood he carries with him, and the way he walks about disdaining iron... perhaps he is a *fomórach* himself. If so, then he has been awake for ages—and yet, he's lingered in the Witchwood in order to serve some terrible lady."

Oliver licked languorously at one paw as she spoke, looking far less concerned with the entire matter than Winnie thought he ought to be.

Winnie let out a sharp breath. "I cannot afford to wait much longer, Oliver," she said. "Mr Quincy is about to have his wish—the dowager will pass tonight, if she has not done already. And what will happen then?" She shook her head. "I am going downstairs. I know you are not fond of boys, but could you guard the hallway for me while I'm gone, in case Master Robert finally falls asleep?"

Oliver paused partway through grooming his paw. Perhaps it was just Winnie's imagination—but she thought she saw his one eye narrow dangerously.

"You may hiss at Robert if he tries to leave the room," Winnie told the cat helpfully. "I need him to stay safe tonight, after all."

Oliver stretched his body with a tiny growl. But eventually, he hopped off the bed and slunk towards the hallway with more than a hint of reluctance.

Winnie leaned down to scratch at his back as he passed. "Thank you very much, Ollie," she murmured softly. "I know how much he frightens you. If he lays even a finger on you, I will make him terribly regret it."

Oliver arched briefly into her touch, taking obvious comfort from her closeness, before he padded out the door.

Winnie sighed heavily, and started for the stairs.

She heard the ruckus in the conservatory well before she reached its doorway. The faeries there had devolved to dancing, despite the crowded furniture and the strychnine trees. An unearthly band of musicians stood upon the tables, piping shrill notes which sounded more like mocking laughter than like music. Beneath it all, the house's warm breath whispered, strangely laboured, stuttering dangerously back and forth across Winnie's skin.

This time, Winnie did not have Oliver with her—and so the faeries did not part for her, as they had done before. Instead, they fixed her with spiteful expressions, going out of their way to block her path and buffet her about the room. Winnie gritted her teeth and tried to focus on forcing her way through, searching for Mr Quincy among the press of violently hateful faeries.

The dizzy crowd of bodies drew closer and closer—and before Winnie had quite realised what was happening, she found herself at the centre of a tight circle, penned in on every side by ominous creatures.

"It is the governess!" crowed a raspy, rustling voice.

"Come and play a game with us, governess!" another laughed.

Strong hands grasped at Winnie's shoulders from behind —another faerie forced a long strip of black crepe around her eyes, winding it tightly over and over until she could see nothing at all.

"Hot Cockles!" a melodious voice called out. "I am sure I know the rules to this one!"

Someone slapped Winnie across the face, so hard that she staggered backwards. She clutched at her cheek, trying frantically to reorient herself.

"Who has slapped you, governess?" the rustling voice laughed.

"I don't know," Winnie replied dazedly. "I don't know any of your names."

"Well, that is hardly *our* fault, is it?" a man's voice taunted. "You never bothered to ask!"

Another hand struck her, hard enough to throw her to the

floor. Winnie forced herself up to her knees, trying to think through her panic. Tearing off the blindfold would only make them angrier... but even if the faeries had been playing Hot Cockles properly, her only means of winning would be to guess a name that she had no reasonable way of knowing.

Someone kicked at Winnie, catching her along the ribs. The air rushed from her lungs as she hit the floor again, gasping desperately for breath.

"Who has kicked you, governess?" asked a breathy voice. "Tell us... or perhaps give us a forfeit?"

Winnie pressed her lips together. Given the vicious mood that these faeries were currently in, she doubted greatly that someone would ask her for a simple kiss upon the cheek.

There were no easy answers to her current dilemma. Sometimes, faerie cruelty was simply inescapable.

"I guess... that an ugly beast has kicked me," Winnie replied breathlessly. "Is that accurate?"

A handful of titters went up among the faeries. The game had offered Winnie an opportunity to insult her assailants indirectly, since her words were merely guesses and not accusations.

The next kick was harder and more punishing.

"Who has kicked you, governess?" an angry voice hissed at her. "Give us a forfeit, foolish mortal!"

"I suspect that a dullard has kicked me," Winnie gasped. "A faerie with no wits about them, who must resort to violence instead of cleverness to have their way. Tell me—have I guessed correctly?"

Long wooden fingers grasped at Winnie's hair, wrenching her up to her feet. She flinched in expectation of another slap... but long seconds passed, and she soon realised that none would be forthcoming.

The shrill, piping flutes had suddenly ceased. The laughter around Winnie had faded, slipping into strange, uncomfortable whispers.

The house's breath caught, stuttering along the back of her neck.

Quiet footsteps sounded in the silence, drifting closer to Winnie. The wooden hand tightened in her hair, but did not drop her, as an unseen figure halted just in front of her.

A gloved hand pressed gently to her cheek, where her skin still stung. The scent of blood and bay berry trickled against her senses—and a sudden, unexpected relief loosened at the knot in Winnie's chest.

"Mr Quincy," she whispered—though no one had yet asked her for a name.

"Well guessed, governess," Mr Quincy said.

The wooden hand in Winnie's hair released her. She staggered slightly in place—but the butler caught her with a careful arm around her waist. A moment later, he tugged the black crepe from her eyes.

The circle of faeries which had tightened around Winnie was now distant and wary. There was fear on the air, Winnie realised. The faeries of the Witchwood Knot watched Mr Quincy as hares might watch a predator, ready to flee at any moment.

Mr Quincy tensed imperceptibly beneath their attention… but one never would have known it from the way that he appeared to ignore them, glancing down at Winnie with those wine-red eyes. "I am owed another game of cards, Miss Winifred Hall," he said. "I do not intend to wait on the whims of your other playmates."

The pronouncement sent faeries slinking warily back to their tables. The dancing, it seemed, had ceased.

Winnie swallowed and steadied herself. As soon as she had done so, Mr Quincy pulled back his arm, settling into a proper posture. He stayed within reach of her, however, as he led her back to his empty table near the white-draped pianoforte and pulled out a chair for her.

Winnie collapsed into the chair, clutching at her bruised ribs. Mr Quincy sat across from her; despite his statement, he had yet to produce his deck of cards.

"You should not have come here tonight," Mr Quincy told her quietly. "If you were wise, you would be halfway back to London."

Winnie studied him with great intensity. There was no obvious, frenetic excitement on his pale features, as was the case with the other faeries here. "You don't seem pleased," Winnie rasped. "I thought you would be. Surely, you know that the dowager is dying. You need no longer try to drive her away. Soon, she will be gone."

"I know," Mr Quincy replied tonelessly. "Sarah Baker sits awake tonight. The lord of Witchwood Manor trembles at what soon will come. But we will not be released tonight, whatever the others may believe. Soon, perhaps—but not tonight." He levelled a serious crimson look at her. "You still have time to flee."

Winnie rubbed at her cheek with a wince. "I cannot flee, Mr Quincy," she said. "Though I am... curious that you worry for my sake. I doubt the other faeries here care much at all what happens to the humans in the manor."

Mr Quincy remained silent—and for a moment, Winnie thought she saw that worry pinching at his narrow face. He forced himself to smooth it over. "I do not crave suffering for its own sake," he said finally. "I have seen too much of it already, and I am weary of its taste. But do not mistake my preferences for weakness, Miss Winifred Hall." His tone sharpened with awful bleakness. "I will not protect you when the Witchwood Knot is broken. I will stand by and be silent as the lady vents her fury upon you for a hundred years and more."

Winnie dropped her hands to the table before her, clasping them together. Whether Mr Quincy was technically capable of lying or not, she *heard* the truth in his voice.

"Let us play a game of Écarté, Mr Quincy," she said softly. "But let it be our last. If you win, then I will answer whatever question it is that you have been craving most—but if I win, then I would like a favour from you."

Mr Quincy's red-eyed gaze sharpened upon her. "A favour will not save you, Miss Hall," he said bluntly. "You should know the limits of what you will have. The others here may fear me, but I am bound by powerful bans; I cannot harm a living thing directly."

"If a favour from you is of such little worth," Winnie reasoned, "then you will not grudge me the chance the earn it." She lifted her eyes to his. "What question will you ask me?"

Mr Quincy gave up his last attempt to persuade her; Winnie saw the desire to do so drain from his features, replaced by an icy hardness. She knew then that the butler would waste no more pity on her. He drew the faerie deck from his pocket. "I would like to know your greatest fear," he said, "so that I may visit it upon you."

Winnie sucked in a soft breath. This, she thought, was not an idle threat. Perhaps Mr Quincy could not directly harm her... but he was more than clever enough to turn her fears into an endless waking nightmare with his other powers.

"I believe that is a fair enough trade," said Winnie. "But my favour from you shall be dear indeed, if I should win."

Mr Quincy shrugged his shoulders and offered out the cards. "Prepare the deck, Miss Hall," he said.

Winnie went through the cards, pulling out those which they would not be using. She lingered over the *Fomórach* for an extra moment when she found it, thinking of the man who currently watched her. The card's ominous fate tickled at her senses, reminding her of horrible, sleeping things which could not die.

Finally, however, Winnie turned over the first card.

"Our trump is Fears tonight," she said. "That does seem fitting." The house's breath tickled at the card, making it flutter halfheartedly.

Mr Quincy did not bother to reply. His manner had grown colder towards her by the second, despite their game.

Winnie dealt them both their first hand of cards in silence. This time, Mr Quincy did not make himself intentionally vulnerable; rather, his play was sharp and skilful, and Winnie knew that any other mortal player would have found themselves in trouble.

He was being relatively kind to me before, Winnie realised. *As much as any faerie is ever really kind.* Despite his cruel tricks, Mr Quincy had not been nearly as terrible to Winnie as was within his capabilities. But that gentle handling had all but disappeared. They were truly enemies now, in a way that Winnie could not yet fully appreciate.

Winnie did not dare to let herself lose the first round—not even to inflate his confidence. Even with her perfect knowledge of the cards on the table, she only managed to win a single point.

"You are a better card player than you pretended to be," Mr Quincy observed, as Winnie collected up the cards.

"I could say the same of you," Winnie replied. "We are both

liars, Mr Quincy, even if you always tell the truth." She glanced up at him as they began their next trick, calculating her next words carefully. "And on that note... I am not entirely certain that you *do* tell the truth. Can the *fomóraig* tell lies?"

Mr Quincy froze, halfway to choosing his next card—and Winnie saw that she had aimed the words well. His face drained of what little colour it possessed, and his jaw clenched visibly.

"That is what you are, then," Winnie said, with exaggerated calm. "That is why these faeries fear you. But you have been here, wide awake, since well before Lord Longfell made his bargain. Perhaps you could have fought the other *fomórach* who trapped you here, if you were not banned from harming living things... but if the *fomóraig* cannot die, then can it really be said that they are alive at all?"

Mr Quincy's grip now tightened so badly that the cards in his hand began to crease. Had the stakes not been so high, Winnie might have felt a pang of guilt at the way the ruthless jab affected him—but he had made it clear that he was no longer in a mood to offer mercy, himself.

"You think yourself so clever, Miss Winifred Hall," he said in a low, dark tone. "Your confidence is born of my benevolence so far. If you truly knew the depths of what you speak about, you would not be so blithe."

Winnie took the round. She had won two points so far. "I do not fear you just because you cannot die," she taunted him. "If you were truly that unspeakable, then you would not be trapped at all."

As she reached out to collect the cards, Mr Quincy's hand flashed out to grasp her wrist. "You suggested before that we should use your deck of cards," he observed. "What sort of governess carries a deck of cards upon her person at all times?" His fingers tightened painfully. "But a magician never leaves her tools behind. You are a diviner, and a cartomancer."

Winnie kept her face calm—but her heart began to pound more quickly, and she knew that he could feel it in her pulse.

"What if I was?" she asked. "We set no rules to do with magic."

Mr Quincy offered her a smile that was far too bland. "We could both use magic going forward," he said. "Or else... we can both agree to play without it."

Winnie pressed her lips together. The threat was clear— Mr Quincy could greatly complicate matters with his illusions, if he was so-inclined. The game might well spiral out of her control entirely, that way.

"I will keep my points," she said, biting off the words reluctantly. "I fooled you fairly, after all. But for the rest of the game, there will be no magic on either side."

Mr Quincy inclined his head at her. "Let us see how well you play without assistance," he said.

Winnie couldn't help the grimace which tugged at her lips as she slowly collected the cards and reshuffled. The feeling of dealing blind was somehow even more unsettling to her than Mr Quincy's dire threats.

This time, the trump suit was Desires. In a truly fortunate turn, Winnie soon realised that she had dealt herself a hand which included the suit's Oracle—the highest of the faerie court cards.

"I have the Oracle of Desires," said Winnie, turning the card around to show it to Mr Quincy. "I mark it for a point."

"You are at three points, then," Mr Quincy drawled. "Good. I expect that you will need them. If you have always relied upon your magic to win, then your skill is likely lacking in its absence."

Winnie let the barb sweep past her. But somewhere in the back of her mind, she began to wonder what she would do if she lost the game.

I can win two points from him, Winnie told herself. *I have no choice but to manage it—so I will do it.*

Despite this exhortation, she lost the next round miserably, while struggling to adjust her thinking. Mr Quincy took four of the five tricks; the only thing preventing him from winning all five was her Oracle of Desires, which no card of his could take.

Mr Quincy soundly thrashed her once again in the next round, for another point. He was so swiftly making progress that Winnie knew she had to take a different tack entirely.

Écarté was all about risk and reward. Mr Quincy was normally an excellent judge of risk... but all Winnie needed to do in order to change that was to remind him of matters which made him hesitate.

"You cannot bring yourself to be as cruel as you would like to Cook," Winnie murmured over her cards. "She has always been kind to you, hasn't she? I imagine that kindness is not a common thing in faerie, especially for you."

Mr Quincy *did* hesitate—so briefly that Winnie might have missed it if she had not been specifically looking for it. He wavered between discards, before finally choosing two.

"Perhaps that is the true tragedy," the butler said, as he arranged his cards in his hand. "She will come to regret it, in the end."

Winnie started the first trick with one of her middling cards. "And will you stand by silently when the Witchwood Knot is broken, and the faeries come for *her?*" she asked.

Mr Quincy stared down at the table, suddenly less certain of his choices than he had been. Clearly, he did not have a card which could win the trick—he was trying to choose which one he would throw away, instead. "I will," he said finally. "I have warned her many times." He forced himself to choose a card, and Winnie took the trick.

The hesitations had cost him. Mr Quincy had misjudged his choices and overplayed his hand. Winnie took another point from him this round, leaving him with two points against her four.

"I am not *strictly* certain that you want to break the Witchwood Knot at all," Winnie observed, as she dealt them both new cards. "That is to say... you clearly want your freedom. But it will also cost you dearly."

"You think I don't know what you're doing, Miss Hall?" Mr Quincy asked in a clipped voice. "Your strategy is obvious."

Winnie arched a brow at him. "I am playing the game as it was meant to be played," she said. "Did you think that humans all sat around in drawing rooms playing cards in silence?" She chose her next card firmly, setting it down at the centre of the table. "Come now, Mr Quincy. Are you upset that I am telling the *truth* now, instead of lying? Do please make up your mind."

Mr Quincy's tail thrashed once against the arm of his chair. Winnie saw him try to calm himself—but she had no intention of offering him the space to do so. "It is your play, Mr Quincy," she said. "You must choose a card—or else, perhaps, you'd care to forfeit?"

The butler met her card with exaggerated stiffness. He had not yet regained himself, despite his best efforts.

The house's breathing stuttered again. This time, it rattled the walls with a rasping sound. The faeries in the conservatory all went silent, focussed on the sound with predatory sharpness.

The gentle breeze rose, just one more time... and then, it died entirely.

The conservatory remained silent... but there was a tight and growing swell of excitement upon the air. Mr Quincy's red gaze stared past Winnie's shoulder at the doorway of the room. The pungent scent of rotting leaves now filtered into the room, growing stronger on the still, dead air. Out of the corner of her eye, Winnie saw a long, thin shadow fall upon the gathering—but she did not dare to turn and look at it directly. Instead, she took the trick in front of her... and with it, her final point.

"I have won the game this time," she said.

Mr Quincy did not respond, as she had been expecting. Instead, he rose slowly from his chair and walked out towards the entrance of the conservatory, with an odd sense of trepidation in his movement. He halted there, and fell into a deep, respectful bow.

"Good evening, Your Ladyship," he said quietly. "We did not know that you would be joining us tonight."

"Good evening, Mr Quincy," a woman's voice replied. It was low and hollow, and mostly toneless—like an echo from a deep, dark well. "I am here to celebrate a death."

Winnie turned very slowly, so as not to draw attention to herself.

The woman in the doorway was tall and rail-thin—too much so even to pretend at being human. Her eyes were wide and coal black, all the way to the edge of her sclera. A tattered mourning gown hugged at her unnatural form, spilling out behind her. Skeletal wooden fingers arched from her black hair in a grasping crown, reaching for the ceiling of the conservatory.

A horrible, sinking realisation came upon Winnie as she took in the sight of the faerie before her. Though she had never seen her before, she had heard her described in perfect, exacting detail.

I have missed the obvious, Winnie thought. *Of all people, I should have known.*

"Will you play a song to liven up our gathering?" Lady Mourningwood asked Mr Quincy, in her flat and joyless voice.

The butler inclined his head deeply in reply and headed for the white-draped pianoforte, pulling the Holland cover from it in a single quick motion.

The pianoforte in the Witchwood Knot was black and twisted, like the faerie woman's crown. Its keys were fashioned out of sickly yellow ivory.

Mr Quincy pulled off his gloves one finger at a time, tucking them into his jacket pocket. He sat himself atop the bench, brushing out his tail behind him... and began to play a familiar requiem.

CHAPTER 9

The sound of Winnie's favourite song echoed strangely through the conservatory, as Lady Mourningwood stood by and smiled.

It had not occurred to Winnie that Mr Quincy might be practiced at the pianoforte. His long fingers flickered across the yellow keys of the piano with the same sort of certainty that she recalled in the Hollow Lady, however—and despite the situation, she found herself staring at him in surreal fascination.

Winnie had once been proud of herself for learning the Hollow Lady's requiem, knowing that it was unthinkably complex by human standards. But the version of the song which Winnie had played was simple compared to the song which the Hollow Lady had performed for her... and *that* song was, in turn, less wild and less beautiful than the one which Mr Quincy now played.

Dark, whimsical elaborations tickled at the edges of the song in places where they'd never been before. The melody sped and slowed effortlessly, building to a new, dramatic crescendo. Winnie found herself desperately taking mental notes, trying to imagine how she might recreate the changes. Very few other people would appreciate the song for what it was, but if she played this new version for Lady Longfell—

—but Lady Longfell would never hear the song, Winnie thought abruptly. Lady Mourningwood was here to celebrate the dowager's death. This requiem was meant to be a signpost for her passing.

Winnie's wonder dimmed, even as Mr Quincy finished the familiar song with a flourish. The last note hung in the air for an extended moment, before it too faded into silence.

Lady Mourningwood sighed with appreciation. "What a happy night this is," she said, in her miserable monotone. "Your years of good work have borne fruit, Mr Quincy. We appreciate all of your efforts on our behalf."

"Humbled as I am by your recognition, Your Ladyship," Mr Quincy said calmly, "I do not believe that our durance will end tonight. This family tree has one more branch. So long as the last blood of Longfell endures, it will continue to feed the Witchwood Knot." His hands remained upon the pianoforte, resting lightly upon the keys.

Winnie tightened her fingers into her palms, where they pressed atop the table. *They are speaking of Robert,* she thought. *He is in graver danger than I imagined.*

Lady Mourningwood tilted her head. The motion sent skeletal shadows skittering across the conservatory, as her crown caught the edges of the room's ghostly blue candle-light. "Then you shall feed upon the last blood of Longfell, Mr Quincy," the faerie woman said. "It is yours, if you can reach it."

And then—though Winnie had begun to hope that Lady Mourningwood had overlooked her presence—the lady of the

Witchwood Knot turned her empty black gaze upon the table next to the pianoforte. "I see that we have human company this evening," Lady Mourningwood observed, in her hollow voice. "You have intruded where you are not wanted, mortal."

A frisson of danger shot through Winnie's nerves. "I am not here by choice, Your Ladyship," she assured the faerie carefully. "The Witchwood Knot disturbs my dreams. And tonight, I sat down to a game of cards to which I was explicitly invited."

Lady Mourningwood's slender shadow shivered minutely —the only obvious sign of her anger. "And who invited you to join our gathering?" she asked.

Winnie kept her eyes carefully upon the dark woman in the doorway. Mr Quincy now owed her a considerable favour, and she was loath to cause him too much trouble until she'd had a chance to use it. A smaller and much quieter part of her observed that he had also done her a good turn earlier that evening... but Winnie could not bring herself to acknowledge a motivation which was so patently naive.

"Will you not speak when you are spoken to?" Lady Mourningwood asked ominously.

"I am not obliged to do so," Winnie replied calmly. "There is no custom which requires guests to answer every question put to them. If that were so, then no one would ever attend a gathering in faerie."

Mr Quincy's crimson gaze burned into Winnie's back, even as she carefully ignored him.

"I invited Miss Hall to cards," the butler announced to Lady Mourningwood. "You have offered me great latitude to decide how it is that I fulfil your desires, Your Ladyship. I only have so many means available to me in order to gather information from the humans here."

Lady Mourningwood returned the heavy weight of her attention to Mr Quincy. "I see," she said slowly. "That is… true. You have brought me many useful prizes with your distractions, Mr Quincy. Perhaps, then, you should introduce your guest to me. I assume that you have won her name?"

Mr Quincy retrieved his gloves from his jacket pocket as he stood again, pulling them back on. Winnie thought she saw a hint of hesitation in the delay—but nevertheless, he cleared his throat. "This is the governess, Miss Winifred Hall," he said. "She is a cartomancer, and a black magician."

Lady Mourningwood smiled her serenely awful smile. "Miss Winifred Hall," she said slowly, tasting the name on her tongue. "As it seems that you are my guest within the Witchwood Knot, I will make you especially welcome."

It was immediately clear, of course, that Lady Mourningwood's 'welcome' would be nothing of the sort. The weight of her power leaned in from every corner of the conservatory, as the blue candlelight flickered. The shadows of strychnine branches reached out for Winnie like fingers, digging phantom claws into her soul, as the faces in the walls widened their jaws and screamed in silence.

"So long as the Witchwood Knot endures," Lady Mourningwood continued, "you will stay here with us, dreaming. Rather than leaving our company, you will continue to sleep, until such time as we have all been freed."

The faerie lady's magic was impossibly powerful—beyond anything that Winnie could have ever summoned, by a magnitude and more. The dire pronouncement settled upon her shoulders with what should have been a terrible finality…

…but Lady Mourningwood had used the wrong name for her curse.

That black faerie magic lost its grip and slipped away,

dissolving into shadows once again. Distressed murmurs rustled between the faeries in the conservatory. Mr Quincy's expression briefly showed his incredulity, before he realised the nature of his previous miscalculation.

Winnie brushed the last cobwebs of ragged shadow from her gown and cleared her throat delicately.

"I fear that I must decline your generous offer, Lady Mourningwood," she replied, with as much sensibility as she could manage. "Though I am deeply honoured to hear that you have claimed me as your guest until the Witchwood Knot has broken."

Lady Mourningwood was silent for a long moment. To Winnie's surprise, there was no sign of fury now; rather, she saw in the faerie lady's features the same calm, terrible calculation which Mr Quincy often showed.

"You have bought yourself a sliver more of time, nameless creature," Lady Mourningwood said finally. "But only that. The Witchwood Knot trembles around us as we speak. And when it breaks, and you are no longer guest within it —I will come for you. Know that when I do, I will weave your lovely hair into brittle leaves, and turn your skin to poisonous bark, and trap your roots beneath the earth forever."

"I trust that you are capable of such a thing," said Winnie quietly.

The Witchwood Knot took another sudden breath. A strong, warm breeze ghosted across Winnie's neck, and the faeries around her murmured in tragic disappointment. Mr Quincy's prediction had come true. Despite the dowager's death, the Witchwood Knot yet lived.

Thunder rumbled in the distance.

"Enjoy the time that you have won, governess," Lady

Mourningwood said evenly, with an inclination of her tall black crown.

Winnie woke in Robert's bedroom, as rain began to tap upon the stained glass window.

～

ROBERT WAS NOT in his bedroom. The realisation drenched Winnie in sudden cold anxiety, as she rose from the small bed and took stock of her surroundings. Though it was clearly morning, the rain outside had cloaked the manor in gloom, such that she found herself stumbling for the door.

Winnie did not need to call for Robert, however; she found him sitting at the bottom of the attic staircase, leaning his chin upon his knees. His eyes were distant and unfocussed. He might have looked like a doll, if not for the faint rise and fall of his chest as he breathed.

Winnie knelt down in front of him, taking one of his hands in hers. His skin was colder than it should have been. "You should not have left your room," she murmured, as she rubbed at his fingers. "But I suppose that's immaterial now. Have you slept at all?"

Robert didn't immediately respond. In fact, Winnie had to repeat her question before he seemed to digest it at all. Finally, he turned his sluggish gaze up to her eyes. "I have not slept," he said in a wooden tone. Then, he added: "We are supposed to join Father for breakfast."

Winnie pressed her lips together at the revelation. But she had avoided Lord Longfell's company for long enough—and she suspected that Robert would benefit from food, in lieu of rest. She straightened slowly, though she kept her grip on his hand. "Come along then," she said.

It was novel to see the dining room with a full breakfast spread—Cook had prepared bacon, eggs, and haddock, along with fresh-baked bread. Lord Longfell had already settled himself at the table, looking just as pale and sleepless as his son. For just a moment, Winnie managed to feel a pang of sympathy for him, as she noted the red rims beneath his eyes. Despite his current composure, he had almost certainly spent part of the night crying.

Lord Longfell rose calmly as they entered. Rather than greet the two of them, he offered out a hand. "Come here, Robert," he said quietly.

The boy next to Winnie shuffled forward listlessly—and for the first time, Winnie saw his father embrace him. Robert rested his head against Lord Longfell's chest, blinking slowly. If the rare emotional gesture had affected him, then the reaction failed to reach his face.

Lord Longfell glanced at Winnie over his son's head. "Thank you for looking after him, Miss Hall," he said. "The evening has been... trying."

Winnie inclined her head, dropping her eyes to the floor. "He's been no trouble," she replied. After a hesitation, she asked: "Her Ladyship..."

Lord Longfell tightened his arm around Robert's shoulders. "My mother passed away during the night," he said stiltedly. "We have called for a tailor, among other things. There is still much to be done. I would be greatly obliged if you could help with the traditional arrangements. Given your closeness, I believe that she would prefer you be involved."

Winnie hesitated. Though her initial instinct was to agree, she knew that seeing to the dowager's last needs would take her away from Robert, right as the faeries had taken extra interest in him. Her eyes flickered to the boy in question.

"Master Robert... may require more of my attention," she said slowly.

"We will all need to balance our responsibilities in the next few days," Lord Longfell replied. His tone implied that there would be no argument, despite the initial phrasing of his request.

Winnie pressed her lips together. "I will ask Margaret for a list of things which still need doing," she said. As she glanced up again, her eyes caught upon Lord Longfell's hand, where it rested at Robert's back. The dowager's knotted ring of wood and iron had joined his signet there.

Lord Longfell released his son, and moved to pull out chairs for the two of them on his side of the table. As they settled in for a deeply subdued breakfast, Winnie couldn't help but note how listless Robert's appetite seemed to be.

"You ought to eat something," she reminded the boy quietly. "You will feel better, I promise."

Robert glanced down at the plate before him, as though he hadn't noticed it there. Nevertheless, he picked at the food with slow, mechanical gestures.

"Your grandmother left me with a last wish, Robert," Lord Longfell announced. "In fact... she asked me to exempt you from going to Eton." He arched a weary eyebrow in Robert's direction. "You will be staying here at Witchwood Manor, after all. I hope that you are pleased."

Winnie stiffened slightly in her chair. "At Witchwood Manor?" she asked. "Surely, his tutors in London would be better equipped to continue his education?"

Lord Longfell offered her a tense smile. "I am sure that your tutelage will suffice, Miss Hall," he said. "I suppose your position here will be permanent, after all. My mother would be pleased."

Winnie had to work to keep the unease from her expression. It was true that most governesses would have been eager to hear that their temporary position had become more secure. But once again, Lord Longfell had made assumptions on her behalf, without ever pausing to ask.

He can think whatever he likes, Winnie assured herself. *I will teach Robert what he needs to know, and disappear when I am ready to do so.*

Gradually, however, it occurred to her that Robert had not bothered to respond to his father's statement. In fact, Robert had returned to staring down at his plate in silence, as though he hadn't heard a thing.

"I suspect that Master Robert may require some rest," Winnie said. "By your leave, I will take him back upstairs for the afternoon."

"Of course," Lord Longfell said. As Winnie rose and helped Robert to his feet, however, the lord cleared his throat to regain her attention.

"I have moved my things into Witchwood Manor," he announced. His dark eyes were oddly penetrating as he considered her. "I will be staying here from this point forward. I expect you will bring Robert down for breakfast each morning, Miss Hall."

Somehow, Winnie resisted the urge to tense her jaw. "I... understand, Your Lordship," she said. "I will see to it."

Robert followed Winnie up to his room mutely. As soon as they had walked inside, Winnie closed the door and leaned her back against it, closing her eyes. Some part of her still felt the weight of Lord Longfell's gaze pressing against the door, as though he were on the other side. An irrational urge rose up within her, insisting that she find a basin and wash the residue of his attention from her skin.

After a long silence, however, she opened her eyes and saw that Robert was still standing in the middle of the room with a blank, unseeing expression on his face.

"Robert?" Winnie asked quietly. "Do you need help with anything?" The dullness in his manner had become more pathetic than it was disconcerting.

Robert didn't look at her. Again, he seemed to struggle with his response, answering only after several seconds. "I don't believe so, Miss Hall," he said.

Winnie stepped forward to settle a hand on his shoulder. Slowly, she guided him to his bed. "I suspect that the Witchwood Knot will take you again when you sleep," she said. "You must stay in your room if it does, and not come out for any reason. Do you understand, Robert?"

"I understand, Miss Hall," Robert replied tonelessly.

Winnie tucked him into bed with an unusual sense of helplessness. It was not the first time she had seen a human being react to tragedy with such a flat affect—the workhouses had more than their fair share of people who found it difficult to function normally. But it *was* her first time seeing a child react that way... and Winnie did not have the first idea of how to address the problem.

"Would you like for me to tell you another faerie tale?" she asked, as Robert stared up at the ceiling.

"No, Miss Hall," said Robert. "Thank you, Miss Hall."

Winnie swallowed. A knot of unsteady emotion had settled into her chest, since speaking with the dowager the day before. Since then, it had grown and grown, devouring all of her sensibilities like some oversized monster.

I cannot fix this, Lady Longfell, she thought. *I am the wrong person to handle it.*

"Sleep, then," Winnie told him. "I will come back and check on you, by and by."

This time, Robert did not respond at all.

DESPITE HER OWN WEARINESS, Winnie knew she would not be able to sleep. Instead, she descended below stairs to the kitchen, where Cook now worked to prepare an afternoon tea.

"I did not see you in the Witchwood Knot last evening," Winnie observed, as she slipped into the half-lit room.

Cook sighed heavily. The circles beneath her eyes were deeper than ever. "I've spent so many years wishing I could sleep the whole night through," she said. "I lay awake last night, expecting I might finally have my wish... after a fashion."

Winnie set the kettle on as Cook continued to work. "That seems a *bit* dramatic," she replied. "I am sure that we can find a better aid for sleep than death by faerie."

Cook stared down at the stove. "Do you know why things continue as they are?" she asked.

Winnie leaned against the wall, closing her arms around herself. "I believe that I might," she said. "The creature who laid this curse upon Witchwood Manor did so using magic born of blood and iron. I do not understand it all completely... but it seems the Knot takes power from the Longfell bloodline. So long as Lord Longfell and his son remain within the manor, the curse continues on."

Lord Longfell's decision to move into Witchwood Manor had been no coincidence. Whatever the man claimed to believe about faeries, he clearly knew the circumstances under which the curse would fail.

The kettle whistled softly in the gloom, breaking the silence which had fallen in the kitchen. Cook offered it out to Winnie, who took it pensively.

"The lady of the Witchwood Knot has charged Mr Quincy with driving out the blood of Longfell," Winnie told her. "The other faeries cannot walk within Witchwood Manor—but the curse has less of a hold on him, I think, because of what he is. He cannot leave the manor; he proved that on the day that I arrived. But neither is he fully trapped within the Witchwood Knot. Because..." Winnie pieced together what she'd learned the evening before. "Because iron does not bind him, as it binds the others."

Cook smiled grimly. "More scones went missing, just last night," she said, with a hint of sideways agreement.

Winnie glanced over at the other woman as she steeped a pot of tea. "What?" she asked. "That isn't possible. I played another game of cards with Mr Quincy. We were together until morning—" Winnie cut herself off, knitting her brow. "Well... there was some time before that, I suppose. I had a conversation with my sister." And Mr Quincy had only arrived in the conservatory partway through that twisted game of Hot Cockles.

"It was earlier in the evening," Cook agreed. "I left to bring some tea to those upstairs. When I returned, the scones were gone."

The revelation left Winnie subtly ill at ease. In all the chaos of the night before, she had lost track of Robert *and* Mr Quincy at separate times.

I cannot afford for that to happen again, she thought. *Robert is directly in his sights now.*

Cook turned to pour them both a cup of tea. "My condolences for your loss," she said quietly. "You seemed close with the dowager."

Winnie's breath hitched in surprise. "Were you not close with her as well?" she asked. "You have stayed here in this cursed house for ages now."

Cook laughed very softly. "I had no special love for Lady Longfell," the other woman replied. "She paid well, but she had little warmth to offer to the servants. I think we mostly puzzled her. She must have seen you differently."

Winnie grimaced. "Lady Longfell suspected that I had blue blood," she admitted. And likely, it was true—though Winnie had never counted that blood to be of any particular importance. Her gaze settled upon Cook more curiously than before, however, and she asked: "Why *have* you stayed, if not for Lady Longfell?"

Cook took a long, slow sip of tea. Grey hairs glimmered on her head in the candlelight. "What would have happened to my village if I'd left?" she asked. "Witchwood Manor can survive without a hundred little things... but it would fold without a cook. I have no magic to my name, Miss Hall, it's true. But I have scones and stubbornness, and I will use them as I can."

Grudging admiration trickled into Winnie's manner as she took her tea. "You are a harder woman than I realised," she admitted. "I am fortunate to have you for an ally."

Cook shrugged her shoulders. "I begin to reach the limits of my capabilities," she said. "But if you still think you can solve our problems, then I can keep you fed."

"I haven't the first idea if I can solve this situation," Winnie told her. "Every time I learn something new about it, I begin to realise how tangled it's become. But I will stay and try."

~

WINNIE LINGERED with Cook over her tea for a short while longer, until Margaret came to join them. As Winnie remembered Lord Longfell's command to assist with the dowager's arrangements, however, she asked the maid what else might yet be done.

Margaret had already stopped all of the clocks in the manor, winding them back to the dowager's time of death; Lady Longfell had passed at two-thirteen in the morning, Winnie heard, according to the physician. The mirrors still required covering, however, and Margaret had started searching for a laurel to hang upon the front door.

Winnie volunteered to handle the mirrors—whereupon Margaret gratefully unburdened a large bolt of black crepe onto her. For the next half hour, Winnie sought out anything in Witchwood Manor with even a hint of a reflection, covering it all with gauzy black squares of the material. The last mirror, of course, was the dowager's vanity mirror—up in the attic bedroom.

Winnie was not surprised to find the dowager still in bed, as she entered the attic; it was still early in the day, and the undertaker had yet to arrive. In death, the older woman was even more drawn and pale than she had been in life; though someone had closed her eyes, she did not look at all like a woman sleeping.

Winnie set aside the small bolt of black crepe which she was carrying, leaving it on a table near the door. Despite everything, she found herself walking towards the bed and settling herself into the chair next to it—as though preparing to converse with the dowager again.

"I certainly hope that you are not still here," Winnie told

the woman. "I cannot send you on, if you are. I am not Bellamira." She fiddled with her skirt uncomfortably, looking down at it. Finally, she sighed heavily. "I am beginning to feel overwhelmed. I have become better at protecting myself since I was young... but even that much is still difficult. I am not yet practiced enough to protect another human being as well, Lady Longfell. We are all so terribly fragile."

The woman in the bed did not respond. Of all people, Winnie knew that she *could* have, under the wrong circumstances. This silence between them was the best possible outcome, even if it *felt* hideously wrong.

"I will try, of course," Winnie said finally. "I promised that I would try. I will use my favour with Mr Quincy to ask about a way into faerie—but I will stay here for a time while my sisters continue on. Once Robert is feeling better, I will continue teaching him everything that he needs to know—"

Winnie cut herself off abruptly. Outside, the clouds had parted for just a moment, allowing a sliver of sunlight to sneak through the twisted ivy of the stained glass window. This light had caught on a quiet silver glimmer at the dowager's neck, drawing Winnie's eyes.

Winnie pushed herself up slowly from her chair, staring down at the woman in the bed. A horrible nausea blossomed in her stomach as she studied the silver chain around the dead woman's neck.

Finally, Winnie reached out to thread one finger through the chain. The pad of her finger brushed the dowager's cold skin, sending a shiver through her body—but she tugged carefully, drawing the weight at the end of the chain into view above the dowager's night gown.

A familiar silver locket gleamed at the end of the chain,

caught in that brief burst of sunlight. It was the very same locket that Winnie had given to Robert.

Winnie dropped the chain as though she had been burned, looking down at it with wide eyes. It refused to change shape, however, no matter how long she stared at it.

She whirled for the attic stairs, ignoring the faint twinge in her ankle as she stumbled down to Robert's bedroom. She found the boy precisely where she had left him, laying in bed and staring at the ceiling.

"Show me the locket that I gave you," Winnie ordered him sharply. "The one with mistletoe inside of it."

Robert blinked very slowly at the ceiling. "I do not have it," he said.

"Why?" Winnie demanded. "Why would you give that locket to the dowager? I *told* you that no magic could keep her from death. I told you that mistletoe only protects children!"

Robert did not reply again. As Winnie took in the blank expression on his face, a terrible suspicion began to bubble up from the bottom of her mind.

She pulled the silver knife from her chatelaine and held it out to him, edge first. "Prick your finger on my knife," she told him. "Now."

The Robert to which Winnie had grown accustomed would never have blindly followed such a demand. *This* Robert shifted upright in his bed, however, looking at the glimmering point of the knife. He reached one small hand out towards her, and pressed his thumb against the blade.

But Robert did not bleed. Instead, a sickly sweet smell blossomed on the air, as amber-coloured sap trickled from his finger.

CHAPTER 10

*W*innie stared down at the Robert-shaped creature in the bed.

"Where is the real Mr Robert Murray?" she asked, with carefully forced calm. Panic had long since forced its way up into her throat—but it was of no use, and so she held it at arm's length.

The false Robert blinked, slow and sleepy, as amber sap bled sluggishly from its finger. "I do not know," it said.

Winnie wiped her silver knife upon her skirts, sliding it back into its sheathe. All morning, she thought, the Robert creature had been perfectly obedient—if terribly oblivious. She rephrased her question with care. "When did you last see the real Robert?" she asked, in a level tone of voice.

The false Robert thought for a very long while. Finally, it said: "I saw him last night, when I replaced him."

"You are a fetch, then," Winnie said flatly. "A puppet made of wood and string."

"Is that what I am?" the false Robert asked. "I did not know." The idea did not seem to concern it overly much.

There was only one person who could have switched the fetch with Robert, Winnie knew. Mr Quincy had taken full advantage of her accidental lapse the evening before. Robert had left Oliver's watchful eye behind while she slept and given away his only protection to a dying woman... and that brief window had been all that Mr Quincy required.

"Robert was already gone by the time Mr Quincy sat down to cards with me," Winnie said dully. "I am such a fool." The last blood of Longfell had not been Robert, after all; the faeries had only to remove Lord Longfell now, and their vengeance would be complete.

The fetch continued staring at her blankly, as though awaiting her next question. Winnie pressed a hand over her eyes, now swaying on her feet.

She wanted to be cross with the real Mr Robert Murray. How badly she wanted to blame him for ignoring everything she'd worked so hard to teach him! After everything that Winnie had done in order to secure his collaboration, he had disobeyed her warnings in the worst way possible.

But for once, Winnie could not muster even a scrap of anger. All she could remember was the frightened, desperate tone in Robert's voice as he begged her to save his grandmother's life.

"I have been treating Robert as an adult," she said softly. "But he is really still a child. I have managed to forget what that is like."

Robert was almost certainly with Lady Mourningwood now. He would be just as frightened and forlorn in her company as the Hollow Lady had been, once upon a time.

Winnie dropped her hand from her eyes, drawing in a breath.

"I assume that you will do whatever I ask you to do?" she

asked the fetch. Whoever had crafted the false Robert had probably had little incentive to teach it disobedience.

"Yes, Miss Hall," the false Robert said. The words came out sluggish, as though oozing through molasses.

"Stay in bed and rest for now, then," Winnie told it.

"Yes, Miss Hall," the fetch said again, in exactly the same tone as before.

Winnie tucked it back into bed, though she was uncertain whether it even noticed the gesture. She turned back for the stairs then, with her heart pounding in her chest.

At least I need not guard the fetch, she thought tiredly. *The faeries made it in the first place. There is no reason for them to harm it.*

Black crepe fluttered around her as she walked through the manor, following at her heels like a ghost. There was no escaping its dour presence—it had worked its way into every corner, drifting on the house's breath.

There were no mirrors in the conservatory, of course. The furniture there was still clad in white Holland covers—a jarring contrast to the rest of Witchwood Manor.

Winnie stalked into the room, projecting more confidence than she truly felt. "Mr Quincy!" she called. "I am here to speak with you. I know that you can hear me."

Thunder rumbled distantly outside. The butler did not answer.

Winnie pressed her lips into a thin, humourless line; she continued to the pianoforte then, and tore the white sheet from it. Dust burst into the air, choking the faint light from the stained glass windows. The deep brown piano beneath seemed shockingly normal now, compared to the twisted black monstrosity which Winnie had seen in the Witchwood Knot—and she sent up a brief prayer of thanks that she would not be required to play upon those keys made of human ivory.

Winnie settled herself on the piano bench, testing its pitch. To her great surprise, the pianoforte was perfectly in tune. Given how little attention anyone at Witchwood Manor paid to it, she suspected that she had the butler of the Witchwood Knot to thank for this.

You will come out of hiding, with the proper motivation, Winnie thought at him.

She laid her fingers upon the keys... and began to play the Hollow Lady's requiem.

It was the simpler version, of course. Winnie could not possibly have recreated the song which Mr Quincy had played the evening before. But the tune was more than recognisable—and Winnie had given it her own little flourishes over the years, of which she was quite proud.

Slowly, the scent of bay berry began to tickle at her senses. Winnie became dimly aware of a figure standing just behind her, casting its shadow upon the pianoforte.

Still, she continued playing—now imitating one of the melodic digressions which Mr Quincy had indulged. The longer that she played, the more quickly his tail's shadow snapped with obvious disquiet.

Winnie drew a certain spiteful reassurance from the butler's confusion. She leaned upon the feeling, transforming it into confidence as she neared the end of the requiem. She added a demanding crescendo where there had been none before—ending on a particularly loud note which echoed through the conservatory.

Silence slowly trickled in, as Winnie rested her hands on the keys once again.

"Where did you learn that song?" Mr Quincy asked from

behind her. For the first time since Winnie had met him, he sounded truly shaken—as though she had struck him violently with each piano key she played.

"Tell me where you learned it first," said Winnie tightly, "and I will match your answer."

Mr Quincy held his silence. There was a strained quality to that quiet this time, as he struggled with some over-whelming hidden conflict.

Winnie was only willing to wait patiently for so long. Finally, she quashed her curiosity and swept past the matter, aiming for more urgent questions. "Where is the real Mr Robert Murray?" she asked shortly.

Her angry tone jolted the butler out of the daze which her performance had inspired. "What makes you think I know?" he asked slowly.

"That is a question and not an answer," Winnie said, staring ahead at the roses in the stained glass windows. "You *are* compelled to tell the truth then, just as faeries are. You know exactly where he is."

Mr Quincy offered a clipped sort of laugh. There was still a shaky edge to the sound. "How clever you are, nameless creature," he said. "And... what will you do with your suspicions?"

Winnie turned upon the bench to fix him with a cold expression. She had to crane her neck to do so, as Mr Quincy had come very close behind her. "You had no right to take him," she snapped. "He's just a child. What has he ever done to you?"

The butler buried his disquiet, refocussing upon her. His red eyes bored down into hers, unrepentant. "I am bound to follow orders, as you already know," he rasped. "Besides which—I had Mr Murray's permission to take him away.

Don't you recall, my precious little liar?"

Once again, Robert's voice whispered through the conservatory, stirring at dusty white linen: *"If I had to choose, then I would rather be abducted than be forced to go to Eton."*

Winnie clenched her fingers into her palms. "Robert's father has said that he need not go to Eton," she replied tightly. "You have therefore abducted him in error."

Mr Quincy shrugged with exaggerated disinterest. "You may make your argument to Lady Mourningwood directly, if you wish," he said. "Assuming you can find her."

"May I?" Winnie asked him, in a dangerous voice. "I think, perhaps, I will." She pushed up from the bench, bare inches from the butler. Mr Quincy did not give his ground—and so she leaned up towards him, pressing the point. "You still owe me a favour, Mr Quincy. And I am calling it in."

The idea of giving up on a way into faerie dropped a leaden weight in Winnie's stomach. But she knew, in that moment, that the Hollow Lady would have wanted it this way. Lady Hollowvale would never have left another child in Lady Mourningwood's care—not for any reason.

Mr Quincy took a step back from her, before he could catch himself. A moment later, his wine-red eyes flashed with anger—though Winnie thought that it might be self-directed. "I will not fetch the boy back for you," he said. "That would be disobedience—and I am bound to do the lady's bidding."

"I never *asked* you to fetch Master Robert back for me," Winnie said, in a deceptively even tone. She reached up idly to straighten the butler's neck cloth, tucking it more firmly into the collar of his waistcoat. Mr Quincy stiffened noticeably beneath her touch. "Here is my favour, Mr Quincy: You will take me to Lady Mourningwood as swiftly and as safely as you can. And then—when I have claimed Mr Robert Murray back from her—you will bring me and Robert safely back to Witchwood Manor, once again."

Mr Quincy's jaw tightened. "There is no safe route through the Witchwood Knot," he said. "Not for mortals."

"You are quibbling!" Winnie snapped at him. "I did not ask for perfect safety. I asked for the swiftest, safest way you know. And now I ask again. Fulfil your oath, Mr Quincy."

Mr Quincy snatched her wrist away from his cravat. "That is a foolish favour!" he hissed. "It will only bring you grief."

"Oh, *now* you care for my grief," Winnie scoffed. She twisted her wrist away from his long, cold fingers. "Tell me the truth, Mr Quincy—did you have a hand in Lady Longfell's death?"

"I did not," he muttered through his teeth. "But I would not have stopped her death if I could do so. This is a war, Miss Nobody, and you have stepped into the middle of it. I have no obligation to my enemy."

"You have an obligation to *me*," Winnie corrected him coldly. "And you will fulfil it. I ask you for my favour, Mr Quincy. Unless the *fomóraig* are known for breaking their word? How pleased will Lady Mourningwood be, if she hears that her servant has forsworn himself?"

Mr Quincy stared down at her, trembling with anger—and perhaps with other emotions which she could not rightly name. But he had promised her a favour... and Winnie had requested it three times now.

"You will regret this," he said finally, clutching at his neck cloth where she'd touched it. "I guarantee it."

"I am your enemy," Winnie shot back simply. "You have no cause to care."

Mr Quincy seemed prepared to speak again—but

suddenly, his reddish eyes flickered towards the door of the conservatory, and his lip curled into a grimace.

Some subconscious, irrational part of Winnie remembered Lady Mourningwood's arrival the evening before, and she found herself turning to follow his gaze with a faint sense of trepidation. But the footsteps which soon echoed down the hallway were far too heavy and too human to belong to Lady Mourningwood, and Winnie's tension eased slightly.

A few seconds later, Lord Longfell appeared in the door-way, and Winnie's sense of relief vanished abruptly. Though the lord of the manor had made attempts to improve his comportment since breakfast, his brown hair was still mussed at the edges—and no amount of work by his valet could hide his bloodshot eyes.

Lord Longfell searched the conservatory with a frown, before his attention fell upon Winnie. "Miss Hall," he greeted her slowly. "I heard someone playing the piano. Was that you?"

Winnie did not need to look in order to know that Mr Quincy had entirely disappeared. Despite the butler's absence, the conservatory seemed to retain a sinister reminder of his interest—shadows pooled too deeply in the corners, and the occasional dark whisper trickled in at the corner of Winnie's senses.

Lord Longfell was affected by that atmosphere; Winnie saw the disquiet behind his bloodshot eyes. The sight of his unease bolstered her strangely, so that she found herself taking comfort in the ominous whispers around her.

For once, Winnie realised, she need not be obliged to entertain Lord Longfell's smothering presence.

"I was not playing the piano, Your Lordship," she lied. She affected a puzzled expression at him. "I thought that I heard someone in the conservatory, just as you did. But there was no one here when I arrived." She smiled at him serenely. "Perhaps it was a ghost. Lady Longfell always said this house was cursed."

Lord Longfell's throat worked as he swallowed minutely. But a hard expression soon came into his eyes, and he steeled himself. "My mother held many silly notions, especially in her old age," he said. "I had hoped that you would be more sensible, Miss Hall."

He was afraid. Winnie saw it in his posture—in the way that his jaw tensed, and the way that his fingers reached for the knotted ring on his hand, worrying it back and forth.

Her courage swelled. "I am very sensible, Your Lordship," she assured him softly. "But there is no one at the piano. And I do not know how it is they might have left. There is only the doorway that you are standing in, after all."

Lord Longfell stared at the pianoforte. "Was that... uncovered, when you arrived?" he asked.

"It was," Winnie lied again. "How curious this all is, don't you think?"

Whispers hissed more loudly on the air, just at the edge of hearing—now reaching out for Lord Longfell. He took a sudden step back into the hallway. "I find my interest waning," he said stiffly. "I am sure that someone has simply played a trick upon us. I will not entertain it. Come away from that pianoforte, Miss Hall."

Winnie's smile inched upwards. "I think that I will study it a bit further," she replied. "But you are right... this does seem beneath your dignity, Your Lordship. Please, do not let my girlish distractions keep you overlong."

If there was a hint too much amusement in her tone, then Lord Longfell was certainly too rattled to notice it. He wavered at the threshold of the conservatory for only one more instant, before turning sharply on his heel and stalking away.

As his footsteps grew more distant, the ominous whispers abated.

"Occasionally, Mr Quincy," Winnie said aloud, "you do manage to be a gentleman."

The butler did not deign to reply.

CHAPTER 11

The undertaker came within the hour to remove Lady Longfell—head first through the front door, in order to confuse her spirit and prevent her from returning. Judging from past conversations with Bellamira, Winnie suspected that this particular ritual was ineffective, even when there *was* a spirit present—but obviously, no one asked for her opinion on the matter.

Thankfully, the family was early to bed that evening, even if the servants were expected to remain awake and working. Robert's fetch was still in his room when Winnie checked— though she was hard-pressed to say whether the fetch actually knew how to sleep. She tucked it in again regardless, since it seemed to possess some modicum of self-awareness. After that, exhaustion settled into the last corners of her body, demanding to be addressed.

By the time Winnie crawled into her blankets, her eyes were already beginning to close of their own accord.

She woke to a knock at her bedroom door. It was a firm,

cool knock which made the cat at her feet sit up abruptly, with his black nose twitching and his ears pinned back.

Winnie pushed to her feet, snatching up her frock and tugging it over her head. The screaming faces of the Witchwood Knot looked on as she strode for the door—but by now, they were becoming strange old friends, instead of troubling apparitions.

Mr Quincy waited on the other side in his crimson jacket and cravat, with an eerie blue-lit lantern in his hand. His manner was stiff and resentful—but as Winnie opened the door and Oliver crept after her, his reddish eyes flickered warily to the cat. The cat fixed the butler with an intense look of interest, twitching his tail in a way that signalled violent intentions.

Winnie scooped up Oliver before the cat could pounce. "How punctual you are," she said. "I do appreciate working with professionals."

Mr Quincy maintained a pointedly cool expression as he turned on his heel and started for the stairs. It was clear that he expected Winnie to follow him—and even clearer that he would not wait for her if she decided to lag behind. Winnie picked up her pace in order to catch up, falling into step just behind him.

"I can come and go within the Witchwood Knot very nearly as I please," Mr Quincy told her calmly. "I rarely need to walk within its corridors at all, as I can cross them in a moment—but you do not have that luxury. If you wish to make it to the centre of the Knot, where Lady Mourningwood resides, then we will need to go below stairs."

As they passed the mirror on the stairs, Winnie saw that the other side was now obscured by black crepe, drifting on the evening air. A sudden thought occurred to her. "You have been spying on the manor through the mirrors," she said.

"One hardly needs to spy on purpose," Mr Quincy told her dryly. "There are so many mirrors in the manor that a walk about the Knot will always reveal *something.*"

Winnie considered the butler critically as she descended the stairs behind him. Her first instinct had been to demand whether Mr Quincy had seen anything inappropriate in the mirrors—but despite her general paranoia, Winnie found herself swiftly dismissing the thought.

"Do you know what I appreciate about you, Mr Quincy?" she asked thoughtfully. "You may evade the truth by miles... but I always know precisely where I stand with you." She smiled to herself. "You have only ever looked at me with frustration and contempt."

Mr Quincy paused momentarily, though he did not look behind him. "I find myself unclear on the matter," he said. "Is that supposed to be a compliment?"

"It is," Winnie assured him. "It changes nothing between us —but it makes our enmity more pleasant."

Lord Longfell felt contempt for Winnie, on some level... but she wondered if he was entirely cognisant of the feeling, given that he'd buried it beneath an interest in her hair and eyes and other features. Mr Quincy's red-eyed gaze had never lingered on those places overlong; rather, he stayed focussed on her face and posture, searching ceaselessly for hints which he might use against her.

It was somewhat flattering, Winnie realised, to be considered as a worthy opponent, instead of as a woman.

"Even your compliments are far from charming," Mr Quincy muttered.

"You continue to make my point for me," Winnie replied,

with a soft chuckle. Oliver nuzzled at the crook of her arm, as though responding to the sound.

Mr Quincy turned them off the stairs towards the green baize door which Winnie normally took into the servants' passageways in Witchwood Manor. He stopped in front of it and turned to face Winnie directly. His crimson eyes fixed upon her, faintly eerie in the darkness.

"This is your last chance, governess," he said. "Choose a different favour, and we will not descend."

Even in the real Witchwood Manor, Winnie had always felt a sense of unease near the green baize door. Here, however, that unease was magnified; the gaping hunger of the earth beneath them radiated through the door, reaching out to grasp at them. If they stepped through it, Winnie knew, then it would happily swallow her up.

Winnie staunchly ignored the feeling. She had already decided that she would not be turning back. She lowered Oliver to the floor just next to her, with one last scratch behind his ears. "You *can* still call me by a false name, if you please," she told the butler lightly. "I do not know your true name either."

Mr Quincy shook his head with resignation. "Let us see if the ghosts here eat you up then, governess," he said, by way of reply.

He pushed open the green baize door. The house drew in a sudden breath, whispering past Winnie's shoulder—and then, Mr Quincy was stepping past the threshold to descend into the earth.

Winnie stiffened her spine and followed after him, with Oliver at her heels.

THE PASSAGEWAYS which led beneath the surface of the Witchwood Knot were reminiscent of those in Witchwood Manor. At intervals, the ceilings were propped up with familiar wooden cross beams, and once Winnie and Mr Quincy reached the bottom of the narrow wooden stairs, they began to tread upon limestone flooring. The walls were close and claustrophobic, tangled with nonsensical copper piping—but the screaming faces had now disappeared, at least, since the passage walls were made of stone.

It soon became clear, however, that the passageways here were far more numerous and twisted than their real-world counterparts. At first, Winnie thought that Mr Quincy was leading them towards the kitchen—but as they reached the end of the first turn and met a solid wall instead of a door, she found herself frowning at his back.

"Have you *any* idea where it is that we are going?" Winnie asked him sceptically.

Mr Quincy's rat tail twitched with annoyance as he turned about, glancing back the way they'd come. The flickering blue candlelight of his lantern highlighted his sour expression. "I do not wander here unless I must," he said. "Besides which, I suspect the passages change when they are of a mind." Winnie began to open her mouth to speak—but he cut her off with irritation. "This is still the swiftest, safest path I know which you can follow. I gave you ample warning."

Winnie closed her mouth again with a grimace. Oliver narrowed his one eye evilly at Mr Quincy, as though suspicious of him—but Winnie shook her head minutely at the cat, and he turned about with a soft feline grumble.

Mr Quincy led them on through the labyrinthine passages, despite his uncertainty. Winnie tried to keep track of the winding twists and turns within her head, but she was soon forced to give up the attempt. There was something naturally disorienting about the underground here which she could not put her finger on.

It was difficult to tell time in the Witchwood Knot... but surely, the house had breathed several thousand breaths already when Oliver shoved himself in front of Winnie's feet with a low warning growl.

Mr Quincy flinched and whirled at the sound, training his gaze upon the cat in expectation of an attack. But Oliver paid the butler little mind—his one eye was now focussed just behind them. Another soft growl rumbled from the cat's throat... and presently, Winnie became aware of heavy footsteps echoing in the halls behind them.

"Who else is in here with us, Mr Quincy?" she whispered warily.

The butler frowned. "I do not know," he said slowly. "I have never encountered anyone else in this area before."

The footsteps, Winnie thought, were perfectly measured. They beat a neat, predictable metronome against the limestone floor. *Clunk. Clunk. Clunk.* She counted carefully, and decided that there was a perfect half-second in between each one.

"Perhaps we should speed up," she murmured.

"Perhaps you'd care to lead instead," Mr Quincy shot back, in an irritated tone. Nevertheless, Winnie noticed that he had picked up his stride, now twice as fast as the half-second footsteps behind them.

The sound of those footsteps faded slowly into the distance as they went... but soon, Winnie heard them again—this time, from somewhere ahead of them.

Clunk. Clunk. Clunk.

Mr Quincy's posture stiffened.

"How have they cut us off?" Winnie asked.

"There is something new ahead of us," Mr Quincy said tightly. "You can still hear what follows behind, if you listen closely enough."

All of them went quiet, and Winnie listened as he'd suggested.

Clunk CLUNK clunk CLUNK clunk went the footsteps now, alternating their march. The louder footsteps were ahead of them, but the softer ones behind were quickly catching up.

Winnie's hand dropped to the silver knife at her chatelaine. "Can we avoid them?" she asked warily.

"Perhaps," said Mr Quincy, "but I would not count on it. We will meet whatever walks ahead of us. Stay behind me, if you can."

Winnie did her best to walk at his heels as they continued on. At one point, she realised that she had begun to hold her breath—*silly*, she thought, feeling irritated with herself—and she forced herself to let it out again.

CLUNK CLUNK CLUNK. The footsteps ahead of them were far louder now. Whatever was making the sound was bigger than Winnie had expected. Just what Mr Quincy hoped to do against something so large was a mystery to her.

As they rounded the next corner, the source of the footsteps finally came into sight, and Mr Quincy's shoulders tightened.

An elongated toy soldier marched along the hallway with creaking wooden legs. The red and white paint of its uniform was faded, just like the abandoned toy soldiers in the classroom—but its bayonet was sharpened like a wicked spear, and Winnie guessed that it was more than capable of injury.

The toy soldier creaked its head about to stare at Mr

Quincy. Its eyes were deep and empty; its jaw gaped open in a silent scream which matched that of the faces in the walls.

"I see the ghosts have found us," Winnie said, in a tone far calmer than the situation likely merited.

The soldier turned to face them, pointing its bayonet at Mr Quincy's chest. It was blocking the only passage before them.

"Back," Mr Quincy ordered. "Now."

Winnie started backpedalling—but Oliver ignored the butler, as cats are wont to do. The tomcat yowled out a furious challenge at the soldier, sprinting ahead through the hallway. As he moved, his small form rippled into shadow, expanding several times over in size.

The creature that ripped into the toy soldier looked only marginally like a cat. Though still four-legged, it was tall and wide enough to take up nearly the entire hallway. Its snout was long and narrow, and its yawning jaws revealed a rictus grin of jagged, wicked teeth. One evil yellow eye fixated on the soldier as the monstrous cat closed his teeth upon the creature with an audible *crunch*.

Oliver shook the soldier about for a few more seconds, as Mr Quincy watched him with apprehension.

"Where *did* you find that terrifying thing?" he muttered at Winnie.

Winnie smiled at him. "A familiar's power is not based on what it was in life," she told him. "Love and loyalty are what lend it strength." She paused, then added: "And spite. Plenty of *that* never goes amiss."

Oliver tossed the splintered remnants of the soldier aside. The pile of painted wood still twitched, as though attempting to rise—but it was ruined enough that it posed little danger.

Slowly, Oliver's form rippled again, receding into that of a ragged, well-muscled tomcat. He smacked his jaws with vague annoyance, as though trying to dislodge a splinter.

Mr Quincy hesitated, instinctively wary of crossing the cat's path. But behind them, another *clunk clunk clunk* was growing quickly, and he forced himself forward regardless.

Oliver's yellow eye followed the butler with amusement as he passed. Winnie reached down to scratch at the cat's ears, and he purred with affectionate pleasure.

It soon became clear that one toppled soldier was the least of their problems, however. The labyrinth was now alive with clunking footsteps everywhere, as though they'd sounded an alarm. With each attempted turn, it seemed, they met a new, unnaturally tall soldier with a screaming face, intent on chasing after them. Oliver tore into the soldiers liberally, as though hunting mice through the passageways... but the wooden creatures were already dead, and it was clear that they did not fear his jaws, even as he felled them handily.

Clunk CLUNK CLUNK clunk CLUNK clunk. There were so many marching footsteps that Winnie could no longer keep track of their direction. As Oliver mangled yet another soldier ahead of them, she backed up quickly—only to find herself in the long, thin shadow of a different wooden form. A twisted, screaming face looked down at her with otherworldly hatred. The soldier raised its bayonet.

Mr Quincy moved before Winnie had fully registered the danger. The butler shoved her behind him with a hiss. The bayonet came down directly, piercing through his right shoulder with almost no resistance. The wooden spear pushed cleanly through the other side, splashing his crimson jacket with fresh blood. He staggered back with a strangled sound of pain—but his knees did not buckle, as Winnie might have expected. He caught himself against the wall with one gloved hand, still clinging to the lantern with the other. The soldier raised its bayonet slowly, lifting him painfully onto his toes.

Some part of Winnie noted the sight with detached horror. But the rest of her acted without hesitation. She drew the silver knife from her chatelaine and ducked past Mr Quincy's other side, reaching out to grasp the bayonet still protruding from his shoulder.

"What are you *doing?*" Mr Quincy rasped. "Run, you blithering fool!"

Winnie raised her silver knife and brought it down upon the wooden bayonet. The small blade glimmered as it fell, cutting through the wood as though it were soft butter instead of polished oak.

The butler staggered back, suddenly freed. The remainder of the bayonet still protruded from his back grotesquely, and he wavered on his feet. The soldier raised its stumpy arms to bring them down—but Winnie curled her other hand around the butler's elbow and hauled him back, as wood slammed against the floor where he had been.

A human being with an injury like Mr Quincy's would have crumpled to the floor in agony, Winnie was certain. But the butler steadied himself against her with a sharp exhalation —and suddenly, there were *several* Winifreds and several Mr Quincys in the hallway, shifting like a strange kaleidoscope around the soldier. A dozen flickering blue lanterns moved with them, twinkling so dizzily that Winnie nearly lost her balance.

The creature swept its blunted bayonet around, attacking the images with violent fury. The splintered weapon passed directly through one crimson jacketed Mr Quincy, striking the floor with an ugly crack of wood. A brief ripple of blue candlelight flared where the bayonet passed, distorting the image—but the illusion soon resolved again into solidity, as several Mr Quincys smiled up at the soldier with grim amusement.

Winnie pulled the butler down the passage with her, towards the downed soldier that Oliver had just discarded like a rag doll. The familiar's large, shadowy form streaked past them for the other soldier that followed them, as Winnie drew Mr Quincy back against the wall to let him pass.

Oliver hurtled through the illusions, pouncing upon the thrashing soldier and rolling to the ground with it. His over-sized claws tore through wood like kindling, sending splinters flying.

The extra lanterns blinked out all at once, as the illusions that carried them collapsed into darkness.

"You somehow... failed to mention that your knife can cut like *that*," Mr Quincy gritted out, as he leaned heavily against the wall.

Winnie stared at the jagged branch still sticking from his shoulder, feeling mildly faint. "I told you it was very sharp," she rasped. "You thought you understood me. The knife is faerie made—it can cut through anything but iron."

"You did not even lie to me about it," Mr Quincy mumbled sourly. "That was another oversight of mine." Despite his lithe frame and sallow complexion, the butler was unnaturally hale. He shoved off Winnie's grip in order to set the lantern down upon the floor... and then, he reached for the broken bayonet still pierced through his shoulder, tugging at it sharply.

Winnie's eyes widened, and she covered her mouth to stifle a nauseous gasp. The wooden shaft came only halfway free, as Mr Quincy stumbled in obvious agony.

"You could help," he spat, between his gritted teeth.

Despite the grotesque sight, Winnie's more practical instincts kicked in. Though Mr Quincy clearly felt the pain, he did not seem to fear it—nor was he being particularly careful with his injury. She forced herself to close her hands around the splintered wood and braced her foot against the wall.

Winnie tore the bayonet loose with one hard tug. The butler gave a strangled cry—then doubled over, breathing hard.

Behind them, Oliver hissed, and wood continued to crack. *CLUNK CLUNK CLUNK.* Another soldier had arrived to join his current victim. It stabbed at the familiar fruitlessly, trying to dislodge him from the soldier on the ground.

Winnie dropped the bloody shard of wood to the floor as though it had burned her. "Are you all right?" she asked him incredulously.

Mr Quincy looked up at her with two raised eyebrows. "Do I *look* all right to you?" he asked hoarsely.

Winnie's mouth worked for a moment. "It seemed the thing to say," she babbled dimly. "Oh God, I hope I have not hurt you."

"You are panicking," said Mr Quincy flatly, as his injury began to bleed more freely. "Where is your level head?"

"I wasn't thinking!" Winnie said, with sudden distress. "I didn't ask my favour with the expectation you would suffer for it. I thought the Knot was safe for you!"

"Safe?" Mr Quincy repeated, as he caught his breath against the wall. "No, governess. I told you I can travel through the Knot as I desire. I can go elsewhere in a heartbeat —that is how I avoid the ghosts which haunt this place. They hate all the living equally... and me, as well, though *some* would say I do not live. I would not come here if you did not need a guide."

The blood at his shoulder had spread into a garish patch of · darker crimson on his jacket, which now dripped down his arm to stain at his white gloves.

CLUNK CLUNK. Another toy soldier sounded ahead of them, searching for their position. How long they had before it found them, Winnie was not certain.

She struggled with a surge of conflicted emotion. "You are too injured to continue," she said finally.

Mr Quincy studied her carefully. "Shall we turn back?" he asked.

CLUNK clunk CLUNK clunk CLUNK. The footsteps were getting closer... but there were now two sets marching side by side, instead of one.

"No, we shall *not* turn back," Winnie snapped back at the butler. "You said that you can travel as you wish here. *You* should turn back—I will continue."

Mr Quincy shook his head incredulously. "Are you releasing me from my favour?" he asked.

Winnie stared at him, trying to make her thoughts work. "I am... releasing you for this evening," she clarified. It was a poor decision, and she knew it. Hastily, she added: "You will only slow me down in your current injured state."

"Hm," said Mr Quincy. He tilted his head with an odd smile. "Then perhaps I *should* stay, after all."

CLUNK clunk CLUNK. Two soldiers rounded the corner ahead of them, in perfect unison. Winnie took a sharp step backwards, pulling Mr Quincy back with her. Behind them, Oliver's shadowy form still tangled with the other soldier who'd arrived. They were quite neatly trapped.

The silent, screaming soldiers marched inevitably

forward, levelling their bayonets at Winnie and Mr Quincy. Their long-legged pace took them down the corridor with terrifying swiftness.

Winnie kept the butler behind her as she backpedalled, brandishing her knife. "Now would be an excellent time for you to leave," she advised him, with a hint of impatient anger.

"Are you *mad?*" Mr Quincy asked her. There was a confused note in his voice, and Winnie realised distantly that he was searching her for deception. "Or, no—you have forgotten, haven't you—"

The bayonets came down. Though Winnie threw them both against the wall, something slammed heavily into her chest, punching the air from her lungs. She doubled over, trying to regain her breath... and saw that a long bayonet had driven through her breastbone.

Winnie blinked slowly, unable to process the sight. Blood oozed from the edges of the injury. *My blood,* she thought dimly. *How queer that is.*

The pain which followed was brilliant, like a light. It was still somehow less horrifying than the feeling of the wood inside her, where it certainly should not have been. Weakness overcame her, all at once, and Winnie's knees buckled.

Mr Quincy caught her by the shoulders. He was swearing, Winnie thought. The words were in a language which she did not understand—but she knew the sound of curses when she heard them.

His reddish eyes snapped up to the soldiers before them... and awful magic twisted on the air. This time, Winnie knew, it was *not* an illusion.

The scent of blood—already thick and sickly sweet— became unbearable. Dark, hungry shadows seeped out from the bloodstain on the butler's crimson jacket, reaching for the toy soldiers and twining around their limbs. Where the shadows touched, wood rotted and gave way, collapsing into a sickening, greasy smoke.

The soldiers tried to stagger forward—but their legs gave out beneath them with a wet, uncomfortable sound. The screaming features on their wooden faces melted and distorted, dribbling like candle wax.

Winnie blinked once—and somehow found herself on the ground, carefully braced against the butler's knee, with the rotten remnants of the bayonet protruding from her chest.

Wine-red eyes burned down at Winnie in the darkness. Mr Quincy's jaw trembled with intense emotion. "I thought you were a sensible woman, Miss Hall," he rasped bitterly. A strange, roiling anger blistered at the surface of his voice, as rotten shadows gathered up around his pale and deathly form. "How wrong I was about *that.*"

Oliver gave a hideous, mournful yowl, nearby. And Winnie thought: *Oh. I am dying.*

The thought didn't bother her as much as it probably should have done. Death had never been her greatest fear.

Mr Quincy peeled away his bloodstained glove and pressed his fingers to the wooden spear. The polished wood withered black all at once, fading into that awful, greasy smoke. Winnie grew colder as her blood began to flow more quickly—but she was grateful to have the bayonet gone, nevertheless.

The butler closed his hand around hers tightly. His skin was cool to the touch, and oddly reassuring. Winnie closed her eyes, as the scent of blood and bay berry tickled at her senses.

There were only so many people she would have preferred to be there as she died. To her great surprise, Winnie decided that Mr Quincy would serve the function well. His clean and honest loathing was not friendship—but it was the dark reflection of a friendship, which was comforting in its own sort of way.

Had she the breath, she might have advised him again to leave. But he was there until the darkness overtook her, and her heartbeat stopped.

CHAPTER 12

*T*here was no reason whatsoever that Winnie should have woken up again. And yet, she did.

She bolted awake in her bed, gasping desperately for air and clawing at her chest. Mr Quincy's scent was gone; his hand was similarly absent. The walls were bare of screaming faces, which comforted her greatly as she slowly caught her breath.

It was still early in the morning, judging from the blackness beyond the windows and the embers which still burned in her fireplace. Winnie blinked slowly, as her pounding heart returned to normal.

I was not really there, she realised. *I was dreaming.*

Despite most folklore to the contrary, dying in one's dreams did not always carry a matching death sentence in the real world. The Witchwood Knot had simply cast her out again. Exhaustion weighed on Winnie's shoulders more heavily than ever before, however, and she suspected that the rude awakening had damaged her in *other* ways.

Mr Quincy was not dreaming, she realised abruptly. *He was injured in reality. Surely, he has fled by now?*

The thought sent a fresh spike of fear through her chest. Winnie bolted out of bed, snatching Oliver's small skull from the mantle and hurrying for the stairs.

Black crepe billowed past her as she hurried past the manor's mirrors. She stumbled several times without a candle to guide her, hissing in frustration.

What *precisely* she was expecting to find in the conservatory, Winnie wasn't certain. But she burst into the octagonal room all the same, searching in the darkness.

"Mr Quincy!" she hissed at the empty room. "Where are you? Are you alive?" Winnie shivered and rubbed at her shoulders. She'd forgotten to throw her house coat over her night gown in her rush. "Mr Quincy!" she called again desperately. "Please answer me!"

Whispers rose along the corners of the room. The scent of blood and bay berry closed in around Winnie—more blood than bay berry, at the moment—and she slumped against the white-draped pianoforte with relief.

"I cannot *die*, Miss Hall," Mr Quincy drawled from behind her. "I thought you were aware of that. Gods save you. Was *that* why you insisted on doing battle with a soldier twice your size?"

Winnie's legs still shook, despite her attempts to compose herself. She sat down heavily on the piano bench, now trembling openly. She closed her eyes, fighting back a bitter mixture of self-recrimination and relief. She had *known* he could not die. But somehow, the reality of that had not connected with her mind, when danger threatened. "I forgot," she said quietly, clenching her fingers in her night gown. "You are entirely correct. I forgot, like a fool."

Nevertheless, at the revelation of Mr Quincy's survival, she curled her fingers around Oliver's skull, calling his spirit back. Yellow light flickered in one of the skull's eye sockets, and she sighed with relief.

Winnie glanced back towards Mr Quincy. The faint moonlight from the stained glass window barely outlined his form—but the scent of blood he carried with him was more overwhelming than usual, and she pressed her lips together with concern. "You are still badly hurt."

Mr Quincy stepped closer with a heavy sigh, and Winnie saw that the ragged gash in his shoulder still remained, dripping blood upon the wooden floorboards. Nevertheless, his hand came down on her shoulder, shaking—and Winnie thought he might be trying to assure himself of her solidity.

"I will heal," said Mr Quincy softly. "I can heal anything, Miss Hall, unless I do the harm myself. That is why the *fomóraiġ* sleep beneath the faerie mounds. The faeries tried to cut us into pieces and bury them in a hundred different graves. But I could heal, even from that."

Winnie stared at him with a sudden knot in her throat. He said the words so matter-of-factly that the horror which they represented only felt redoubled.

"That is... *awful*," Winnie rasped. "By God."

Mr Quincy smiled an oddly chilling smile. Blood still speckled at the corner of his lips. "It was merited," he said. "You really don't know half of what you have pretended, do you?"

Winnie closed her arms around her shoulders. She had erred so many times tonight—and now, she continued to do so. But dying, even in a dream, had thrown her so off balance that she couldn't find her dignity again.

"I know you don't deserve *that*," Winnie said. She stared down at her lap. "No one does."

"We both know that's not true," Mr Quincy told her gently. "There are monsters in this world, Miss Hall. I could have been one, but for happenstance. I would tear my siblings into pieces personally, if I believed that it would bury them forever. But sleep is still the only remedy."

Winnie swallowed slowly, as old workhouse memories scratched at the bottom of her mind. "Yes," she said finally. "I suppose I *have* known people who deserved it. I have spent too long in the company of people who pretend those monsters don't exist. It becomes easier, eventually, to adopt the lie again."

Mr Quincy looked down at her in silence. For once, there was something other than hardness in his red eyes—though she could not quite identify it. "Innocence is so offensive, isn't it?" he asked her finally. "It is never content in its existence. It must force itself upon the rest of the world, insisting that true horror is a fiction."

For some reason, the words pricked at something deep within Winnie, drawing tears to the corners of her eyes. "You are only the second person who has ever said something like that to me," she rasped.

It was so easy, Winnie thought, to feel alone in her convictions—belittled for her impolite fears. She was too cold, too paranoid, too quick to assume the worst of everyone she met. But she had been hurt already. Why should she be obliged to pretend that it had never happened?

Mr Quincy offered out her glimmering silver knife, hilt first. Winnie took it from him, though her chatelaine was still upstairs.

"The world would be more comfortable without us, Miss

Hall," he said. "But I have never troubled myself overmuch with making other people comfortable. I would rather carry a knife."

Winnie clutched the weapon tightly. "I doubt very much that you require a knife, Mr Quincy," she mumbled. "I saw what you did to that soldier. That magic was no illusion."

The butler glanced away—but not before Winnie caught a flicker of dark shame in his crimson eyes. His rat's tail had stilled itself behind him. "The creature was already dead," he said tonelessly. "My ban does not apply."

"That was magic drawn from blood and iron, then," said Winnie quietly. The Witchwood Knot had been woven from a similar fabric.

"I was already bleeding," Mr Quincy told her stiltedly. "The magic was close to hand."

"But you were bleeding earlier," said Winnie. "You could have used it sooner."

"I do not *like* to use it," Mr Quincy replied stiffly. "Not even on the dead."

"Why use that magic at all, then?" Winnie murmured. "You cannot die. And you knew that I would wake again."

Mr Quincy considered that question for a good long while. Something sad and tired crossed his face. "You released me from my favour for the evening," he said. "I stayed in order to complicate matters for you, Miss Hall, since you decided to defend me. I expected you to die, and I did not move to stop it—though as you note, I knew that you would wake again."

His hand tightened on her shoulder.

"But I am just as nonsensical as you are," the butler admitted hoarsely. "It was... very difficult to watch."

Winnie stared at him. *Of course he let me die on purpose*, she thought distantly. *He was no longer obliged to protect me. I offered him a loophole, and he took it.*

They were both knaves. The cards had warned her—Mr Quincy had warned her, as well. There was no reason she should feel so unaccountably betrayed.

Sentiment would not stop either of them from pursuing their needs. Mr Quincy was loyal to Lady Mourningwood. If Sarah Baker could not break him from that loyalty after decades of constant friendship, then Winnie surely had no chance.

Winnie twisted away from the hand on her shoulder. "You have accomplished what you wanted," she said evenly. "What will happen when I fall asleep again?"

Mr Quincy drew back his hand. "The Witchwood Knot will take you, as it always does," he said. His voice turned colder as he once again controlled himself—but his rat's tail still flicked apprehensively behind him. "You will be whole and unharmed, once again. But we shall have to start the labyrinth from the beginning."

He fixed her with a grave expression. "You are tired—I can see that. You will only grow more weary. Your sleep will be less restful, as you travel deeper into the Knot. If this goes on too long, you will go mad."

Winnie shoved back to her feet, still clutching Oliver's skull in one hand and her silver knife in the other. Her knees still shook—but she schooled her face into a frigid expression.

"Fear not, Mr Quincy," she said icily. "I will not pity you again. I know that it was foolish in the first place—but I learn from my mistakes."

Mr Quincy watched her from behind the careful mask he'd made of his expression. His tail moved ceaselessly behind him, restless with unnamed emotion.

"I will escort you back to your room, if you would like," he told her finally. "Other things prowl through this manor now, as you well know."

Winnie's stomach turned at the reminder. The idea of running into Lord Longfell in her nightgown did not appeal to her at all—even with her knife in hand.

But she shook her head at the butler stiltedly. "I have spent several years surviving without escort, Mr Quincy," she replied. Her throat was tight upon the words. "And how silly would I be to trust you twice in the same night?"

Winnie stalked for the exit of the conservatory, unwilling to look back at him as she departed. Nevertheless, she felt as though the words had struck him soundly, leaving some incomprehensible injury behind.

Ah well, thought Winnie dully. *I am sure that he can heal that injury, too.*

Winnie did not sleep again that night, though Oliver's phantom weight settled at her feet. Her nerves were alight with tension, and her fingers kept straying to her chest, where there should have been a gaping wound. Eventually, she rose again and paced to the door which separated her bedroom from the classroom.

The painted toy soldiers still stood in their neat lines on the shelf, staring blankly ahead. Winnie shuddered at the sight.

On impulse, she swept the soldiers into her skirt, carrying them back into her bedroom. There, she tossed them into the embers of her fireplace one by one, watching as their wooden faces melted and their faded paint curled.

She sat there next to the fireplace until the sun came up again.

～

BREAKFAST WAS A HORRIBLE, maddening affair. Despite a strong dose of coffee, Winnie's limbs still felt faintly leaden, and her nerves were stretching thin. Her paranoia was so strong now that it tickled at her throat.

She was not in the best frame of mind to be dealing with Lord Longfell.

"You are still very quiet, Robert," said lord observed, partway through the meal. "Have you nothing to contribute to the conversation?"

Robert's fetch barely glanced up from his plate. "No, sir," it responded slowly. Again, the fetch had barely eaten without regular prompting from Winnie.

What a bright lot of people we are this morning, she thought tiredly. The atmosphere at the table was palpably bleak. Though Lord Longfell seemed better rested than the day before, even he had yet to fully recover from the long vigil at his mother's side.

Flowers and notes of condolence were already accumulating at the opposite end of the dining room table—sent by villagers or vague acquaintances. There had been no visitations yet, though Winnie suspected that some local busybodies would soon show up at the door in search of gossip. Lord Longfell had set the funeral in three more days, which meant that the household had yet more to do in order to prepare.

"I will expect you back at your lessons after the funeral," Lord Longfell told his son. "You cannot sulk forever, Robert."

It has been barely more than a day, Winnie thought with irritation. She bit down on the inside of her cheek in order to suppress the words, rephrasing them carefully in her head.

"Master Robert is still weary," she said slowly. "I worry for his health, in all of this excitement. But given further rest, I'm sure that he'll be back to normal, Your Lordship."

Lord Longfell glanced her way. "You look unwell yourself, Miss Hall," he observed, with a hint more kindness in his tone. "Perhaps I should send for the physician."

Winnie forced her thoughts to move as she swallowed down the last of her coffee. A physician would not solve what ailed the house—nor would medicine solve what ailed her personally. Unnecessary drugs, she thought, might make her *truly* sick. "I have had... nightmares," she said finally. "They are distressing, but I hope that they will pass. I expect that I will feel much better after the funeral."

I hope I will have Robert back by then, she thought uneasily.

"I will call the physician regardless, if you are not soon improved," Lord Longfell said. Somehow, Winnie felt the words as though they were a threat.

"Of course, Your Lordship," she muttered. Inwardly, she began to wonder if she could find some compound to cover up the growing shadows beneath her eyes. She'd seen a ghastly white bottle of it on the dowager's vanity.

Winnie carefully excused herself along with Robert's fetch —but rather than take him back to his bedroom, she led him down to the scullery, where Cook and Margaret were doing dishes.

Margaret, who currently had her hands half-submerged in a sink, startled as Winnie slipped through the doorway with Robert's fetch in tow. Cook maintained her calm composure by comparison, reaching out to catch the pan which Margaret had nearly fumbled.

"I did not see either you or Master Robert last evening, after I fell asleep," Cook observed to Winnie.

"I had cause to go ahead without you," Winnie admitted. She glanced between the two women, weighing her words. "The faeries have taken Master Robert, I'm afraid. This is his replacement, made of wood. I am attempting to bring back the actual boy, but the task is difficult so far."

Margaret stared at the boy currently standing next to Winnie. "He looks... so real, though," she whispered fearfully. "Is he dangerous?"

Winnie glanced down at Robert's fetch, who did not seem to react to this statement. "I don't believe he is," she said. "In fact, he is far better behaved than Master Robert was. I see no reason to blame him for his own creation, so long as he causes no trouble."

The fetch looked up at Winnie with the same slow manner it had exhibited thus far. There was, for once, a flicker of something other than ennui in its distant gaze. "Thank you, Miss Hall," it said. "I promise, I will cause no trouble for you."

Margaret seemed unconvinced. But Cook accepted the explanation and moved past it rather practically. "What might they want with Master Robert?" she asked carefully. "Or has he simply been a naughty child?"

Winnie sighed. "The curse which keeps the faeries bound has something to do with the blood of Longfell," she said. "The dowager never left the manor, you recall? And now Lord Longfell will not leave, himself. The faeries aim to strip this family tree of leaves. Lord Longfell's ring will protect him, but I do not know the particulars of its magic. Whatever the faeries want with Master Robert, it is clear that we should want him back."

Cook nodded at her. "You have come to tell this to us for a reason, I expect," she said.

Winnie smiled wearily. "I do require a bit of help," she

admitted. "It will involve facing down the faeries in the conservatory. I can send Oliver with you—but the task might still be dangerous."

Cook shrugged and set aside her towel. "It would not be the first time I have scrapped with them," she said. "Tell me what it is you need, and I will do it."

CHAPTER 13

*T*hat evening, when Winnie descended to meet Mr Quincy at the green baize door within the Witchwood Knot, Cook was walking next to her. The two of them cast skittering shadows ahead of them, backlit by the guttering candle which Winnie held in her hand.

Mr Quincy's reddish gaze fixed instantly upon Winnie, weighing her attitude with wariness. Irrational betrayal flared again in Winnie's stomach—but she did not deign to show it to him. Instead, she buried it beneath a business-like exterior.

The butler's eyes shifted next to Cook. "Surely, you will not be coming with us, Sarah Baker," he said slowly.

"I will not be coming with you," Cook assured him. "Though I hope to speed you on your way, regardless." The older woman cradled Oliver absently in her arms. Though Winnie had been concerned that the cat might snub her, she needn't have worried; Cook had brought a pocket full of cat mint with her into the Witchwood Knot tonight. Even as they spoke, Oliver rubbed his cheek against Cook's chest and purred.

Winnie gestured towards the door with her candle. "Shall we try the labyrinth again?" she asked calmly. "We will need to make do without Oliver tonight, I fear. I am leaving him with Cook."

Mr Quincy frowned at the two of them, attempting to puzzle out the situation.

"I have asked Cook to play the pianoforte for us, while we navigate," Winnie explained. "The other day, Lord Longfell could hear the music from upstairs. I expect that we will also hear it from below—I hope that we can use the sound to orient ourselves. If we can go swiftly, then perhaps the soldiers will not catch us."

Mr Quincy's mouth thinned with displeasure, and his wine-red eyes fixed upon Cook. "You should not enter the conservatory without me," he said. "The faeries there will not play cards with you, as I do."

Cook smiled at him. "I've noted your concern," she said, with nearly as much insolence as Mr Quincy often used. "But Mr Oliver will keep me safe—won't you, my sweet boy?" She scratched beneath Oliver's chin, while the cat closed his only eye and purred more loudly.

Mr Quincy's jaw twitched. "I do not trust that creature," he muttered. His rat's tail thrashed once, just behind him.

"He is the *only* trustworthy creature in this entire cursed manor," Winnie informed the butler sharply. "You are simply prejudiced."

Mr Quincy did not offer a rejoinder, this time.

Cook let Oliver back down to the floor and took the candle from Winnie, who turned back towards the green baize door. "The night is wasting, Mr Quincy," Winnie said curtly, "and I must make up for lost time. Let us get on with it."

The butler offered one last reluctant glance at Cook,

before he took up his flickering blue lantern once again. Winnie pushed open the green baize door, and led them down into the darkness.

The earth eagerly swallowed them up into its belly once again. This time, Mr Quincy was far more alert—his reddish eyes shifted back and forth as they went, and his tail flicked with barely suppressed tension. Winnie, too, strained her hearing, listening for the telltale sound of clunking footsteps. But all she heard was the uncanny breath of the house, moving in and out like an ocean tide.

Many minutes later, however, a distant ringing sound began on the air—a single piano note, played over and over.

Mr Quincy turned his head in the direction of the sound. His lips twitched with reluctant humour in the flickering candlelight. "I do not believe that Sarah Baker knows how to play the pianoforte," he observed. "The faeries in the conservatory are not likely to enjoy her performance."

Winnie raised an eyebrow at him. "You don't seem terribly upset on their behalf," she observed.

Another dull, repetitive piano note sounded through the corridors, and Mr Quincy hid a smile behind his free hand. "Most faeries are not accustomed to things which they cannot control," he said. "I will admit—I take some pleasure in knowing that they will be forced to learn some patience. How should I put this? It might… build character."

Winnie narrowed her eyes at him. "You are not like them," she said slowly. "They dance and frolic every evening. But you are truly a servant here—bound by oaths and bans."

"Such is the price that I have paid in order to remain awake," said Mr Quincy staunchly. The humour fell away from his expression as he walked beside her. "The lady of the Mourningwood agreed to let me live in her domain, despite the danger I present... but I must serve her in return."

"And yet, none of the faeries here trust you," Winnie said. In that light, she was no longer terribly surprised that Mr Quincy could not bring himself to drive away his only friend, regardless of the looming tragedy he knew to be at hand.

"Why should the faeries trust me?" Mr Quincy asked. "I do not care for them. But I will never break my oaths. If I did, then Lady Mourningwood's protection would expire, and all of faerie's power would turn against me. Longshadow, in particular, would hunt me down and cast me into slumber."

Winnie did not look at him. She could not help but think that this explanation was something of an apology. It did not overcome what he had done—but now, at least, she knew that he was fighting for his own survival.

"Another faerie could take you in," she observed slowly. "Perhaps... one who owes you a favour."

Mr Quincy sucked in a soft breath. "I wondered where it was you learned that song," he whispered. "I have only ever taught it to one person."

A piano note echoed down the hallway, painfully discordant.

Winnie stopped in her tracks. "Of course you did," she breathed. She turned her head to stare at him. "You were the shadow at the pianoforte. You helped the Hollow Lady leave the Mourningwood. No little girl composed that music—it belongs to *you*."

Mr Quincy flinched. "It is my composition," he said stilt-edly. There was, Winnie thought, a hint of embarrassment in his voice before he steeled it forcibly.

The idea struck Winnie with a sudden insecurity. How could her favourite song belong to someone other than the

Hollow Lady? The revelation cast so many of her memories into a jarring light. All of the strength and satisfaction she had drawn from her mastery of the requiem had been born of Mr Quincy's sentiments and talent. How much work had he put into the song? What did it truly mean to him?

Oh dear, thought Winnie suddenly. *I dared to play his own song in front of him.*

A horrified flush crept into her cheeks at the belated realisation. Mr Quincy had been so off-balance after her performance. Her version of his masterpiece had been crude and clumsy in comparison to his own. She had paid him such a disastrous insult at that pianoforte—she was surprised now that he had not taken the opportunity to immediately repay it.

Mr Quincy cleared his throat. "Do not mistake me, governess," he said carefully. "I only did what was necessary. No human being should have ever set foot within the Mourningwood—not even half of one. Faeries are so foolish, just like men. They forget their danger, given too much time."

The declaration reminded Winnie of more immediate concerns. She pressed her lips together. "The dead thing which slept beneath the earth," she murmured. "It was a *fomórach*, like you. The Hollow Lady's human blood made it stir. And now, the *fomórach* is loose once more."

The piano key struck again, wavering awkwardly on the air.

"And now, the mortal world will suffer," Mr Quincy agreed softly. "Perhaps you will be happier as a tree after all, Miss Hall."

The observation struck Winnie uncomfortably, as she remembered Lady Mourningwood's promise to turn her hair to leaves and her skin to bark. "Is that what Lady Mourningwood meant?" she mumbled.

"That is what she meant," Mr Quincy sighed. "It is her punishment of choice. For many centuries, Lady Mourningwood has kept the Witchwood as her mortal garden. Each time the villagers cut down one of her prized trees, she crafted a new tree from one of *them*, in turn."

A nauseous chill raced down Winnie's spine at the implications of those words. "Oh," she whispered. "Mr Quincy. You can't possibly mean…"

A grim silence fell between them as she looked up at the wooden crossbeams above their heads.

"Witchwood Manor required such an abundance of white oak," Mr Quincy said finally. "Lord Longfell took only the finest specimens for his new house."

Winnie shrank back from the ceiling. Her stomach churned as she thought of the white oak floorboards she had walked upon—the walls which surrounded her as she slept—the vines and flowers carved into the manor's wooden moulding. All of the faces in the walls now made a horrifying sort of sense.

"Does Lord Longfell know what he has done?" Winnie asked hoarsely. She'd thought herself a hardened cynic… but the idea of this particular crime was still enough to shock her.

Mr Quincy tightened his jaw. "Perhaps I am ungenerous," he said, "but I believe that he knew all along. It is part of the magic which keeps the Witchwood Knot intact, after all. Magic born of blood and iron, Miss Hall." He stared ahead of them with a serious expression. "I warned you that he was a monster."

Lord Longfell and Lady Mourningwood are both monsters, Winnie thought. But she did not dare to besmirch Lady Mourningwood's character aloud, in front of Mr Quincy. Instead, she said: "The *spirits* feel that both Lord Longfell and

Lady Mourningwood are to blame. They are angry with a lord and with a lady."

Mr Quincy did not reply to this assertion. But the fact that he did not deny it made Winnie think that he agreed with the idea.

A fresh, uncomfortable thought occurred to Winnie then. "The toy soldiers in the classroom," she said. "They were carved from Witchwood oak, weren't they?"

"Of course they were," said Mr Quincy calmly. "Why should they not be?"

As the butler spoke, Winnie stumbled sharply over something in the darkness. The floor rose up to meet her with alarming swiftness—but Mr Quincy snapped out his arm to catch her, hauling her back to her feet.

Winnie clutched at his arm, briefly disoriented. For a moment, she found herself struck by the feeling of Mr Quincy's closeness and by the sight of his wine-red eyes looking down at her, dancing with the light of that blue lantern. A queer, fleeting *something* stirred in her chest—so entirely foreign that she could not properly identify it.

A memory snagged at Winnie's mind: She was a girl again, settled at the foot of a piano bench in faerie, as the Hollow Lady played her requiem. Winnie had often sat there in her dreams, looking up with unspeakable awe at the lovely, terrible faerie lady, with her mismatched green and grey eyes and her wild rust-red hair. Though the Hollow Lady was a monster, she was *Winnie's* monster, tucked away into a precious place within her heart.

Mr Quincy was a monster, too. That, she thought, was why his latest betrayal had hurt so keenly. For some reason, Winnie had begun to tuck him into that same corner of her heart, until he'd torn himself free once again.

That was not his fault, thought Winnie. He had never volunteered to walk beside her. Quite the contrary—Mr Quincy had done everything he could to see her banished from the manor. He had his own impossible problems to deal with... and she was just his latest complication.

Mr Quincy released her again, without another word. He was so quick to help, Winnie thought, and so quick to let her go again.

"I am sorry," Winnie told him quietly, brushing off her skirts. "I have held you to a higher standard than I hold myself. I would have done the same thing, in your place."

"I don't believe you would have," Mr Quincy murmured back. "I think you wish that were the case." A tinge of frustrated guilt slipped past his guard—and Winnie found that she'd forgiven him. "What is that at your feet?" the butler asked, before Winnie could pursue the matter. He raised his lantern to illuminate the obstacle which Winnie's foot had caught upon.

A twisted pile of blackened wood sprawled before her. Winnie blinked down at it, trying to make sense of what she was seeing. As she did, her eyes caught upon a lingering splash of red paint among the wreckage.

"Oh," she whispered.

Mr Quincy frowned at the charred remains. "Is that..."

Winnie pressed her lips together. "I think I was the one who did this," she mumbled. A gut-wrenching guilt flooded her as she looked down at the twisted wooden soldier. She had not meant to torment the house's spirits any further. "I threw all of the toy soldiers upstairs into the fireplace."

Another monotonous piano note chased itself along the labyrinth, bouncing along the walls. Mr Quincy turned his crimson eyes upon her, studying her intently. "Did you know?" he asked.

"Did I know... what?" Winnie asked him slowly.

The butler nudged experimentally at the pile with his foot, as though testing it to see if it might rise. It did not move. "It was a *fomórach*'s magic which trapped these spirits here," he said. "That magic is traditionally undone by hearth fire."

Winnie blinked at him. "I had no idea," she admitted. "I was simply upset at the time."

Mr Quincy rubbed at his narrow chin. "And did you burn them all?" he asked. At Winnie's hesitant nod, he managed a wan smile. "I believe that you have cleared our way, Miss Hall," he said. "The spirits are not gone—but they will need to find new forms." He looked up at the sound of another ringing piano note. "The pianoforte is growing fainter. We are headed in the right direction."

Mr Quincy grew more confident in his bearing as they went now, winding through the servants' passageways with increasing speed. Soon, the sound of the pianoforte had faded away almost entirely—just as they came to a strangely familiar set of stairs.

"These are the attic stairs," Winnie observed in surprise. "But they are headed downwards here."

"So they are," said Mr Quincy. "The centre of the Witchwood Knot lies further down, in this direction." He considered the stairs with renewed wariness. "I will go first. Nothing in this place can kill me." He glanced back at her, then added: "I felt I ought to remind you of that specifically, for some reason."

Winnie flushed again. "You needn't tease me about it," she said.

Mr Quincy arched an eyebrow at her. "You are correct," he

said. "I do not *need* to do so. But I take great pleasure in it, nevertheless." He held the lantern out before them, and started onto the stairs.

Unlike the servants' passageways, the attic stairs did not extend beyond their usual length. Instead, Mr Quincy soon came to the dowager's bedroom door. A bundle of black crepe hung upon the door handle—the very same crepe which Winnie had put there herself. The sight struck her with sudden uneasiness, and for a moment, she stopped breathing entirely.

"There is a new apparition here," Mr Quincy observed grimly.

Winnie clenched her hands, digging her fingers sharply into her palms in order to force another breath into her lungs. "You mean... the dowager's spirit is still here," she said.

"Did you really believe that the Witchwood Knot would let her go in peace?" Mr Quincy asked. His tone was softer than Winnie might have expected—perhaps, in fact, it held a mild note of sympathy.

Again, Winnie found herself longing for Bellamira's help. But she had kept her sister at arm's reach for good reason; she would have to make do with bits and pieces of the necromantic mumblings which she had overheard from Bellamira over the years.

"The dowager is freshly departed," Winnie murmured. "She will be confused, and likely terribly distressed. I am sure that the Witchwood Knot has not been kind to her, either. She could harm either one of us by accident."

Mr Quincy raised an eyebrow sardonically in Winnie's direction, and she corrected herself. "She might harm *me* by accident," she said. "The freshly dead sometimes draw the living with them into death. And they have great power here, in dreams. I am not sure that I would wake again if Lady Longfell dragged me after her." She hesitated. "If you had not given that bay berry perfume to your lady, it would be the perfect protection."

Mr Quincy's free hand dipped into the pocket of his crimson jacket. In the next moment, Winnie saw that he was holding a familiar vial of perfume.

"You still have it?" she asked in surprise.

"I decided to keep it for myself," Mr Quincy replied. He offered Winnie a slow, sly smile. "Would you like your perfume back, Miss Hall? I could make a gift of it to you."

Winnie narrowed her eyes at him. "And I would owe you a debt, of course," she said shortly. "There are no true gifts in faerie, Mr Quincy. We both know that."

Mr Quincy swirled the perfume vial absently, and Winnie caught a fresh whiff of its bay berry scent. "I could perhaps be persuaded to part with it," he offered.

"And what would you like in return?" Winnie asked him flatly.

"I would like the answer to my question," Mr Quincy said. "Your worst fear, Miss Hall. That is a worthy trade, I think."

Winnie's heart sped up at the very thought. She shook her head. "You will not have it," she told him in a tight voice. "Keep the perfume, Mr Quincy. It suits you well."

She snatched the lantern from the butler and strode past him for the attic bedroom's door. Winnie set her hand upon the black-swathed silver handle, pushing it open before her.

The attic bedroom was very nearly as Winnie had left it. A familiar small table and chairs were set out before the oak and ivy stained glass window—though the world beyond the window was dark and dull. Black crepe covered the mirror at the vanity, drifting on the house's breath. The cold oven at the back of the room offered no heat, leaving the entire room uncommonly frigid.

Above the dowager's bed hung a photograph which Winnie had never seen before: a portrait of Lady Longfell in a dark, stiff gown. Though the older woman's head turned towards the unseen camera, her eyes were closed, as though she were sleeping. Her mouth had fallen open in a silent, gaping scream.

A human figure was laid out upon the bed—now draped in the same black gauze which covered so much of the rest of the manor.

Winnie took a sharp step backwards, nearly colliding with Mr Quincy. The butler stumbled back in turn, grasping blindly at her shoulder.

Winnie swallowed down the shock of fear which had assaulted her, forcing herself to straighten. To her consternation, however, shivers still wracked at her body as she stared at the screaming portrait.

She had hoped—she had convinced herself, somehow—that Lady Longfell was at peace. But clearly, that was not the case at all.

"That is a horrid portrait," Mr Quincy observed from behind her. His tone was perfectly sedate—as though he were discussing a bitter cup of tea. "Imagine painting such a thing on purpose."

Winnie let out a shaky breath which frosted on the air. The trembling in her limbs, she realised, was partially from the cold air in the room. Her feet refused to move her forward.

"That is no painting," she said hoarsely. "It is a photograph —a memento mori. We are supposed to take a picture of her, just before the funeral. But we have not done so yet. That picture should not be here."

And of course, no photographer with any common sense would pose the dowager in such an agonised state.

Mr Quincy's gloved hand still rested on Winnie's shoulder as she stood in the doorway. Each moment that passed made her shivers increase more violently, however... and finally, he cleared his throat.

"Will you be going inside?" he asked. "There is only so much time before you wake, Miss Hall."

Winnie clenched her jaw... and forced herself to take a step into the attic bedroom.

The figure on the bed was still and silent beneath its black shroud—but Winnie knew what she was expected to do. Slowly, she made her way to the chair next to the bed, settling down into it as though she were visiting the dowager once again. Mr Quincy settled himself against the doorframe at the edge of her senses, watching on with careful interest.

Winnie set the lantern down upon the table and threaded her fingers tightly together in her lap. She could not bring herself to look directly at the apparition in the bed.

"I'm so sorry, Lady Longfell," she whispered shamefully. "I have lost Robert to the faeries. I understand if you are furious with me. I am... trying to get him back."

No voice rose up to answer her. But the house's breath stuttered and shifted, and a strange knocking sound creaked along the walls. The lantern's flame wavered in the breeze.

Winnie shuddered in her chair. "I made you a promise," she said in a tiny voice, "and I will keep it. I will not stop until he is home again... or else, I suppose, until I have joined you here."

The knocking sound repeated, as the house shifted softly.

Winnie glanced around herself. "I need to find my way deeper into the Witchwood Knot if I am to rescue your grandson," she whispered. Her teeth chattered slightly as she spoke now. "Do you know which way I ought to go?"

The knocking grew erratic and insistent—nearly panicked. Winnie knitted her brow. "I d-don't... understand," she admitted. "You wish to tell me something important. I'm sure that's why you're here. But I'm not Bellamira. I don't know any necromancy—"

A thought occurred to Winnie then, and she sucked in her breath. "Wait just a moment," she said quickly. She fumbled in her pocket with numbed fingers, searching out her deck of cards. "Just tell me what you are about," she said, as she shuffled the cards with shaking hands. "Can you choose a card, Lady Longfell?"

Winnie reached out with her magic, offering it to the spirit like a lifeline.

"Don't!" Mr Quincy said sharply. He straightened abruptly in the doorway, with alarm flashing in his reddish eyes. "You will hurt yourself this way, governess."

Something brushed against Winnie's magic—cold and terrible and familiar, all at once. Like a frigid hand, it closed upon her soul, seizing her directly.

The remaining warmth drained from her body, all at once. Winnie's shivers redoubled, now so violent that she nearly dropped her cards. As she opened her eyes, she saw that the figure in the black shroud had sat up in place, and was now staring straight ahead.

Mr Quincy's hands were on her shoulders again, Winnie realised—but she could not feel them any longer. He was cursing softly now, in that other language which she did not recognise. "Stop!" he demanded. "Whatever you are doing—put an end to it!"

Winnie forced herself to ignore him. Instead, she tore the top card from her deck and set it down onto the bedside table in front of her. Blue lantern light flickered along a dark feminine figure on the card.

"The Queen of S-Spades," she chattered. "That was your card, Lady Longfell. This is something to do with *you*, and not with Robert."

The knocking sound rose up again. This time, Winnie was *certain* that it meant she'd guessed correctly.

She picked another card from the deck. "The Nine of Spades," she rasped. "A death. But that is obvious. I still don't understand." A chill beyond all reason was creeping slowly through her veins, winding its way towards her heart.

"You are too pale," Mr Quincy said urgently. "Do you understand that she is killing you?" Winnie had the impression that his grip had tightened on her, though she could not feel it.

Winnie tried to answer—but a rattling cough tore its way from her throat, and she doubled over, gasping for breath. When she brought her hand away from her mouth, she saw blood on her fingers.

The sight made her draw back from the table in alarm. She tugged at the spirit's grip on her magic, trying to loosen it—but Lady Longfell's ghost was too confused, too blindly distressed to let her go again.

"I can't make her release me," Winnie gasped.

"I cannot help you!" Mr Quincy said. A strange, helpless fury tinted the words. "Death is foreign to me. I have never learned to touch it. Take the perfume, Miss Hall. What could you possibly fear more than death itself?"

"There is much to fear apart from d-death!" Winnie snapped at him breathlessly. "You cannot die, Mr Quincy. Does that make you fearless?"

The butler stilled behind her.

"I must decipher what it is she w-wants," Winnie said, forcing steel into her voice. "She will relent then, I am certain." She fumbled for another card, as that dread chill reached the edges of her chest. Though Winnie nearly dropped the card, Mr Quincy snatched it from her fingers, setting it onto the table in front of her.

"The... K-King... of Spades," Winnie mumbled. "A dishonest man. An enemy. He is... s-someone to be feared."

"She is telling you about her murder," Mr Quincy hissed. "She wants you to know who has killed her."

The black-draped figure turned its head towards the butler with a keen and penetrating interest, as the knocking in the walls grew louder.

"Who—" Winnie coughed again violently. "Who is the King of Spades? How did he kill you?"

A shrouded hand flashed out to grasp at Winnie's wrist, tightening there sharply. Winnie cried out in pain, looking down at it.

The black crepe had drawn tight against the dowager's dead hand, so that it was nearly transparent. Beneath that material, Winnie saw a putrid black ring of skin encircling the corpse's thumb.

"The r-ring," Winnie said. Her heart leapt into her throat. "It was the ring that killed you. The ring that Lord Longfell gave to you."

The knocking ceased abruptly. The dowager's hand relaxed. As it did, the grip on Winnie's magic loosened, and the chill in her chest receded. The house let out a rattling breath... and settled into silence.

The black crepe shroud fluttered down to the bed, which now held no body at all.

Winnie sagged against the back of her chair, briefly unable to speak.

"That was foolish," Mr Quincy said. His hands still clutched at Winnie's shoulders, as though he could pin her physically to the world of the living. He sounded oddly shaken.

"You knew," Winnie said hoarsely. "You knew all along what was killing her. And you said nothing." She trembled with misery and confusion. "You could have saved her."

Mr Quincy looked down at her, suddenly uncertain. Very slowly, he released her shoulders and drew back from the chair.

"That ring is tied up with the magic of the Witchwood Knot," he said quietly. "It feeds upon the blood of Longfell in order to sustain itself. Had the dowager left the house, as I intended, then perhaps she would yet live."

Winnie curled in upon herself, trying to regain some warmth. She pressed her forehead to her knees. "And the Witchwood Knot would fall apart," she mumbled. "And Lady Mourningwood would take her vengeance on the dowager regardless. There is no happy ending to this story—is there, Mr Quincy?"

The butler looked away from her. "One last Longfell wears the ring," he said. "His heir is gone. Unless he has another child, he has no recourse. The Knot will come unravelled once the ring is done with him."

Winnie glanced up from her knees as a strange thought occurred to her. "You... stole Master Robert away," she said slowly. "You took him before the dowager had died." She studied Mr Quincy's pale, narrow features, searching him for hints of emotion. "You believe the worst of Lord Longfell. That is what you told me. Did you believe that he would give his son that ring?"

If that were so, Winnie thought, then Mr Quincy might believe that he was saving Robert's life—despite the other awful consequences.

Mr Quincy's face betrayed nothing. He was cold and distant, once again. "Once Lord Longfell dies," he said, "the fetch will become the new lord of these lands. It will obey the faeries; the village will no longer cut down Witchwood trees. Lady Mourningwood shall have her garden back."

"There will be no village left," Winnie told him quietly. "Not when Lady Mourningwood is through with it. You know that."

Mr Quincy smiled bitterly, and Winnie knew that he believed the same. "You are correct, Miss Hall," he replied softly. "There is no happy ending to this story." He gestured towards the stained glass window of the attic bedroom—and Winnie saw that it had disappeared. Darkness yawned beyond the hole in the wall, stretching out into the unknown. "Regardless, we continue. I have no power to change what lies at the centre of the Knot... and you yourself refuse to walk away."

Winnie closed her eyes again, bone tired. She knew that she needed to rise to her feet and continue. But every inch of her still shook with cold and weariness.

"Give me just a moment," she whispered. "I will get up soon, Mr Quincy."

But when she opened her eyes again, she was back in her bedroom, staring at the white oak ceiling.

CHAPTER 14

*E*xhaustion weighed down Winnie's limbs, even in the waking world. It was several minutes before she could even bring herself to rise from bed—and yet, somehow, she did.

I must go down to breakfast with Lord Longfell, she realised, with a sickening twist of her stomach. Every time that she had faced the man so far, she had deplored the experience... but until this very moment, she had felt herself reasonably capable of handling him.

The knowledge of Lord Longfell's many possible crimes had begun to stack up to such heights, however, that Winnie was no longer certain of her ability to extract herself from his grip. If Mr Quincy's suspicions were correct, and Lord Longfell had done all of these things while fully cognisant of their consequences, then surely he was capable of *anything*.

Winnie saw no reason to offer him the benefit of the doubt. But still, she was within his power so long as she remained at Witchwood Manor. Somehow, she had to hide all of her fear and revulsion of the man, until...

Until what? she thought dimly. Perhaps, if she was very clever, she would rescue Robert from one monster—only to immediately hand him back to an entirely *different* monster.

What would the Hollow Lady have done in her place?

The Hollow Lady is a monster too, Winnie thought wearily. *She would bring the others to their knees and laugh at their misfortune.*

But Winnie was not a powerful monster, no matter how she sometimes wished to be. She could not be the Hollow Lady.

"I must take this one step at a time," she whispered, trying to shore up her courage. "I cannot solve everything, all at once."

The remnants of Lady Longfell's chill still plagued Winnie as she dressed; her fingers trembled on the buttons of her threadbare frock, and she nearly tore one of her stockings pulling them on. Despite this, she composed herself, straightening her shoulders and pushing open her bedroom door.

The door caught upon something in the hallway.

Winnie glanced down in confusion. A large white box had been set outside her room, tied up with a heavy black ribbon.

She brought the box inside and settled it upon her bed, pulling the ribbon loose. Inside, someone had folded a heavy gown of black silk, along with several petticoats—and a matching pair of slippers.

The dowager said that she would leave me some of her gowns, Winnie remembered belatedly.

The gown was certainly fine enough to belong to the dowager. The stitching was impeccable—though the collar was somewhat lower than Lady Longfell had preferred in her advanced years. Winnie found herself wondering whether this was one of the woman's old mourning gowns, worn after her husband had passed away.

Either way, Winnie had promised the dowager that she would wear what she was given. In fact, the gown was something of a welcome reassurance—Winnie's good clothing was all still with Margaret, in desperate need of washing, and she'd yet to replace her only pair of slippers. At least this way, she would no longer walk about the house with only stockings on her toes, so painfully aware of Lord Longfell's gaze upon them.

Winnie replaced her frock with the mourning gown and tugged the slippers onto her feet. She took a moment to consider herself in the mirror, frowning at her reflection.

She had hoped that the dark gown would offer her a stern and unapproachable air—but alas, it did nothing of the sort. It hugged her curves a bit too nicely, and displayed the column of her neck in an inviting way.

"You were too daring in your younger years, Lady Longfell," Winnie muttered at the mirror. "You must not have been terribly displeased with your husband's death, if this is what you wore to mourn him."

Winnie plucked a dark woollen shawl from her things and threw it over her shoulders in order to blunt the gown's appeal. She headed then to Robert's room in order to collect his fetch for breakfast.

"You look very lovely today, Miss Hall," the false Robert told her, as they headed down the stairs.

Winnie shot a surprised glance at the fetch. Robert's double so rarely spoke at all—and she could not recall it ever doing so without plenty of prompting.

"Thank you, Master Robert," she told the fetch. "It is kind of you to say so."

The false Robert did not respond again for a long while as they walked. Just as Winnie had assumed it would not speak again, however, it said: "You do not give me lessons anymore."

Winnie frowned at the construct. Its expression was wooden and unreadable... but the words had some important purpose, she knew, since the fetch did nothing without great deliberation.

"I told Lord Longfell that you are ill," she murmured. "And you are resting." She hesitated. "But... I cannot recall ever giving *you* lessons. I did not know you craved them."

Robert's fetch was quiet again for several moments.

"I do not like to be alone," it said finally.

The toneless words struck Winnie with unusual weight. She tightened her hand on the fetch's instinctively. *Somewhere in the Witchwood Knot,* she thought, *Robert is likely very frightened and alone.* Despite her best efforts, a hint of pity crept beyond her stiff defences.

"I'm sorry," she said softly. "I have ignored you, haven't I?" She smiled tiredly at the fetch. "I have been awfully overwhelmed of late... but if you would like something from me, then you must not be afraid to tell me. I promise, I will listen." She paused, then added: "I will tell you more stories today, if you would like."

Robert's fetch did not react to this overtly. But she thought, perhaps, that its hand tightened on hers in return. "I would like that, Miss Hall," it said. And though its tone was unenthusiastic, she suspected that the words were true.

Lord Longfell was absent from the dining room when they arrived, though Margaret had set out a spread. For a while, Winnie managed to relax, hoping that he would not show his face—but partway through the meal, the lord's steps sounded in the hallway, and he came into the room.

The lord of Witchwood Manor was now dressed in mourning. His waistcoat was all black, with subtle ebony stitching showing along its front. His jacket was sombre but fashionably cut, and his hair was freshly trimmed. The dark colours made his skin seem far too pale by comparison—but this only offered him a tragically handsome sort of air.

"Miss Hall," he greeted her warmly, with a tired smile and an inclination of his head. "I find my wretched morning instantly improved by your presence."

Winnie's gaze dropped instantly to the knotted ring of wood and iron on his index finger. The sight of it now chilled her—but she did not dare to look at it for long. "Your Lordship," she mumbled. "A good morning to you, then."

Lord Longfell ignored his son's fetch entirely, pacing close to Winnie's chair. He paused just behind her, looming over her place at the table. His fingers brushed gently across her shoulder, and she stiffened with a sudden inhalation.

"You are wearing the gown I bought for you," he murmured. "I knew it would look lovely on you."

Winnie's stomach twisted with a sudden, sickening panic. Her heart leaped into her throat, now beating so swiftly and so loudly that she wondered if the room could hear it.

"I... thought this gown belonged to the dowager," she rasped. "She asked me to wear the clothes which she had left for me. It was her final wish."

"How kind of her," Lord Longfell said. "But we have not read her will yet, Miss Hall. I would not know what she has left to you." His hand lingered on Winnie's shoulder with a new hint of possessiveness which made her tremble with revulsion. "But you must have *something* better to wear to my mother's funeral, in the meantime. That old frock does not suit you in the least."

If Winnie had not been in front of him, she knew, she would have torn the gown from her body in a heartbeat. The hand on her shoulder was nearly as awful as the black silk against her skin—as though someone had stitched Lord Longfell's covetous gaze into every inch of the fabric where it touched her.

Winnie knew that she should keep her voice calm and her manner polite. She knew, as well, that she should stay for breakfast. But her trembling had grown worse now, and hot tears had begun to prick at the edges of her eyes.

She bolted out of her chair and sidestepped his grip abruptly, with a hand pressed over her mouth.

"I'm sorry," she gasped. "My stomach has turned, Your Lordship. Perhaps I have taken ill, after all."

Winnie fled the dining room, stumbling up the stairs on shaking legs. She staggered through the door to her bedroom until she had reached the chamber pot near her bed—whereupon her stomach *did* betray her, casting up what little food she had managed to eat that morning.

She dry heaved for a few more seconds, shuddering violently. Even as she did, she tore the slippers from her feet and unbuttoned the collar of her new gown, intent on removing it from her body.

But it was too late, she knew. She had accepted a gift from Lord Longfell. Just like a faerie, he would never forget. Already, he had mentally assumed her in his debt. She could not take back her mistake—not even if she tore the gown to shreds or forced it back upon him. Rejecting his gift now would only raise his ire.

Footsteps fell upon the stairs... and Winnie knew then that he had come after her. Fresh panic whited out her thoughts, even as she tried to recover her breath.

Do not come in, she thought at those footsteps. *It is wildly inappropriate for you to enter my bedroom, and you know it.*

But Lord Longfell cracked open the door behind her and stepped across the threshold, offering Winnie a look of grave concern where she knelt upon the floor. He crossed the distance between them, reaching out to press the back of his hand to her forehead.

"This is too much, Miss Hall," he scolded her. "You should have said something sooner. I am calling the physician."

Winnie jerked back from his touch. Her vision swam, and her head began to spin with dizziness. She was cornered in her own bedroom now. "I do not wish to see a physician," she replied in a shaking voice. "Please leave me be."

Lord Longfell ignored her entirely. He slipped an arm beneath her shoulders instead, hauling her to her feet and settling her onto the edge of the bed. He was close, too close—his cologne was sickening and overpowering. Winnie thought suddenly of the silver knife upon her chatelaine, and her hand clenched in her lap just next to it.

Lord Longfell set his fingers beneath her chin, tilting her eyes up to his. There was an expression of solemn concern on his face. "I have just lost my mother, Miss Hall," he told her. "I will not lose you too."

You do not have me! Winnie screamed internally. *I am not yours!*

But some shred of hard-won self-preservation had finally clawed its way to the front of her panicked mind. There were ways to make him leave. None of them, alas, involved *demanding* that he leave.

Winnie could not calm her trembling. But that was for the best. She allowed the tears into her voice. "I am... so upset by everything," she admitted hoarsely. "I have been trying to be strong and sensible. But I am not strong—I am surviving. It is the simplest, most difficult thing in the world, because I have no choice."

Lord Longfell smiled sympathetically. "Oh, Winifred," he sighed. "Didn't you think that I would understand? I am upset as well. You do not need to bear this all alone." He pulled her into an embrace, while Winnie's heart tried to escape her chest. The cologne was sickly sweet now, and she thought that she might suffocate as it crawled down her throat.

Leave, she begged him silently. But he would not do so without careful handling, she knew. Lord Longfell would not leave unless she found a way to force him.

"Thank you," Winnie croaked. "You have been more generous than you should be." She shivered again, and he tightened his grip. "I... I think that you should call the physician, then. I will rest until he comes, if that will reassure you."

Lord Longfell pulled back to look down at Winnie. Very slowly, he reached out to brush her long blonde hair behind her shoulder... and Winnie knew then that he had desired to touch her hair since the very first moment he had seen her.

"That would greatly reassure me, Winifred," he said, with far too much affection in his voice.

Then—blessedly—he let her go again.

The smothering cologne lifted, and Winnie gulped in a desperate breath of fresher air, clutching at her chest.

Presently, she became aware of Robert's fetch standing in the doorway of her bedroom, staring in at her. No one had ordered it to go upstairs, she thought dimly... but it had come after her, all the same.

"Are you well, Miss Hall?" it asked her in a small voice.

Winnie offered it a weak smile. "I fear I have been better," she replied. On sudden inspiration, she added: "But I would love to have your company, Master Robert. Your presence always cheers me."

The fetch padded slowly over to the bed, while Lord Longfell considered it with a paternal sort of puzzlement.

"I had not realised just how fond you are of Miss Hall, Robert," the lord said slowly.

Winnie patted the bed. "Will you sit with me?" she asked the fetch gently.

The false Robert joined her—and Winnie *did* feel better with it there nearby. Lord Longfell did not often linger when his son was present, she had noticed.

"I will see to the physician, then," Lord Longfell said finally. "Take good care of your governess in my absence, Robert."

The fetch did not respond this time. As Lord Longfell turned for the hallway, Winnie found herself relaxing, hoping that he would now depart.

But he paused with his hand still on the doorframe, staring out into the hallway.

"...it had occurred to me earlier," Lord Longfell said slowly, "that you should have something of your grandmother's, Robert." He turned to consider the boy, and his hand dropped to the knot on his index finger, twisting at it anxiously. "I have her ring, if you would like it."

Winnie stared at him—and she knew, in that moment, that Mr Quincy was entirely correct about Lord Longfell. Every step of the way, she thought, the man had known exactly what he was doing.

You truly are a monster, she thought silently. *But I always knew that; I felt it when I met you. I always, always know.*

"I would like the ring," said Robert's fetch, in a quiet, even tone.

Winnie sucked in a breath. *The fetch does not have Longfell's blood*, she thought suddenly. *The Witchwood Knot will fail if Lord Longfell gives the ring to a false Robert—and I will have a different monster to confront.*

"I do not think that wise," she said.

Lord Longfell glanced at her quizzically. Winnie swallowed, searching for a way to phrase the truth which would not trigger his contempt.

"Since the dowager's passing," Winnie said slowly, "Master Robert has been almost like a different person. I do not think that he requires another reminder of her at the moment."

Lord Longfell's dark eyes slid towards Robert's fetch, lingering upon it for several seconds. He was a cunning man, Winnie thought—and though he'd protested all this time that Witchwood Manor was not haunted, she now suspected this to be a mere excuse. It was, she thought, a way in which he had contrived to avoid all discussion of the ring and the curse and the manor itself.

His fingers twisted at the ring again. But finally, Lord Longfell drew in a breath.

"Perhaps not," he said.

He turned back for the hallway then, and closed the bedroom door behind him.

In the resulting silence, Robert's fetch stood up from the bed. It walked somewhat mechanically across the room to pick up Winnie's folded nightgown from the top of the dresser, and then walked back again in order to offer it out to her.

"Shall I bring you some tea, Miss Hall?" it asked her. "You have always brought me tea when I am upset."

Winnie took the nightgown gratefully, clutching it to her chest. But this observation managed to penetrate the haze of sickened panic which had so fully consumed her until now, and she frowned at the construct. "You are not referring to the last few days," she observed slowly.

Robert's fetch blinked at her sluggishly. "I have many memories," it said. "I do not know why."

Winnie studied it intently. A construct made entirely of wood and magic should not have had those memories. "I wonder," she said softly, "do you have a piece of Robert's soul within you? That would make you more convincing."

Robert's fetch tilted its head, contemplating this. "There is something like that in me," it admitted. "A little sliver, deep beneath my bark. It is uncomfortable."

Winnie set the nightgown aside and reached out to take the fetch's hands. Though they were cold, like polished wood, she thought that there was something vaguely human in the way that Robert's fetch closed its fingers around hers.

"If there is any part of you that can hear me," she whispered, "please know that I am coming for you. I will not abandon you to faerie, Master Robert."

The fetch looked down at her hands blankly. "I am afraid," it said. "But I believe in you, Miss Hall. You always seem to know what you are doing."

Winnie smiled at it unsteadily. "That is because I am an excellent liar," she whispered back.

Robert's fetch looked back up to meet her eyes. "I am sorry to have caused you so much trouble," it said. And though its voice was toneless, Winnie thought that it was painfully sincere. It released her hands again, and stepped back from the bed. "Please rest, and I will bring you tea. And perhaps you could tell me another story when I get back, if you are feeling well enough."

"I will do that," Winnie promised it.

Once the fetch had departed, she tore away the gown she had been given and replaced it with her nightgown. The false Robert soon returned with tea, and Winnie let it climb onto the bed just next to her.

She told the fetch a faerie tale. It was a lovely faerie tale, with an uncommonly happy ending.

There was another faerie tale which Winnie might have told to Robert's fetch, which was not very happy at all. But she kept this faerie tale inside herself, as she had always done, instead of burdening the construct with it.

This was the faerie tale which Winifred did not tell.

CHAPTER 15

Once upon a time, a beautiful little girl was abandoned at a London workhouse.

Her name was Winifred—though she did not recall her surname, since she was too young to know it. Unlike the other children at the workhouse, Winifred was soft and lovely; everyone there was envious of her porcelain skin and her long blonde hair. Winifred was also a well-mannered little girl, who had been taught to curtsy and speak softly and avoid other people's eyes.

The other children were cruel to Winifred—or at least, that is how she recalled the situation when she was older. But the workhouse master found Winifred to be very charming, and he told her so most every day that she was there. In fact, Master Green often brought chewy caramels for Winifred, and he let her keep him company in his office, where it was safe and quiet. Every time he offered her a caramel, he asked her for a hug and for a kiss upon his cheek—which she politely gave him.

There was a curiosity in Master Green's office, which

Winifred often noted. One day, while she was sitting in his office chair, she asked him why there was an iron horseshoe nailed above his door.

"It is there in order to keep dangerous faeries at bay," said Master Green, as he looked over the workhouse bills. "The Lord Sorcier is supposed to protect us from faeries, among other things—but he is always concerned with the nobility, and so the rest of us must protect ourselves."

Winifred found this terribly unjust, and she was not shy to say so. Master Green smiled at her and patted her on the head, and offered her another caramel. "You are such a good girl, Winifred," he told her. "I wish I had a daughter just like you."

He bent down then, and Winnie kissed him dutifully on the cheek, exactly as he had taught her to do.

The other children also talked of faeries, especially at night. In particular, they told stories of the Hollow Lady, who supposedly stalked the hallways of London's workhouses, dragging away unwary workhouse masters. The other children thought that this was grand—they did not much like Master Green—and Winnie found herself in arguments with them. "You would be sorry if the Hollow Lady dragged Master Green away," she scolded them. "Who would take care of us *then?*"

The next day, Winifred awoke to find that the other children had cut off all her lovely hair while she was sleeping. For the first time in her life, she raged and cried and screamed— and when Master Green came to see what had happened, he badly punished all of the other children and took Winifred to his office in order to comfort her. It was a crime, he said, that the rest of the children had ruined her beautiful hair. But as he stroked his fingers through Winifred's short curls, she found herself uncomfortable... and when he asked her for a kiss upon his cheek, she tried to turn him down.

Master Green was terribly upset with her at this. "I have protected you, Winifred," he said. "I have brought you candies and been kind to you. The very least that you owe me is a kiss."

Winifred felt ashamed at the words—and so, she leaned up to kiss his cheek again. But this time, Master Green turned his head, and she was forced to kiss him on the lips.

From then on, Winifred did not like to visit Master Green's office at all. But she knew that it was impolite to turn down the caramels that he brought her, because she had accepted them before. And because he had punished the other children on her behalf, they were even less kind to her now, so that she had little choice but to hide in his office.

Now, when Master Green saw Winifred, he demanded that she kiss him on the lips. And though Winifred did not like this—though it made her feel miserable and unclean—she did not know what else to do. He was still kind to her, and doting like a father, and she had been taught that she should be polite to people who were kind to her.

But soon, Master Green asked Winifred to sit in his lap while he worked—and she did not want to do that at all. When she refused, he accused her of wickedly manipulating him. He hauled her out of his office with a grip which left bruises on her arms, and sent her to bed without any supper, warning that he would punish her until she apologised.

That night, when Winifred was crying, another little girl named Clarimonde came to see her. "You should call the Hollow Lady," Clarimonde whispered. "Don't you know that Master Green is afraid of her? All of the workhouse masters are. Call her name three times, and maybe she'll appear."

But Winifred knew that Master Green was in no danger from any faeries, so long as he kept that iron horseshoe nailed above his office door.

For many days, Winifred went without supper, until her stomach gnawed with hunger. When still she refused to approach the workhouse master, however, Master Green came to her with a caramel in his hand and told her gently to come with him to his office.

And Winifred made a terrible decision.

"You are busy, Master Green," she told him. "I will go and wait for you in your office until you are done with your work."

Master Green smiled at her and patted her on the head. "I knew that you were still a good girl, Winifred," he said.

Winifred went to his office and searched his desk until she found a letter opener. She dragged a chair to the office door and stood upon it, prying out the nails and tearing the iron horseshoe from the wall.

She hid the horseshoe underneath Master Green's desk and whispered the Hollow Lady's name three times. In fact, she said the faerie's name over and over, in case the Hollow Lady was distracted. Winifred repeated the name to herself until it felt dull and clumsy in her mouth—and only fell silent once she heard Master Green's steps approaching his office door.

When Master Green entered the office, he did not notice the missing horseshoe. He was terribly distracted by Winifred's lovely hair, and by the kiss she placed upon his cheek.

"Will you not kiss me on the lips, Winifred?" he asked her with a frown.

Winifred stepped back from him, wringing her hands in

front of her. Inwardly, she was frightened—halfway uncertain of whether she wanted a dangerous faerie to appear or not.

"Are you afraid of the Hollow Lady, Master Green?" Winifred asked him finally, rather than answering his question.

This was not the response that Master Green had been hoping for. In fact, he *did* appear afraid—but he covered his fear with anger. "You should stop listening to faerie tales, Winifred," he told her sharply. "If you continue to be wicked and disobedient, then one of those monsters will drag you away forever."

Winifred thought, in that moment, that she wanted to be dragged away. She would have preferred to be anywhere else —even in the clutches of an awful monster.

"If that is the case," said Winifred, "then I would be happy if the Hollow Lady dragged us *both* away. I would pay that price, Master Green."

The workhouse master's eyes caught on the empty spot above the door then, and his fear increased. But even as he reached for Winifred's arm again, the light in the office darkened, and the window fogged with frost.

The Hollow Lady came like a winter wind, appearing just behind the workhouse master. She was exactly as wild and terrifying as Winifred had hoped, with her rust red hair— almost like blood—and her tattered grey gown, and her mismatched green and grey eyes.

"Oh!" the Hollow Lady cried, in a lovely, lilting voice. "I am so glad to see you, Master Green!" She embraced the workhouse master from behind with obvious joy. "I have been hoping to speak with you for ages now!"

The workhouse master's skin went pale, and his fingers were now faintly blue. He shivered and cried and begged for mercy—but the Hollow Lady did not have any mercy for him. She laughed at his tears and stroked at his cheek, leaving painful frostbite where she touched him. And though Winifred was terrified, she realised that she was not terrified for *him*.

"Away with you, Master Green!" the Hollow Lady declared, with another trickling laugh. "I will see you back in Hollowvale, and we will finally become acquainted!"

She shoved the workhouse master into his office chair... and then, both he and the chair were gone.

Winifred stood there in silence with the faerie lady, uncertain of what she should say. But the Hollow Lady turned to Winifred and clasped her hands together, still full of wild delight. "How clever you were!" the faerie lady enthused at her. "What is your name, my darling?"

Winifred did not know that it was dangerous to give her name to faeries, and so she said: "My first name is Winifred. But I do not remember the rest of it."

The Hollow Lady offered Winifred a smile full of danger. "Then you must *choose* a name," she said. "That is what faeries do, you know."

As Winifred looked at the lady, a cold dread closed around her heart. "What will you do with me?" she asked. "What must I pay you for your help?"

The Hollow Lady tilted her head and narrowed her mismatched eyes. "You have given me something which I greatly desired, Winifred," she said. "But it is true that there are things I want from you."

She took a dancing step towards Winifred and drew a silver knife. Winifred stepped back in fear—but the Hollow Lady seized her blonde hair and slashed a lock of it away, curling her long fingers around it.

"I will take your hair," said the Hollow Lady, "so that I can find you wherever you go. Tomorrow, Winifred, you will receive a visitor—and when he orders you to go with him, you will do it. That is the payment which you owe me."

Winifred trembled—but she had been taught to pay her debts, and so she nodded her head. "I will do it," she promised the Hollow Lady.

The faerie lady disappeared with that lock of Winnie's hair in hand. The frost that she had brought with her lingered on the window, however—and when the matron of the work-house came to see what had happened, she could not help but see it. The matron called immediately for a priest, who asked Winifred about the devil she had seen.

Winifred did not tell the priest that she had summoned the faerie herself. Instead, she lied and said that the Hollow Lady had come for Master Green all on her own.

That night, Winifred and the other children slept more soundly than ever before.

The next morning, a well-dressed man with pale hair and eyes like golden embers stormed into the workhouse, stirring all the occupants. He demanded to see the office, and the frost that still lingered on the window glass.

"That awful faerie has struck again!" the matron cried at the man. "You must put a stop to her, please!"

The strange man fixed the matron with a chill expression. "I am not here to capture a faerie," he told her. "I am here to find a child. Where is the little girl who saw the Hollow Lady?"

The matron directed him to Winifred—and though Winifred knew that this was the man of whom the Hollow Lady had spoken, she shrank back from him, all the same.

"What is your name?" he asked.

"I have not yet decided," Winifred whispered.

The man nodded at her, unsurprised. "You are coming with me," he told her. "You will never return to this workhouse again."

Winifred did not *want* to go with him, now that he was here. But she had promised the Hollow Lady... and so, she followed him away from the workhouse and into his carriage.

"Don't you wonder where it is that we are going?" the man asked Winifred, as she sat across from him in silence.

"I do," said Winifred. "But I was not certain if it was polite to ask."

"Oh bother," said the man. "I am exhausted with politeness. Half the world would walk off a pier if someone told them that it was polite." But he answered the question which Winifred had not asked, regardless. "We are going to a private orphanage run by a woman named Mrs Dun. It is better than the workhouses, I like to think." He frowned at Winifred darkly. "Why did she come this time?" he asked.

Winifred looked down at her lap. "You mean the Hollow Lady?" she replied.

"Yes, the Hollow Lady," said the man impatiently. "'Lady Hollowvale' is what magicians call her."

Winifred pressed her lips together. But since the man was so belligerent, she decided for once that she would match his tone. "I asked her to appear," she dared to say. "And I am glad that I did."

The man sighed heavily, running his fingers back through his hair. "I'm certain it was well-deserved," he said. "But I often wish that she would be less obvious about it all. I suppose she knows that I will always tidy up her messes."

Winifred glanced up at him. "You know the Hollow Lady?" she asked him in surprise.

"I do," said the man. "Oh—I suppose I don't. It's awfully complicated, and I don't enjoy explaining it."

Winifred considered him warily. "If you do not know the Hollow Lady well," she said slowly, "then why do you tidy up her messes?"

The man shot Winifred a wry smile. "I am in love with her," he said. "As she is well aware."

The Lord Sorcier, Elias Wilder, did not deign to elaborate further upon the matter.

When Winifred fell asleep that evening in a fresh new bed, she dreamed of a distant manor, lit by chilly blue candlelight. She walked along the halls in a daze, following the sound of distant piano.

Eventually, she came into a large black-and-white chequered ballroom which held a grand pianoforte. The Hollow Lady sat at the bench, playing a lovely, maudlin song. Winifred stood and listened, absorbing the sound with wonder.

When the Hollow Lady had finished, she turned and saw that Winifred had joined her. She leapt to her feet and laughed with pleasure. "Ah, you are here, nameless lady!" she said. "Won't you come and play the pianoforte with me?"

Winifred joined the faerie lady at the piano, running her fingers along the ivory keys. "I do not know how to play the pianoforte," she admitted.

"Of course you know how to play it," the Hollow Lady scoffed. "Press a key and make a sound!"

Winifred hesitated one more moment, before dutifully tapping a key. The sound rang throughout the manor, and the Hollow Lady clapped her hands together. "There!" she said. "You have played it!"

Winifred smiled uncertainly. "I did not play it *well*," she pointed out.

The Hollow Lady sat down at the piano bench, tapping one of the other keys idly. "No one said you had to play it *well*," she replied. "Someone forced me to play the pianoforte once, until I learned it perfectly. I never forgave them for that. Now, I play the pianoforte however I please—and that is how you should play it, as well."

Winifred spent some time tapping clumsily at the pianoforte, as the Hollow Lady clapped for her. When she awoke again at Mrs Dun's orphanage, she decided that it was the loveliest dream that she had ever had. But she could not help feeling guilty about her apparent good fortune—and so, she begged her new caretakers to bring Clarimonde to Mrs Dun's, where they became as good as sisters.

In the years to come, Winifred learned much at the foot of the Hollow Lady's pianoforte. Other things, she learned from the Lord Sorcier, though he was always terribly impatient and aloof.

On the day that Winifred was ready to leave Mrs Dun's orphanage, however, she dreamed of Hollowvale again—and this time, the Hollow Lady offered Winifred the silver knife which she had used to cut her hair.

"If you are going out into the world again," the Hollow Lady said, "then you should take this with you."

Winifred accepted the knife with great uncertainty. "It is very wicked looking," she said carefully. "What if I hurt someone with it?"

"Oh, I should hope that you *will* hurt someone with it!" said the Hollow Lady cheerfully. "That is exactly why I am giving it to you!" She smiled at Winifred with a violent glitter in her mismatched eyes. "The world is full of monsters, darling. Alas, you cannot always take a knife to them—but if you *should* require a knife, I will be glad to know you have one."

Winifred tightened her hands around the silver knife... and to her very great surprise, she discovered that it *did* make her feel safer.

"I have decided what my name will be," Winifred told the faerie lady.

"Oh?" the Hollow Lady asked her curiously. "Well, what have you decided?"

Winifred drew in a deep breath. "I have no mother and no father," she said firmly. "But you have been my mentor—and that is more important, I should think, than family." She smiled at the Hollow Lady. "I will be Winifred of Hollowvale... if that does not offend you."

The Hollow Lady was always prone to sudden and intense emotion—and so, it did not terribly surprise Winifred when the faerie broke into sobs, now reaching for her tattered handkerchief. "Oh, that is lovely!" cried the Hollow Lady, as she dabbed at her eyes. "I am *exceptionally* fond of that name, Winifred of Hollowvale."

And that is how Winifred of Hollowvale earned her wicked silver knife and learned her name.

CHAPTER 16

*L*ord Longfell reappeared in Winnie's room with the physician after only a few hours of waiting, ordering Robert's fetch away with a succinct command. The physician, Mr Burrell, was a distinguished older man with a balding pate, dressed all in sombre black as though he were attending Lady Longfell's funeral. And perhaps he *would* be attending the funeral, in just two days—Winnie suspected that he had been the same physician to attend the older woman on her deathbed.

"A mild case of hysteria," said Mr Burrell authoritatively, as he finished examining Winnie's eyes and skin and mouth. "Not uncommon in women after a traumatic event. I would advise strict bedrest and no intellectual activity for the next few days. Some laudanum for the nerves, as well."

"Perhaps rest alone would be sufficient?" Winnie asked him guardedly. "I have a physician in the family, and he normally reserves laudanum for more serious cases."

Mr Burrell offered her a look of such offence that Winnie knew she had erred. "Perhaps you should have called your family then, Miss Hall," he said. "I have offered my professional opinion on the matter."

Winnie bit the inside of her cheek in order to prevent her next protest. The physician would not change his mind—she would be better off pouring out any laudanum in secret.

"Mr Burrell is an excellent physician," Lord Longfell told Winnie. "I trust his opinion implicitly. Besides which—I would feel much better if you took some medication."

And since Lord Longfell's opinion was, in fact, the only one that mattered, Winnie soon found herself presented with a cup of awful, medicinal-smelling tea, while both men stood by awaiting her compliance.

I will vomit it up later, Winnie promised herself, as she drank down the tea. Her stomach, so recently abused, did not enjoy the concoction—but she held it down for now, unwilling to be dosed a second time.

Mr Burrell soon departed... but Lord Longfell lingered at her bedside, as her head swam dizzily and her limbs grew heavy and her eyes began to close.

Distantly, she felt him take her hand in his, stroking it in what he must have thought to be a reassuring manner. Winnie's stomach might have threatened to revolt again... but soon, she found herself in a distracted state, as her eyes opened on a different ceiling.

Screaming faces wavered at the edges of her senses, somehow less distinct than usual. Winnie shoved clumsily at her bedsheets, stumbling to her feet. The Witchwood Knot lurched around her, swaying precariously as she pulled on her frock and her silver chatelaine.

Something was scratching at the door.

Oliver let out a high-pitched whine on the other side and scratched again. Winnie opened the door for him—but the ragged cat only sat down at the threshold, looking up at her mournfully.

"You can't come into my bedroom," Winnie mumbled dazedly. Her tongue felt thick in her mouth. "Is something keeping you out?"

Oliver stared at her with his one remaining eye, unable to convey his difficulty. The edges of his black fur were oddly foggy, drifting on the air.

Lord Longfell's ring, Winnie thought. *It is keeping Oliver at bay, along with all the other spirits of the house.*

"Don't try to go inside," she murmured. "That ring might harm you. Come with me instead."

Oliver paced dutifully after Winnie as she stumbled down the stairs, leaning heavily upon the railing. Halfway down, she found herself face-to-face with Mr Quincy and his blue lantern. The butler had a grim expression on his pale, narrow features.

Mr Quincy offered out his arm. Winnie accepted it somewhat more tightly than usual, with her head still dizzy and her heart still lurching nauseously in her chest.

"The Witchwood Knot has already exhausted you," Mr Quincy observed. He supported more of Winnie's weight than usual as he helped her down the stairs, with Oliver walking warily behind them.

"No," Winnie mumbled. She had to pause after each stair, even with his assistance. "Well… yes. But I have been dosed with laudanum. I did not want it. I had little choice."

Silence fell, as they reached the bottom of the stairs. Mr Quincy walked with her to the green baize door—and Winnie nearly cried as she realised that she would have to walk the labyrinth all over again. She stared at the door, swallowing hard.

"What will I do with you?" Mr Quincy muttered tightly. "You will not stop. You will not leave. What is the point of this, governess?"

Slowly but surely, Winnie worked to draw the shreds of her strength together, trying to convince herself to continue forward again. "You know the answer," Winnie told him tiredly. "Stop pretending that you don't."

Mr Quincy turned to look down at her. His wine-red eyes sharpened in the darkness. "I have never deigned to believe that I could read your mind, Miss Hall," he said. "You are infuriating at the best of times."

Winnie focussed on those red eyes, willing them to anchor her unsteady world. "I want to save someone," she told him quietly. "Just one person, Mr Quincy. I have spent all of my life just trying to save myself—and I am tired of it. If I cannot save the Hollow Lady, then I will at least save Master Robert. Or else the Witchwood Knot will have me, or Lord Longfell, or Lady Mourningwood."

Mr Quincy's fingers tightened on her arm, and Winnie smiled bitterly at him. "You know *precisely* what I mean," she observed. "You have spent all of this time trying to save Sarah Baker—but you cannot even manage that. We are both throwing ourselves against the impossible, because... what else is there to do? Now that I have finally decided to save someone, I can't admit that I am powerless, Mr Quincy. It would break me."

The butler said nothing in reply. His jaw clenched, however, and his red eyes darted away from hers.

Winnie turned back to the door, drawing in a deep breath. "It seems that we must start again. At least we are going more swiftly each time." She glanced down at Oliver, currently leaned against her leg. "And I have Ollie with me again. That is reassuring."

The cat rubbed his cheek against her in reply, as she opened the green baize door.

Without the sound of the pianoforte to help them navigate, the way was still less certain. Winnie had to stop several times, as the world tilted and phantom sensations assaulted her—the awful warmth of Lord Longfell's hand on hers made her rub insistently at her palm, and she found that she couldn't allow herself to think too much about it for the sake of her stability.

The laudanum will keep me trapped within the Knot for longer than is usual, Winnie thought. *I may not have wanted this, but I must take advantage of it while I can.*

The house's breath tickled at her neck as they walked— and now, with Lord Longfell's hand on hers, Winnie could not help but think that it was *his* breath, far too warm upon her skin. The idea made her shudder more violently than any screaming ghost had done.

Time twisted strangely in her head, as the laudanum did its work. It was an eternity before Mr Quincy managed to bring them to the attic bedroom once again—or perhaps it was an eye blink. The dowager's distressed portrait stared down at them, still screaming silently, as they considered the hallway beyond the attic bedroom's empty window.

Mr Quincy's blue lantern illuminated trees. Tall and dark and twisted, they grew within the claustrophobic hallway—as though someone had picked up an entire forest and forced it inside of the manor, heedless of the consequences. Pale moonlight illuminated everything ahead of them, though the ceiling still blocked out the sky. Mirrors lined the walls, all covered in drifting black crepe.

Oliver hissed at the hallway. His fur stood on end, and his yellow eye narrowed.

"Is that our path?" Winnie asked tiredly.

"There is no other path," Mr Quincy replied. "Even if we took a different route to get here, that is the centre of the Witchwood Knot. The Mourningwood itself is trapped here, along with all its faeries."

Winnie nodded slowly. "I doubt that those mirrors mean anything good for us," she murmured. "Do you know if they have always been there?"

"They have," said Mr Quincy grimly. "Though they are usually uncovered. I avoid this place whenever I can." He offered out his hand. "Hold onto me, and do not let me go. Keep your eyes closed, and ignore everything that you might hear."

Winnie took his hand slowly. The butler's touch was cool and reassuring, she thought, against the nauseous warmth of Lord Longfell's hand.

"What might I hear?" she asked. "I would like to prepare myself accordingly."

Mr Quincy met her gaze evenly. "I haven't the first idea, Miss Hall," he replied. "You refuse to tell me what it might be."

A long, instinctive shiver wound its way through Winnie's body at that answer. "My worst fear," she whispered.

Mr Quincy watched her for a long moment. He did not ask her this time if she would turn back. Winnie found herself wondering whether that was because he was tired of asking, or else because he had more faith in her than she had in herself.

But either way, the butler was watching her with such resigned expectation—such absolute assurance that Winnie was going to continue forward, no matter what he said—that she found herself drawing strength from the idea.

"I will not let you go," she told him, with more courage than she truly felt. "Lead the way, Mr Quincy."

The butler drew her through the empty window, into the forested hallway beyond. Winnie closed her eyes as she passed the threshold, clinging to the poisonous, drifting feeling of the laudanum in her veins. Though the drug had dulled the edges of her anxiety, it had also heightened the uneasy feeling that something terrible was hovering just out of sight.

Dead leaves crackled underfoot as Mr Quincy wound them slowly between trees. Winnie's heartbeat pounded far too quickly, as her mind whirled with the awful possibilities of what she might soon hear.

But the first thing that she *felt* was a finger which brushed ardently along her cheek.

Winnie halted in place with a strangled breath. Mr Quincy stumbled—but he had an iron grip upon her hand, and he did not let her go.

"Keep moving," he advised her in a low voice. "Whatever it is, it will pass."

"What a blessing it is to have you here, Winifred," Lord Longfell's voice sighed. The house's warm breath trickled across Winnie's skin, raising uncomfortable goosebumps. *"At least there is one beautiful thing in this wretched house of mine."*

"No," Winnie whispered with horror. "I am hearing something real. It's coming from out there—in my bedroom."

"Keep moving, all the same," Mr Quincy snapped at her. "We cannot linger here—"

His voice cut off abruptly, and Winnie opened her eyes.

The black gauze had slipped from one of the mirrors. Mr

Quincy's crimson gaze had caught upon its reflection; now, he stared at what he saw there, unable to look away.

At first, Winnie thought he must be seeing something which she couldn't; the reflection in the mirror *was* Mr Quincy. But the other Mr Quincy was smiling with an edge that Winnie had never seen before—a deeply off-putting expression which did not belong on his lips. His gloves were gone; his pale fingers now dripped with red. Every inch of his crimson jacket had been soaked in blood, dying it a deep and ugly brown. A familiar crown of black brambles rose from his brow, reaching for the sky like skeletal fingers.

An overwhelming copper scent tinted the house's breath as it trickled past Winnie's shoulder.

The awful creature in the mirror reached through the glass for Mr Quincy. Blood dripped onto the leaves as it clasped its long fingers around his forearm.

Mr Quincy stumbled back with a hoarse cry, and let go of Winnie's hand. But the reflection dragged him forward, pulling him halfway through the glass and into whatever lay beyond it.

Winnie lunged at the apparition, grasping at its fingers in an attempt to pry them away from Mr Quincy. At her touch, the reflection *did* release him—but Winnie soon found herself tossed unceremoniously to the floor. Her head slammed into a twisted black tree root, and stars flashed before her eyes.

The lantern crashed to the ground and went out. Darkness flooded in, as Lord Longfell's fingers drifted over Winnie's hair, combing through it fondly.

Winnie scrambled back clumsily on her hands, slipping in the rotten leaves as she struggled between the impulse to flee and the impulse to claw at her hair.

Footsteps crunched lightly after her, as Mr Quincy's

reflection advanced on Winnie with his usual calm grace. She found that she could barely see his outline, as her eyes adjusted to the sudden dearth of light.

"What will I do with you, governess?" he asked, with cold amusement. His voice drifted on the darkness, just above her.

"You will do nothing," Winnie said tightly. "You are not real."

"Is *that* what you believe?" he asked her archly. "But I have walked next to you, all of this time."

A high, horrible yowl split the darkness. Oliver streaked past her, slamming into the reflection. The two figures tumbled fitfully to the ground, as Mr Quincy's voice hissed with dark fury.

"I must admit it, finally," Lord Longfell sighed. *"My loneliness."* His warm breath ghosted across Winnie's cheek, and she curled up with a gasp, trying to hide her face. *"I feel as though you understand that loneliness. I see it in your eyes, sometimes."*

Mr Quincy's silhouette struggled for another moment with Oliver—and then, he was back on his feet, shoving the monstrous cat against a mirror. Oliver yowled again—but this time, the sound came as though from a great distance, muffled by the mirror's glass. His claws scratched wildly at the barrier, making a sound that set Winnie's teeth on edge.

Mr Quincy's shadow stalked for Winnie. Bloody fingers wrenched at her hair, dragging her back to her feet. She stumbled, trying to ignore the warm breath on her face and the wrenching pain in her scalp in order to fumble for her silver knife.

"You are a nuisance," Mr Quincy's voice whispered in her ear, faintly laboured from his struggle with the cat. "One of the many crawling insects which infests my house. I will take this realm, as is my birthright. I will rule this place with blood and iron—and there is nothing you can do to stop me."

"*I could give you a home*," Lord Longfell murmured lovingly. "*I could give you safety. You could be mine, Winifred.*"

Winnie lashed out blindly with a terrified cry, slamming her knife into the reflection's chest. The weapon sank in easily, all the way to the hilt. But the other Mr Quincy did not flinch or cry out in the darkness. The only thing that her savage blow gained her was a disconcerting trickle of warmth against her hands.

The reflection laughed, grasping Winnie's wrist and prying her fingers away from the knife. Oliver scratched more insistently at the glass where he'd been trapped, howling with caged fury.

"I cannot die," Mr Quincy's reflection reminded Winnie with a dismissive sneer. "Will you cut me into pieces? That has been tried before."

Winnie laughed back at him desperately, clutching at her head. She could not tell, suddenly, whether her body was leaden and incapable of moving from her bed or else thrashing against this other Mr Quincy's grip. Everything was such an awful blur. But suddenly, she knew that the phantasms in this corridor would not show her anything at all. Her worst fear had already come for her—in fact, it had cornered her in her bedroom, helpless and alone.

"This is *your* fear, Mr Quincy!" she called out hoarsely. "I cannot fight it for you! You can heal anything at all—unless you deal the injury *yourself!*"

The reflection grasped at Winnie's throat, shoving her against the tree behind her. Wine-red eyes pinned her into place, as sharp-edged bark bit into the back of her frock. "You are afraid of me," the butler hissed. "I hear it in your voice."

Winnie sucked in a rattling breath. "I am not afraid of you, Mr Quincy," she choked out helplessly. "I am afraid of Lord Longfell. I am afraid of men who think that my eyes and my lips and my hair are something they can own. I doubt you even *know* the colour of my eyes."

Mr Quincy's red eyes glittered, and his reflection leaned in closer. His lips brushed very lightly against her ear. "Your eyes are blue," he corrected her softly. "And I could own you if I wanted. Everything I covet could be mine... if only I reach out to take it."

Winnie froze—and for a moment, there was no difference at all between the leaden weight of her body in the bedroom and the way that she trembled in his grip.

The scent of copper surged abruptly on the air, turning rank and pungent, as the blood which trickled along Winnie's silver knife flared with dread, rotting magic. The reflection staggered and released her with an awful choking sound. Winnie dropped to the ground again, gasping for breath, as another silhouette approached.

"That is... *more* than enough," Mr Quincy's voice said tightly. It was the real Mr Quincy, she was certain—there was a horror and an anguish in his tone which Winnie doubted the reflection would have understood.

The reflection did not speak again. Winnie could not see what was left of it, in the darkness... but then, she suspected that the sight would do her stomach little good, judging from the lingering stench upon the air.

The real Mr Quincy pried Winnie's silver knife from his reflection's corpse, whirling to slam the weapon into a nearby mirror. Glass shattered—and suddenly, Oliver was there again, rubbing his nose against her hand with urgent affection. And though Winnie could have sworn that she could not bring herself to move again, she found herself petting him with trembling fingers and scratching behind his ears.

Mr Quincy stumbled back from the broken mirror. The brief burst of anger which had fuelled him disappeared, and his shoulders slumped. He pressed a hand to his face, breathing in sharply.

It was several moments before he seemed to gather up his strength again. Finally, he turned for Winnie, kneeling beside her with a soft rustle in order to offer out her knife. For some reason, though she could not see him well, she had the impression that he was shaking too.

"I have your knife, Miss Hall," Mr Quincy said. It was the gentlest and most fearful tone that she had ever heard from him. "I expect that you would like it back."

Winnie nodded, slow and silent. Mr Quincy must have thought her truly blind, for he pressed the hilt of her knife into her free hand. He drew his hand back shortly afterwards, as though he had been burned.

"We must go quickly," he said, in that strangely subdued tone. "But I... will not touch you without your permission, Miss Hall. I will not."

Winnie drew in another forceful breath. Oliver licked at her hand, and she blinked away her paralysis.

"That was a part of you," she whispered. "The part you fear." Her hand tightened on the hilt of her knife, though she had just been reminded yet again that it would be no use against him. "It spoke the truth... didn't it? What do you covet from me, Mr Quincy?"

Mr Quincy fell into silence, unable to look at her. For a moment, the warm breath of the house was all that Winnie heard. But she felt Lord Longfell's fingers in her hair, on the other side of the manor.

"I would have you play my songs until your fingers bled," he confessed hoarsely. "I would compose new music, just to hear you play it with such passion. I cannot bear it, governess —how dare you love my music more than I do?"

The words sent an unexpected, tingling chill down Winnie's spine. The pleasant reaction stole her breath and muddied her mind. There was a terrible possessiveness in Mr Quincy's voice which she had heard from other men before— but it came with such uncertainty, such fear, that she knew he would not act upon it. Even now, he was afraid to touch her.

It was the distance, Winnie thought—the obvious self-imposed reticence—which made the revelation pleasant, rather than terrifying.

Winnie turned her head towards Mr Quincy, though she could barely see him. "I ought to thank you," she rasped. "You have helped me realise something." She lifted her other hand from Oliver's head, offering it out to the butler. "I am *still* not afraid of you—I am not even afraid of being desired. I am simply afraid of what desire becomes whenever I dare to decline it."

Mr Quincy's hand took hers, so careful and so measured that a tiny spark of reassurance lit itself against the drugged and fearful thoughts which trickled back from Winnie's bedroom. He helped her back to her feet.

"After all of this time," he murmured bitterly, "your worst fear does me little good. It is the one thing which I cannot bring myself to act upon, even if I were to harm you in some other manner."

Winnie's legs trembled as she stumbled after him. Mr Quincy paused, and she knew that he was thinking of helping her further—but he was still too shaken to touch more than her hand.

"I would appreciate your assistance, Mr Quincy," Winnie reassured him dimly. "I am not... well." A thread of fear leaked back into her voice, despite her best efforts. "In fact, I wonder if I should not find a way to die so that I can wake up. I would have let your reflection kill me, except that I was worried for you and Oliver."

Mr Quincy halted, with a hand now hovering uncertainly at her shoulder. "What do you mean by that?" he asked.

Somewhere distant from the Witchwood Knot, Lord Longfell's lips pressed gingerly to Winnie's forehead, as she stared stonily ahead. The idea of speaking the truth aloud made her body shudder with irrational shame.

"What do you mean by that?" Mr Quincy repeated, with a fresh edge to his voice. His reddish eyes flickered back towards her.

Winnie did not dare to look at him, though she could only see his silhouette. "He is in my bedroom," she said quietly. "And I am drugged with laudanum. I cannot make him leave."

Mr Quincy's hand tightened on hers.

"You should have said something sooner," he told her in a clipped voice. His body had begun to coil with a rare, cold fury.

Winnie shook her head slowly. "Lord Longfell's ring protects him," she said. "The manor's ghosts can't reach him, and its magic keeps Oliver at bay. If *you* could harm him, I expect that you'd have done so long before today."

"I am capable of *many* things, Miss Hall," the butler told her darkly. "I have been unable to harm any living thing for centuries now, and I have managed mostly without trouble." He pressed her hand carefully into his arm, in order to help her move more quickly. "Put your knife away. I must leave you somewhere safer than this place."

CHAPTER 17

*T*he forested hallways at the centre of the Witchwood Knot slowly opened up, as Mr Quincy led Winnie deeper into the trees. Though she remained aware of distant walls closed in around them, the twisted black roots and rotten leaves had now overcome the limestone floor entirely.

"You said that we were going somewhere safer," Winnie mumbled to Mr Quincy, as she leaned upon his arm. She found she could not help the dubious tone which filtered into her voice.

"I did say that," Mr Quincy murmured. "And I do not lie, Miss Hall. You know that."

Presently, Winnie became aware of the soft trickling sound of water nearby. Oliver's ears pricked up, and the cat padded ahead of her in order to investigate.

The forest floor inclined upwards, and the way became a bit more challenging, especially in Winnie's laudanum-addled state. Mr Quincy slowed for her—but Winnie could still feel

Lord Longfell's too-warm hand and the house's breath upon her neck, and she sped her pace despite his efforts, stumbling up the hill.

As they crested the top, a strange, shimmering ribbon of water came into view below. The sight was so instantly arresting that Winnie came up short, staring down at it.

It was a river, clearly—but the reflection on the water was of endless twinkling stars, all glimmering in the darkness. It was as though someone had raked down all of the stars which should have hung in the sky beyond the ceiling and poured the light into the creek before them.

Beyond that water was a shocking burst of greenery, tucked into the centre of the dying forest. White flowers blossomed on the trees; their fresh scent floated on the breeze, intoxicating against the stale and rotting air which so infested the rest of the Mourningwood.

A weeping willow arched above the other trees, leaning close against the starry river. Its long branches draped across the water, as though drinking from the light.

Winnie had seen many beautiful things in faerie—but something about that willow tree arrested her entirely. She now believed Mr Quincy's promise of safety in a visceral way. If she could only hide herself beneath those branches, Winnie thought, then even Lord Longfell's touch would seem unimportant.

As Winnie stared down at the tree, Mr Quincy carefully released her arm in order to remove his crimson jacket, draping it over one arm. Without it, he seemed suddenly much tamer and more harmless—dressed only in his crisp white shirt and simple black waistcoat.

He turned to offer the jacket out to Winnie, with a sombre expression on his narrow features.

"If you put on my jacket and sit beneath that tree," said Mr Quincy softly, "then nothing in this place will dare to harm you. You have my word, Miss Hall."

Winnie looked down at the crimson jacket uncertainly. "Is that not a gift?" she murmured. "What will I owe you for it, Mr Quincy?"

"It is not a gift," Mr Quincy assured her, with that new, uncommon gentleness. He met her eyes with level calm. "I am loaning you my jacket. You must give it back to me when I return."

Very slowly, Winnie took the jacket from him, with a hollow feeling at the bottom of her stomach. "You are leaving, then?" she asked, clutching the coat against her chest. "Well—of course you are leaving. That is a silly question, isn't it."

"I will return," Mr Quincy assured her again. "I do not leave you here lightly, Miss Hall. I have never allowed another soul to set foot in this place before. But it is appropriate that you should stay here, in particular."

The strange new look behind his eyes was sadness, Winnie thought. Mr Quincy had grown terribly dark and melancholy as he gazed down at that river.

Winnie tightened her arms around the butler's jacket. The coat was suffused with an overwhelming scent of blood and bay berry perfume; it should not have comforted her nearly as much as it did. Very slowly, she unclenched her fingers from the fabric in order to pull the jacket around her shoulders. It was larger than she was, but not uncomfortably so. And though she knew that Mr Quincy was generally cool to the touch, his jacket kept her warm.

"Wear the jacket as you cross the water," Mr Quincy told her. "I fear that your familiar cannot join you. You must tell him to remain on this side of the river, or else he may court danger."

Winnie glanced down at Oliver, sitting next to her feet like a proud sentinel. She reached down to scratch at his ears, and he leaned into her hand with a soft purr.

"You will wait for me here, Ollie?" she asked softly. "I promise that I will come back for you."

The cat tilted his head at Winnie, and she knew that he was not pleased at the prospect. But very slowly, he hunched down to settle his chin upon his paws, staring down at the tree below.

"Wait for me, Miss Hall," said Mr Quincy. "I will not be long."

It took more strength than Winnie would have liked to admit in order to leave the butler's side. But she clutched his crimson jacket more tightly about her shoulders, and forced herself to descend.

As she waded carefully into the creek, she found that it was shallower than it had first appeared. The water barely kissed her ankles, even at its deepest. The stars in the water brushed past her dizzily, leaving behind cold tingles on her skin—and suddenly, Winnie had the impression that they were less wholesome than they'd first appeared. The scent of blood on Mr Quincy's jacket grew abruptly stronger, though, and the lights in the water soon rushed onward without care.

Winnie stepped out of the water onto lush green grass. She could not help but turn her head to look up at the hill, searching for Mr Quincy's shadow there—but his figure had already disappeared. Instead, she saw Oliver's single yellow eye glowing down at her in the darkness.

The willow tree's long branches swayed before her—though the house's breath seemed distant and less smothering in this place. The tree was so delicate-looking that Winnie almost could not bring herself to touch it. But Mr Quincy had been clear that she should sit beneath it—and so, she slipped between the branches gingerly, in order to press her back against its trunk and settle herself among its roots.

Inside the willow tree's embrace, the rest of the Witchwood Knot felt less important and less pressing. And though Lord Longfell's fingers raked through her hair again, Winnie found that she no longer cared. His presence was a distant and inconsequential dream.

She was hidden here, completely, in a secret world of safety. A lovely, warm, unfocussed feeling enveloped her—and slowly, Winnie came to realise what it was.

There was love here—soft and sweet and unassuming. It did not belong to her, though. Rather, it was focussed on the jacket which she wore around her shoulders.

Winnie leaned her head back against the tree, closing her eyes. Though the love was not for her, she felt it keenly nevertheless. It had been so long since she had felt its likeness; the closest she had come to it was Oliver's soft nose against her palm and his purr against her skin. Perhaps, she thought, it was akin to the ache which sometimes struck her when she caught a whiff of the bay berry perfume which Clarimonde had given her.

In that stillness, she became aware again of Lord Longfell's nauseating warmth, and his shivering breath. But there was something else, as well—a murmur of piano, drifting up from the conservatory.

It was Mr Quincy's fingers on the pianoforte. She knew it in her soul with utter certainty, the same way that she would have known his footsteps or his whisper. No one else could manage those delightful flourishes or those wandering digressions.

The song was something new—an ominous, creeping lullaby. Its notes curled upon the air, echoing with faintly sinister intent. But Winnie smiled as she heard it, nevertheless.

Lord Longfell's touch froze as he heard the music. His breath stuttered, and his pulse sped with panic. With every slow, advancing note, his dread increased—even as Winnie's fearful tension eased. Her attention drifted slowly away from the man at her side, focussing instead upon the rise and fall of that song so that she might commit it to memory.

Eventually, the song died away into stillness again. Lord Longfell held his breath, shivering, as he waited to see if it would resume.

Instead, there were soft footsteps on the stairs.

The wind picked up throughout the manor, drawing a long, slow creak from its walls. Dark whispers rose along the edges of Winnie's bedroom, hissing with otherworldly anger.

It was real anger, Winnie thought. Mr Quincy's fury was a palpable, smothering thing, where it closed in around her bedroom.

Lord Longfell stood abruptly.

"Whatever you are," he spoke hoarsely, "you will not have Miss Hall. She does not belong to you, monster." His tone wavered unconvincingly, and Winnie smiled again.

The stained glass windows rattled softly. The whispers rose to greater volume. And presently, there came a loud knocking sound—exactly like the one that Winnie had heard while she was in the dowager's attic bedroom. Mr Quincy had repurposed it, she thought, on behalf of his own devices. Again, she found herself admiring his resourcefulness.

"Begone, apparition!" Lord Longfell ordered. His voice was now high-pitched and thready, though—far from the confident and dismissive tone which he so often used with Winnie.

A lone whisper rose above the rest, in a familiar cracking voice.

"Robert!" cried the dowager. *"My traitorous son!"*

Lord Longfell collapsed into a shocked and terrified silence—and then, all at once, he fled the bedroom, sobbing as he fumbled with the iron door handle. He stumbled into the hallway with frantic, thudding footsteps which receded into the distance.

The whispers receded with him, very slowly. Winnie's heart eased, and her body relaxed.

New footsteps sounded in her bedroom—soft and light, and walking with deliberation. Though Winnie could not open her eyes, she knew that it was Mr Quincy; the scent of blood and bay berry was everywhere now, drifting on the air of her bedroom even as it curled around her shoulders.

"Run while you can," Mr Quincy whispered after the absent lord, with loathsome promise in his voice. "Someday, you will set aside my brother's ring... and then, I will show you what it is you have been truly dreading, all this time."

The butler's steps took him to the mantle over Winnie's hearth, and she heard him set something down atop it. He walked to Winnie's bedside then, and paused there—though still, he did not touch her.

"I will go emphasise my point, I think," he told her. "Be patient, governess. I will return when he has cried enough to suit me."

Mr Quincy did not make a sound this time, as he departed.

But Winnie knew that he was gone, as the last of the whispers died and the scent of blood slowly faded.

~

FOR A LONG WHILE, Winnie drifted out of thought, leaning her head against the willow tree. Eventually, however, she became aware of Mr Quincy's shadow on the willow branches.

The butler brushed aside the leaves with careful reverence. There was a grim satisfaction on his narrow features—but already, the hard edges of that emotion began to soften at the willow's touch, and Winnie knew that he was far from immune to the love which now enfolded him.

Mr Quincy knelt down next to her. "The lord is in the manor's chapel," he informed her dryly, "praying for salvation. I doubt that he will pry himself away from the altar before the sun rises."

Winnie could not help the soft, desperate laugh which trickled from her throat. "You are so cruel, Mr Quincy," she told him. "I admire it intensely." She pulled the crimson jacket more tightly around herself, leaning her shoulder into the tree. "What is that song you played on the pianoforte? I have not ever heard it before."

The butler settled his back against the tree, taking care to leave a respectful distance between them. "I have only just composed it," he murmured back, as he looked away from her. His manner had softened greatly now, with the willow's branches swaying so gently around them. "It is yours, if you would like it."

Another pleasant shiver raced down Winnie's spine, akin to the one that had struck her before. The feeling had grown stronger now—she found that she did not know exactly where to put it. She drew in a long, slow breath, floating on the scent of blood and bay berry which tickled at her throat.

"And what would I pay for it?" she whispered unsteadily.

Mr Quincy glanced over at her. "Nothing," he said quietly. "It is yours." His wine-red eyes lingered on Winnie, and she saw that the cold contempt in them was gone—replaced with tired helplessness.

Winnie smiled at him softly. "If only I had the time," she told him, "I would play it 'till my fingers bled."

Mr Quincy stared at her. His fingers closed into his palms beside him... but Winnie reached out slowly to take his hand in hers. His gloves were still gone; his skin was cool against her warmth. As she touched him, his breath paused with uncertainty.

"I doubt that I could ever fear you more than you already fear yourself, Mr Quincy," she assured him gently. "Whatever thoughts you have been hiding from me... you have hidden them so well that I believe in your restraint. You have always let me go before I even think to ask."

Mr Quincy drew in a shivering breath. Gradually, his fingers closed around hers, though Winnie had the distinct impression that he still teetered on the edge of snatching back his hand again.

"I know what I am," he told her. "I know what I might do, if I forget my place. That version of me once existed; only simple accident prevented me from becoming something worse than even the monster of Witchwood Manor."

Winnie shifted closer, leaning her shoulder lightly against his. "I believe you," she assured him. "But you are something different now. Your reflection would not have been quite so startling if I had not met you first."

Mr Quincy let his head fall back against the tree. "I will tell you, if you want to know," he said. "One way or another, you should know the story you have stumbled into."

Winnie closed her eyes. "Tell me," she murmured back.

Mr Quincy related to her then a faerie tale which she had never heard before, as they leaned against the willow tree.

CHAPTER 18

*O*nce upon a time—long before most faerie tales begin—a dread king of the *fomóraiġ* known as Balor of the Evil Eye conquered yet another realm, and took yet another wife.

Balor's wives were several. Though his first was willing, the rest were trophies, taken from his battles with the humans and the faeries. These wives bore Balor many children, and he doted on the strongest of them, raising them to be his champions and successors. The weaker children, he tore from their mothers' arms and threw into the ocean—a crime which would someday undo him, as his own blood was fated to defeat him.

The children who remained were all of different stock—but the blood of Balor ran most strongly in their veins, and so they were called *fomóraiġ*, regardless of their origin. The oldest was a boy of human blood, whom we shall call Secundus. After him came a lovely girl of faerie blood, who will be known as Tertia. Twins came next, born from a faerie woman whom Balor had torn from the realm of Mourningwood. One of the twins, a girl we will call Quarta, was drowned beneath the waves. But the other twin, a boy whom we may know as Quintus, grew up at Balor's knee.

Quintus was a vicious, clever creature, always quick to please his father. The dreadful magic which he had inherited from the king was strong enough to wither living things with but a touch; once Quintus was older, said Balor, he would surely conquer his own realm.

Quintus sometimes met his mother, who loved him dearly despite the way in which he had been born. She tried to teach him faerie tricks and fleeting illusions—but Quintus was contemptuous of both his mother and her magic. For many years, he spurned her cruelly, resenting that he should be forced to speak with her at all.

Had Quintus been allowed to grow into his power, then perhaps this story would be different. But he was still a boy when Balor's grandson—born of Prima, who was thrown into the ocean and thought dead—led a host of humans and faeries against the *fomóraig*, overthrowing the dread king's reign at last.

Balor and his children could not die, however—and so, the faeries wove powerful curses around them, laying them each to sleep beneath a different faerie realm. Lord Longshadow, who was considered most powerful among them, agreed to lay Balor of the Evil Eye to rest beneath his own lands. In the years to come, a great tree sprouted from the king's sleeping body, bearing silver apples which could cure any illness and restore life to the dead.

But as the faeries prepared to lay Quintus to sleep, his faerie mother begged that he might stay awake. Because of her long suffering, and because her first child had been taken from her, the faeries took pity upon her and left Quintus awake—on the condition that some faerie lord or lady must accept responsibility for him.

Since Quintus's mother was a faerie of the Mourning-wood, Lady Mourningwood took on this task. She made young Quintus swear to serve her, and placed a ban upon him so that he could never harm a living thing. In order to enforce her will, she stabbed his finger with a sliver from her favourite tree, which he could not remove himself. "If ever you betray me," Lady Mourningwood intoned, "I will ignore your mother's cries and drive you from the Mourningwood, and let the other faeries hunt you."

Quintus lived within the Mourningwood for many centuries with his mother—and slowly, he began to under-stand the love she bore for him, and the terrible things which his father had done to her. He learned to love her in return, playing music and composing faerie songs for her enjoyment; and though the other faeries were afraid of him, he drew comfort from her company.

Because Quintus could no longer use his father's magic to harm living things, he learned illusions from his mother and deployed them in the service of Lady Mourningwood. There were humans on the other side of the Mourningwood, in England, who often vexed her. On occasion, she sent Quintus to abduct those who displeased her—and since the sliver in his finger yet remained, he did her bidding.

But one day, Lady Mourningwood brought a little human girl to her realm and forced her to embroider until she pricked her fingers and bled upon the Mourningwood's dark earth. The scent of blood made something stir, and Quintus remembered that his brother Secundus had been laid to rest beneath their feet. With human blood enough, he knew, his brother would return.

Quintus went to the little girl in secret, and helped her to escape. But the damage had been done, and Secundus soon stopped dreaming—though the faeries did not know it.

When Secundus awoke, he went in secret to the avaricious human lord who lived on the other side of the Mourning-wood, in England. Secundus promised to rid the lord of Lady Mourningwood—he required only that the lord cut down specific trees within the nearby woods and build a manor from their bones.

The villagers feared to cut down Lady Mourningwood's trees, knowing that her reprisal would be terrible—but the lord soon starved them into compliance, and they did as they were told. The villagers paid a heavy price while the lord built his manor; and when it was complete, Secundus bound the Mourningwood within it, burying the realm within the very tomb where he had slept himself.

Secundus gave the lord a ring of wood and iron, and warned him that a member of his bloodline must always wear the ring and stay within the house, or else risk Lady Mourn-ingwood's escape. And though the lord knew that the ring would drink its wearer's blood and someday kill them, he took it all the same, and gave it to his mother.

Secundus visited the Witchwood Knot, where the faeries were all trapped, in order to reveal his vengeance to them. But he went more quietly to his younger brother, Quintus, and told him that the Mourningwood would be his kingdom. Surely, Secundus said, clever Quintus would find a way to escape his bonds to Lady Mourningwood and conquer the realm. Because Quintus was a *fomórach*, the Witchwood Knot would bind him loosely, and the lady of the realm would be forced to rely upon his service in order to disrupt it.

Quintus had changed greatly as his brother slept, and the

idea of a kingdom all his own no longer sounded grand. But he was still a clever creature—and so, he let his brother believe that they were allies, even as Secundus departed for other faerie realms in order to release his siblings.

Quintus went to return to his mother's side—but no matter how he searched the Mourningwood, he could not find her. At the revelation that the *fomóraig* would soon awaken once again, she had thrown herself upon the lady of the Mourningwood and begged the faerie lady to help her disappear. Thus, Lady Mourningwood turned Quintus's mother into a weeping willow tree deep in the heart of the Mourningwood, where she could hide away forever.

And there she remains at the centre of the Witchwood Knot until the *fomóraig* sleep safely beneath the earth again, no longer able to touch her.

innie sat next to Mr Quincy for a long while beneath the willow tree, absorbing the story that he'd told her. Out of every awful thing which she had heard, however, there was one detail which she could not shake.

"Mr Quincy," she said quietly, "I fear that I know where Secundus has gone."

The butler turned his head to look at her, now warier than before.

"I lived in London well before I came to Witchwood Manor," Winnie said. "All of the faeries there have disappeared, and the ways that once led into faerie are gone." She tightened her grip on his hand. "The new Lord Sorcier is hunting down low-born magicians. I have not met him personally—but I have heard him called Lord Cassius Secundus."

Mr Quincy pressed his hand across his eyes, breathing in sharply. When he spoke again, his voice was strained. "He is making certain that no mortal magicians will be able to offer their help, this time," he said. "The faeries could not throw down Balor of the Evil Eye until they offered their magic to humans in return for their assistance."

Winnie's heart thudded in her chest. "Secundus has already done something to the Hollow Lady," she said. "I do not see her in my dreams, as I once did."

"It was Lady Hollowvale's blood that woke him," Mr Quincy rasped. "Secundus would have gone to find her first of all. But I doubt that he has slain her."

There was an ominous fear in his voice which implied that perhaps it would be better if he *had* slain Lady Hollowvale.

Winnie steeled herself against that thought. *The world is full of monsters,* she reminded herself grimly. *I knew that all along. What can I do, except to fight them?*

"Who knows what has happened to the faeries?" Winnie sighed quietly. "Perhaps they are all hiding, with their doors closed. Perhaps they are defeated. Either way, I cannot sit here while he conquers everything I care about."

She turned Mr Quincy's hand over in hers, looking over his long fingers. There was, on closer inspection, a thin red line along his index finger, where a painful-looking splinter had been buried.

"You can't remove this on your own," said Winnie. "I could remove it *for* you, I am certain... but you will not ask me, will you?"

Mr Quincy closed his eyes, drawing in a breath. "I will not," he whispered.

Winnie looked away from him, though she kept her grip on his hand. "You are afraid you will become exactly what your brother thinks you are," she said, "and exactly what your mother fears. You are frightened you may be a tyrant, Mr

Quincy—but in trying to avoid your fate, you have instead resigned yourself to *serve* a tyrant."

The butler smiled bitterly. "There are no happy endings, Miss Hall," he reminded her. "I have chosen the least terrible of many awful paths. That does not make it pleasant."

Winnie curled her fingers around the crimson jacket at her shoulders. "I understand," she told him softly. "I wish that I did not. You will stay here with your mother, as you promised her you would."

Mr Quincy did not offer a reply. But Winnie knew that she had guessed correctly. Try as she might, she could not bring herself to blame him. His mother had been the first to show him love, and he had wronged her. There were some debts which one could never properly repay, even here in faerie.

Winnie leaned her head against his shoulder, swallowing back the knot which had tightened at her throat. "I would like to stay here with you for a while," she told him. "If that is… quite all right. I do not have it in me to go further. But this is such a lovely dream."

Mr Quincy was silent for a moment, next to her. "Everything you hope to find is very close," he said. "You are nearly there, Miss Hall."

Winnie blinked back irrational tears. The weariness inside her was bone-deep now—but that was not why she could not move. "I know," she said. "But I do not dare to speak with Lady Mourningwood until I've warned my sisters of Secundus. If she traps me here, then they might never know what we are fighting." She offered him a watery smile. "So I would like to stay with you until I wake again."

At first, Mr Quincy did not respond. But he drew his

thoughts together... and finally, he said: "I would be glad to have you here."

~

WINNIE DID NOT KNOW how long she spent beneath the willow tree, leaning her head on Mr Quincy's shoulder. She drowned herself in peace and let herself forget the road ahead, while trying to regain some modicum of strength.

When the dream finally ended, and she opened her eyes upon the ceiling of Witchwood Manor, a horrible emptiness settled into her stomach. Slowly, she became aware of Margaret kneeling at the fireplace, sweeping ashes into her bucket.

Winnie shifted upright, clutching at her head. Her mouth was dry, and the laudanum's dizziness had yet to fully fade. Margaret rose from the fireplace, moving quietly towards the bed.

"I've brought a letter for you, Miss Hall," the maid whispered. She kept her voice low and furtive. "I'm told it came in yesterday." She reached into her apron to retrieve a rumpled letter.

Winnie took it from her with a weak, instinctive "thank you", still blinking back unsteadiness as she tore the envelope open with shaking fingers.

Dearest Winnie,

said the letter.

I am so upset with Bellamira. She has pushed herself too hard and had another attack. Hugh is watching her, and she is recovering, but we both know that might change at any moment.

I did not like the tone of your last letter. I wanted to come visit you, but there is trouble at the shop, and I remain uneasy. The Lord Sorcier has taken a sudden interest in the business. His people claim that someone here is doing magic. I do not want to think there is a black magician here... but maybe they are on to something.

Please be safe. I hope to see you soon.

All my love,

Clarimonde

Winnie stared down at the letter with growing dread, as she read between the lines what Clarimonde had carefully not written.

Lord Cassius Secundus had realised that there was a magician at the perfume shop where Clarimonde worked. At this rate, he would surely pin her down—and Clarimonde had no idea what he truly was.

Winnie could not write to Clarimonde with everything that she had found. Her sister was clearly worried that her mail might now be intercepted.

At least Clarimonde had managed to warn Winnie before she sent another letter back. She would have to send a reply to someone else entirely, and hope that they might get the message to her family.

"Margaret," Winnie said quietly, "I must write a very important letter. Will you post it under your name, instead of under mine?"

The maid shifted uncertainly on her feet, wiping a smear of soot from her cheek. "You make it sound as though it's dangerous," she said slowly.

Winnie nodded at her listlessly. "It is very dangerous," she said. "I hope your name will make it less so. But it might yet come back on you, I will not lie."

Margaret bit at her lip. "D'you believe that it might... help us?" she asked carefully.

Winnie pressed her palm against her eyes. Her hands were shaking now on Clarimonde's letter. "I truly do not know," she admitted. "I am doing my best to solve this, but everything here is against me. This letter might do nothing for the manor or the village—but maybe it will help someone *else* put up a better fight, in the case that I don't leave this house."

Margaret hesitated noticeably. She returned to the hearth to sweep another pile of ashes into her bucket as she chewed the question over.

"...I'll post your letter," the maid said finally, into the fireplace. Her voice was small. "I can't even bring myself to sleep here. It seems the least that I can do."

The reply should not have surprised Winnie quite so much. But the obvious fear in Margaret's voice touched her for a moment.

Even if Mr Quincy will not help me further, she thought to herself, *I am not here entirely alone.* Cook and Margaret had done what they could, which was not nothing. Winnie's sisters had sent help, at times, and Oliver would never leave her—

"Oh!" Winnie breathed. "Oliver." She stumbled out of bed,

still swaying on her feet as she hurried to the mantle to retrieve Oliver's skull and call him back. Margaret watched her, blinking in confusion.

A yellow light soon burned in the cat's eye socket, and Winnie smiled down at him. "I am here, Ollie," she told him softly, as she leaned down to kiss the skull. "Thank you so very much for waiting."

The yellow eye blinked once, very slowly, as though to reassure her. Winnie clutched the skull gently to her chest, taking in a breath. As she did, however, she saw that something else was laying on the mantle.

A familiar perfume vial had been tucked away, just behind Oliver's skull. Winnie reached out for it slowly, halfway certain that if she dared to touch it, it might disappear.

The scent of bay berry wafted up towards her, before she'd even opened it.

"Oh," Winnie sighed.

Technically, she *had* told Mr Quincy her worst fear. And he had kept his promise to give back Clarimonde's perfume, in return for it.

Winnie closed her fingers around the vial, as fresh hope struggled up into her chest. It would be simpler by far to walk the Witchwood Knot with Clarimonde's perfume to keep away the ghosts and faeries. Despite everything, her sister's gift would help her reach the centre.

The thought stirred something sluggish in Winnie's mind, even as she clung to it. She turned it over slowly, examining it with what little energy remained to her.

A gift, Winnie thought.

"Margaret," she said suddenly, as she set down Oliver's skull again. "There is something else that you can do—something which will help you, in fact." Winnie opened the small vial of perfume and dabbed a few drops at her collarbone. The sweet scent of bay berry suffused her, instantly strengthening and reassuring her.

Winnie offered out the perfume vial to Margaret, who crept closer to inspect it. "Wear this perfume today," Winnie told her, "and make sure that all the other servants do, as well. Once you've given some to all of them, you should take the perfume down into the village and use it up on everyone you find."

Margaret took the vial gingerly, frowning down at it. "What does it do?" she asked.

"It is a magical perfume," Winnie told her. "If you wear it, it will protect you from evil things—but you should not tell the others that, or else you might get into trouble with the vicar. Tell a different lie to everyone you meet, if that is what you need to do." Her thoughts spun now through plans and complications. "I will give you until noon. At that point, something terrible might happen here. But if the village is protected, then you might have the chance at least to flee."

Margaret rubbed a drop of perfume awkwardly across her neck, now openly apprehensive. "I can do that much, Miss Hall," she promised, in a tone that wavered only slightly at the edges. "Should I... give some to His Lordship?"

"Absolutely not," said Winnie sharply. Her voice was harder than she had intended—and she winced as Margaret stepped back from her in surprise. "What I mean to say is... I will handle him directly."

The idea did not thrill her. But it was what she had to do.

Winnie shook the cobwebs from her mind. "I will write this letter," she said slowly. "Please build up my hearth fire while I do—I will need it burning high today. When I am done, you must go quickly with the perfume."

Winnie sat down at the writing desk to stumble through the most disordered letter she had ever set to page. When she had finally finished it, she sealed the message and marked it to be posted to Mrs Henrietta Lowe, a family friend of little note who lived outside of London.

Perhaps, Winnie hoped, the letter would go far enough afield that no one offered it a second glance.

~

ONCE MARGARET HAD LEFT, Winnie retrieved the black gown from the corner of her room, where she had crumpled and discarded it.

She laid it out upon her bed, staring down at it with grim determination. To her surprise, the more she looked at it, the more the nausea in her stomach soon receded.

This gown is a weapon, Winnie thought. *Just like my knife. It belongs to me now, and I will use it as I wish.*

She dressed in the black mourning gown, with its low collar and enticing neck, and pulled on the black slippers. Instead of pinning up her long and lovely hair, she left it loose about her shoulders. She cinched her silver chatelaine about her waist and looked into the mirror.

The woman in the mirror looked like Winnie. Her blue eyes were harder, though, and there was something wilder about her, lurking just beneath the surface.

"Today," Winnie told the mirror calmly, "I will be wicked and manipulative. And I will not feel guilty for it—not even for a moment."

She whirled for the hallway and went to retrieve Robert's fetch from his bedroom, in order to go down to breakfast.

Winnie was not terribly surprised to find Lord Longfell

missing from the table. Perhaps he was still in the chapel, praying—or perhaps he had finally managed to fall asleep, now that the sun had risen. Either way, he did not show his face.

"I am going to solve this awful tangle today, one way or another," Winnie informed Robert's fetch, as they headed upstairs afterwards. "You have been marvellously patient. I hope the rest of you is holding up."

Robert's fetch considered her as they reached Robert's bedroom. "Will it be dangerous?" it asked her, rather than answering the question which Winnie had implied.

"Inordinately so," said Winnie grimly. "But that is how it sometimes goes. I believe that I can save you, and that is what most matters." She opened his door for him and smiled reassuringly. "I know that it is not ideal... but you should stay in your bedroom until things have settled. Can you manage that for me?"

"I can," said Robert's fetch tonelessly. "Though I wish that I was better at disobeying." It padded obediently inside and sat upon the edge of Robert's bed, looking out at her with flat brown eyes. "You must be safe when I return, Miss Hall. I think I would be sad if you were not."

The statement left a pang in Winnie's chest. "I believe that I will come through safely," she lied.

She closed the door behind her, aware that Robert's fetch was probably still staring after her.

There was still a precious bit of time before the afternoon —and Winnie found she had decided how to spend it. She walked for the conservatory, where she knew Lord Longfell would not go, and pulled the white sheet from the pianoforte.

Even as she settled onto the piano bench, she caught the scent of blood.

"I would like to learn my song, Mr Quincy," Winnie told the butler evenly, as she settled her fingers against the piano keys. "Will you teach it to me?"

She felt his figure just behind her, hesitating once again.

Winnie rested her palm against the piano bench just next to her, in invitation. "I do not have all afternoon," she said. "I hope you have not changed your mind."

Very slowly, Mr Quincy settled himself on the piano bench just next to her, draping his tail behind him. His wine-red eyes glanced over at her, taking in her dress and figure.

"What *are* you wearing today, Miss Hall?" he murmured with perplexion.

Winnie smiled at him. "I am not wearing this gown for *you*," she said. "Though I suppose you may enjoy it if you like." She tapped a piano key and frowned. "I think it started here. Am I correct?"

Mr Quincy reached out to touch two other keys. "You are correct," he said quietly. "But you will need the rest of the chord, as well."

Winnie stretched her fingers out to join his, brushing against his gloved hand. At the contact, Mr Quincy hitched his breath uncertainly... but did not pull away.

"I do not mind you touching me," Winnie murmured to him, as she played the chord. "In fact, I think I would prefer it. Restrain yourself if you would like... but I enjoy your fingers on my skin."

It was a bold and vulgar thing to say. But Mr Quincy absorbed the words with equanimity. His hand trembled briefly against Winnie's... and then, he pulled it back, in order to strip off his gloves.

Winnie shifted on the piano bench, into the circle of his arms. Mr Quincy laid his fingers over hers, at the keys of the pianoforte. His touch sent a breathless shock of pleasure down her nerves, and Winnie's eyes fluttered closed. There was no avoiding now his breath against her neck—but that was pleasant, too.

"Do you remember the progression?" he whispered at her ear. His voice was notably unsteady.

Winnie shifted her hands beneath his, searching for the keys which she remembered. His fingers gently guided hers, until she had the next part of the song. Several times, his breathing stuttered—as did hers.

"If everything was different," Winnie mumbled hoarsely, "I think that I might do this every morning."

Gradually, Mr Quincy led her fingers through a melody. Though his movements were restrained, his heart was beating madly at her back. "I must confess to something, governess," he told her tightly. "Perhaps it will upset you."

Winnie opened her eyes, staring down at their entangled hands. "Perhaps it will not, Mr Quincy," she said breathlessly. "Perhaps you should confess it."

His body had coiled behind hers, now stiff and careful—as though he had caught himself a wild animal and did not know quite what to do with it.

"I am fond of your eyes and your lips and your hair," he whispered shamefully. "I did not think of them before. But when you swindled me at cards, I noticed that your eyes were blue. And when you played my requiem... I thought your hair was lovely."

Each word caressed at Winnie's nerves. Her breathing quickened, and she flushed with warm, embarrassed pleasure.

"You may be fond of all those things, if you would like," she whispered back to him. "I do not mind, as long as it is you."

Mr Quincy shivered violently, clearly caught off-guard by

the words. His thumb brushed carefully along the back of Winnie's hand—deliberate, as though to test for her reaction. She leaned back into his chest, brushing her cheek against his.

They had both stopped playing the pianoforte now, as Mr Quincy looked down at her with dark desire in his wine-red eyes.

"I am done with trying to deceive you," Winnie told him softly. "I am tired of it, Mr Quincy." She threaded her fingers through his, drawing his arms closer around herself. "I must do something very difficult today. Before that, I would like to kiss you—but I worry it would only hurt you later."

Mr Quincy stared down at her, struggling with openly conflicting thoughts. His arms tightened around her.

"I know it does not change a thing," Winnie assured him gently. "It's just that... I have kissed men before. But I have never kissed someone because I *wanted* to. I thought it would be nice, just once, to try it."

Mr Quincy closed his eyes. "You need not worry about hurting me," he told her, in a shaken tone. "I am already hurt; and I have done it to myself. It will not heal."

Winnie shifted in his arms to face him, bringing a hand up to his cheek. She brushed her thumb along the sharp edge of his cheekbone. "I do not blame you, Mr Quincy," she promised. "I do not lie. I told you, I am done with that—at least where you're concerned." She offered him a tired smile, as his reddish eyes slitted open once again. "I did not have your help before. I won't rely upon it now."

Mr Quincy swallowed thickly. There was still guilt in his expression. Winnie wished that she could wipe that guilt away—but she knew she did not have the power.

Either way, he reached for her. He brushed Winnie's hair aside with trembling fingers, which lingered at the column of her neck. He closed the last bit of distance between them, and caught her lips with his.

A blissful shiver blossomed where he kissed her. It caught her like a wave, washing over her from head to toe. It tingled in her fingers and along her skin, suffusing her like numbing laudanum. Winnie closed her arms around his neck and kissed him back, so dizzy she could barely think.

There was nothing dutiful or polite about the way she kissed him. It was wild, thrilling, and enjoyable. It stole her breath and offered something better in its place. She did not want to stop.

Mr Quincy pressed her back into the pianoforte, which jangled at her back. Winnie kissed him harder—kissed him again and again—letting her hands wander along his ghostly skin and into his dark hair. She kissed along his jaw, and up his neck, enjoying the faint tang of copper which she tasted there.

His fingers twisted in her hair. His breath was hot against her, as he kissed her jaw in turn. And all of it was *good*.

But Winnie knew, despite herself, that it was unfair to continue. She had stolen *several* kisses now, each better than the first. And he would feel them all acutely, in just an hour or so.

She pulled away to rest her head against his, breathing hard. A foolish smile had overcome her, but she did not try to stifle it. "Thank you," she whispered. "That was lovely."

Mr Quincy laughed. "I think it was my pleasure," he said hoarsely.

Winnie breathed in deeply. His fingers were still tangled in her hair, and she did not want them gone. But she had one more thing to do, and time was moving on.

"I release you from your debt to me," she told him. "I will not see you in the Witchwood Knot tonight."

Mr Quincy froze. A distant panic slipped into his wine-red eyes, and his fingers tightened in her hair. "Tell me you are leaving Witchwood Manor," he begged softly.

Winnie's smile faltered. "You know that I am not," she said. "I am about to break the Knot, Mr Quincy. I know that it might bring you grief. But I have warned off everyone I could, and all the servants here are wearing my perfume, if they have any sense. I will ask Cook to leave, though I suspect that she would rather stay."

A terror unlike anything she'd ever seen before now over-came his features. Winnie's heart twisted as she saw another dozen desperate pleas threaten to escape him—but they all died upon his lips before he spoke them. Neither of them had ever managed to dissuade the other.

"There is no happy ending, Mr Quincy," Winnie reminded him gently. "But there must be an ending, all the same. I cannot blame you for the choice you've made—but I have promises to keep, as well."

He did not hold her back, as she slipped away from him and stood again.

Winnie straightened her gown self-consciously, and combed her fingers through her hair. "You have a little bit longer," she told him softly, without turning around. "If there are things you must prepare, then there is time."

She forced herself to leave the conservatory, though her heart ached more with every step she took. Mr Quincy did not try to stop her.

CHAPTER 20

*W*innie had intended to go find Cook in the kitchen—but for once, the older woman had intruded on the house, already waiting for her at the green baize door.

"Well," said Cook. "I'm wearing perfume for the first time in my life. What is all this, Miss Hall?"

Winnie grimaced at her. "I am about to let the faeries out," she said. "That perfume will protect you long enough that you might leave, if you were so inclined."

Cook arched an eyebrow at her, and Winnie sighed. "Won't you *consider* leaving?" she asked softly. "You have fought well—but there is nothing more for you to do after today. And Mr Quincy is already grieved enough."

"Nothing more?" Cook asked sardonically. "I suppose that's so. Who needs a cook to face a faerie?" She offered out a tied-up handkerchief, which Winnie accepted with a frown.

Inside the handkerchief, Cook had tied up two freshly baked scones.

"One for you, and one for Mr Quincy," she said. "The last

he'll have from me, if things go as expected. But I won't leave, Miss Hall. I've already come this far—I see no reason to start running now." She smiled sharply at Winnie. "You've gone soft on Mr Quincy. He is a grown adult whatever-he-is, and he'll need to face the consequences of his choices, either way."

Winnie looked away from the other woman, as she tucked the scones into her pocket. "It is not often I go soft," she admitted. "I like the feeling, I am finding—just a little bit." She swallowed hard. "If you are staying, then there is one more thing which you can do for me. Please find Lord Longfell and inform him I am waiting for him in my bedroom. Tell him I am desperate to speak with him."

Cook pressed her lips together. "I hope you know what you're doing," she warned.

Winnie's fingers closed around her silver knife. "I know what I am doing," she assured the other woman. "Will you tell him?"

Cook inclined her head. "Good luck, Miss Hall," she said.

Winnie headed up the stairs to her room, leaving the door cracked open just behind her. She settled onto the edge of her bed and consciously calmed her heartbeat, as she waited for the monster of Witchwood Manor to appear.

LORD LONGFELL'S steps soon sounded on the stairs, thudding into Winnie's stomach like a hammer.

The man who appeared in her bedroom doorway was no longer tragically composed. His brown hair was wild, and his eyes were blood-shot and exhausted. Though he had made an effort to straighten his clothing, it was clear that he was still wearing yesterday's attire.

Nonetheless, a smile flickered to his lips as he saw Winnie wearing the gown which he had bought for her. His eyes lingered at the low-cut neckline, and Winnie hardened her nerves against the feeling. "Winifred," he said, "you are looking so much better this morning. It seems the laudanum was called for, after all."

Winnie rose from the edge of her bed, affecting a look of concern. "You look so awful," she replied. "Did you watch over me all night?"

Lord Longfell offered her a sheepish laugh. "Not the *entire* night," he said. "But much of it, I would suppose."

Winnie swept towards him, reaching up to touch his cheek. Inwardly, she thought of Mr Quincy's lips on hers, and his fingers in her hair; the memory stilled the nausea in her stomach as she felt Lord Longfell's feverish warmth beneath her hand.

"I think it is your turn to rest," she told the lord sweetly. "Please... come lay down here, and I will keep you company. There is a healthy fire in the hearth."

Lord Longfell leaned into her hand with a long and heavy sigh. His fingers strayed to Winnie's hair, which was still loose about her shoulders, and he turned to press his forehead against hers. But Mr Quincy had touched Winnie first, in all those places—and Lord Longfell could not wipe that thought away.

"I know that I should rest, Winifred," Lord Longfell whispered. "But suddenly, I do not want to do so." His hand curled around Winnie's neck, and a sickened shiver struck her as the iron ring pressed at her skin.

Winnie had halfway expected this. She shoved her fluttering alarm away and forced a smile, steeling herself for what came next.

"Do not rest, then," Winnie told him.

She reached up to grasp Lord Longfell's hand, threading her fingers through his and pulling it down between them. She leaned up on her toes to press a kiss against his lips.

Lord Longfell groaned softly against her. His eyes fluttered closed, and his other arm wound tightly around her waist. Before he could fully pin her, Winnie fumbled for her silver knife with her free hand, drawing it from the sheathe on her chatelaine.

Winnie opened her fingers to stroke along his palm, coaxing his hand open. Then—all at once—she seized upon the knotted ring and cut away his finger.

At first, Lord Longfell did not even notice what had happened. The knife was so unnaturally sharp that it did not truly pain him. But as hot blood trickled down his hand, he pulled back to look down at it, staring blankly at the sight.

The knotted ring remained in Winnie's palm, now slick with blood. She felt the ugly magic within it like a heartbeat, shivering against her tightly closed fingers.

Lord Longfell let out a hoarse, belated cry—and before Winnie could move, he had her on the ground. Her silver knife clanged across the floor, now out of reach, as his remaining blood slick fingers closed around her neck.

"What have you done?" he demanded wildly. There was a maddened, desperate light behind his eyes now, and his body trembled with violence. "No—what *are* you? You are not Winifred at all! You are some ghastly creature, left here to replace her!"

Winnie tried to gasp for breath—but his grip was tight, and no air trickled past it. She kicked and scrabbled at him, all to no avail. But she had kept her grip upon the knotted ring, and that was all that mattered.

Presently, she became aware of frenzied dark whispers rising up around them. The fire's shadows leapt and screamed with fury, reaching out for Lord Longfell with unnatural, grasping hands.

The lord snatched his hands back from Winnie in a panic, and air rushed in to fill her lungs. She gasped desperately, as one of those shadows hurled itself upon Lord Longfell, driving him onto his back. A monstrous cat-like apparition pressed against his chest with a low, horrible growl. One yellow eye fixed upon him with malevolence, as Oliver's shadowy paws held him down on the floor. Lord Longfell coughed, staring up at the familiar with wide eyes as Oliver's weight began to slowly suffocate him.

Mr Quincy stalked in from the doorway, fixing a cold stare upon the lord. The butler held Winnie's gleaming silver knife at his side, still slick with Lord Longfell's blood.

The entire weight of Witchwood Manor seemed to lean itself upon them, as Mr Quincy's wine-red eyes blazed and his rasping voice spoke. "Every time I see you, you are mewling like a coward," he hissed at Lord Longfell's prone form. "All the power of the *fomóraig* will not change what you are inside. My brother laughed at you in secret as he offered you that ring. You are the most pathetic monster I have ever seen."

Lord Longfell whimpered helplessly, unable to articulate an answer to this accusation. And though Winnie knew that Mr Quincy could not harm a living thing, she saw his fingers tighten on the silver knife as though he badly *wished* to do so.

Winnie struggled painfully to her knees, with spots still dancing in her vision. She had the strength she needed, though, to hurl the cursed ring into the hearth fire.

The flames leapt high and hungry, as the ring's magic began to burn away. A thousand agonised screams went up around them as it burned—and Winnie saw the faces in the walls again, their mouths agape with pain and fury.

Mr Quincy snapped his gaze to hers—and for a moment, Winnie saw the fear in his eyes all over again, as he realised what was happening.

"Lady Mourningwood," Winnie rasped at the fire, "I have a gift for you. Lady Mourningwood. Lady Mourningwood."

The third and final repetition of the faerie's name echoed on the air beneath the screams. The shadows on the wall shivered… and the walls began to dribble away like smoke.

Black, twisted trees stretched up around them, bathed in sourceless moonlight—no longer contained by the walls of Witchwood Manor. An inky void yawned overhead, as the pungent scent of rotten leaves overtook everything else. Where the hearth fire once had been, just behind Winnie, there was now a great oak throne. Lady Mourningwood's pale, unnatural form slowly resolved upon it, with her crown of woven branches reaching up like fingers at the sky. Her coal black eyes were fixed upon Lord Longfell, struggling on the ground.

There was a smile on the faerie lady's lips.

"The Mourningwood is free," she said, with calm serenity. "And now, mortal lord, I take my due. You should not have dared to spite me."

The shadow of Lady Mourningwood's crown reached out to close around Lord Longfell's helpless form. At first, Oliver's wavering silhouette hissed and swiped at the encroaching darkness, intent on finishing the job which he had started—but Lady Mourningwood's power here at the centre of her realm was dreadful indeed, and the cat was forced to backpedal away from Lord Longfell's chest. The lord drew in just one ragged breath, staring up in horror at the faerie lady on her throne.

The darkness embraced him—and soon, his voice rose into a long, high scream which joined those of the manor's spirits.

New roots clawed into the earth in an agonised crawl. Lord Longfell's body twisted upwards, reaching for the sky. His hair wove into brittle leaves, and his skin hardened into an ugly black bark.

Finally, all of the screams cut off into an eerie silence. All that remained of Lord Longfell was a twisted, dying tree, with the distinct impression of an agonised face upon its trunk.

Winnie reached up for her throat with trembling fingers, wiping at the blood which Longfell's hands had left there. Very slowly, she turned to face Lady Mourningwood's throne and bowed. "I am... so pleased that you enjoyed my gift, Lady Mourningwood," she said, with a rattling cough.

Oliver prowled closer to her, watching Lady Mourning-wood with one careful, baleful yellow eye. Mr Quincy took several wary steps towards the throne, until he had knelt down respectfully before it.

The faerie lady regarded Winnie in the sudden stillness. Coal black eyes bore into her soul, leaving behind a shiver. "Your... gift," Lady Mourningwood murmured.

Next to Winnie, Mr Quincy's reddish eyes fluttered closed, and he exhaled in obvious relief.

Winnie sucked in a ragged breath and straightened. "I broke the Witchwood Knot," she said, "and offered you Lord Longfell. I warned you that he was a gift. And yet, you still accepted him."

Lady Mourningwood tilted her head in dour contempla-tion. "You have... trapped me, nameless creature," she observed. "What debt will you demand of me, in order to repay your gift?"

Winnie forced one last bit of steel into her spine as she stood before that throne, fighting back exhaustion. "I have given you your vengeance," she replied. "Is it not complete? I would like for you to spare the Honourable Mr Robert Murray, and the servants, and the village. And myself, of course."

Lady Mourningwood laughed. It was the first time Winnie had ever heard the sound from her.

"One mortal man is not worth more than my entire precious garden," the faerie lady said. "You are too bold, governess." Her black eyes somehow darkened further, drawing in the paltry light around them. "I will spare just one person, in exchange for just one man. I recommend that you choose wisely."

Winnie pressed her lips together. Lady Mourningwood clearly expected that Winnie would spare herself, and have done with it. Mr Quincy turned his head to fix his reddish gaze upon her, and Winnie felt him urge her silently to do just that.

Winnie reached slowly into her pocket to pull out the scones which Cook had given her. She nibbled at one as she delayed her answer, choosing her next words carefully.

"I have other gifts to offer you, if you would like," Winnie continued finally. "Gifts you might find valuable enough to spare a village." She swallowed down a bite of scone, now feeling just a bit steadier. Everything was always easier when you had food at hand. "I am a magician, as you already know. My sisters are magicians, too. Secundus will come back for you eventually, Lady Mourningwood. But we would ally with you, as magicians did before when you defeated Balor of the

Evil Eye. We will be glad to do so, if you will spare the people I have named."

Lady Mourningwood's gaze remained flat and empty as it leaned upon Winnie before her throne. "What need have I of human magicians?" she droned. "I have a *fomórach* to serve me." Her eyes shifted to Mr Quincy, who still knelt before her, holding Winnie's bloody silver knife. "I know the magic which you brought here with you, governess," she announced. "I know the lady who has sent you with that knife. But you will not be the instrument of her victory against me. Spare yourself, and flee from my domain while you still can."

Winnie tightened her jaw, fighting back impotent fury. Lady Mourningwood was too cruel, too paranoid, too contemptuous to see her obvious danger. But what had she expected? There was a reason that the Hollow Lady hated her so deeply.

"I am not here to harm you," Winnie said. "We have a common enemy."

"And why should I believe you?" Lady Mourningwood intoned. "You are a liar, nameless governess. You have already drowned us in deception; I have no cause to trust your word. Now choose the person you will spare, before I lose my patience."

Winnie clenched her teeth. But part of her had known all along that this might be the end, no matter how she argued.

If Margaret had done her job, then the servants and the village would have time to flee. Winnie had found the truth about the Hollow Lady's disappearance and sent it to her sisters. She had a way to fulfil her promise to the dowager. There was no happy ending, here—but she could choose the unhappy ending which most suited her. That had to be enough.

Winnie offered out the remaining scone to Mr Quincy, next to her. "Cook has sent this for you," she informed him. "I should give it to you now, while I still can."

Mr Quincy's wine-red eyes flashed with alarm as he parsed through the implications of that statement. His fingers tightened on the silver knife. "Do not do this," he whispered under his breath. He did not reach out to take the scone.

Winnie set the handkerchief down on the rotten leaves at her feet, with the scone atop it. She straightened again and faced Lady Mourningwood, as Oliver offered the handkerchief a curious sniff—and then pulled back in disgust. "I will not spare myself," Winnie said. "If you insist that I choose just one person, Lady Mourningwood... then I choose the Honourable Mr Robert Murray."

Mr Quincy shoved abruptly to his feet, taking one step closer to the throne. The movement placed him directly between Winnie and Lady Mourningwood.

"Have I served you loyally, Your Ladyship?" he asked, in a low and urgent tone. "Will you acknowledge that I have?" His tail thrashed with frantic tension.

Lady Mourningwood looked down, so that the shadow of her crown now fell upon him. "You have kept our bargain admirably, Mr Quincy," she agreed tonelessly.

"Then please spare one more person, for my service," he begged. "Let the governess go free. I will help you fight Secundus, in any way I can."

The crown's shadows shivered around him with subtle displeasure. Lady Mourningwood's expression darkened. "You are already bound to do so, Mr Quincy," she said slowly. "Your shelter is your payment. Do you demand yet more from me?"

Winnie smiled wanly at Mr Quincy's back. He had known

already that the faerie lady would not listen, she was certain. But his attempt still warmed her, even so.

"You misunderstand the situation, Mr Quincy," Winnie said softly, as she ran her fingers through Oliver's ragged, monstrous fur. "I have decided on the value of my life. I throw it away in order to save the people I have chosen. You may absolve yourself of any guilt—I count you on that list."

Mr Quincy whirled on her. His reddish eyes were wild, and his jaw trembled. "How dare you," he whispered hoarsely. "After everything that I have done... why must you and Sarah Baker torment me so? I did not ask for your kind regard. I spurn it actively, you foolish woman." He dashed the scone on the ground with his polished shoe, crushing it deliberately beneath his heel. "I will stand by. I warned you."

"And I listened," Winnie assured him quietly.

The lack of anger in her voice only seemed to strike the butler harder; he stumbled back as though she'd slapped him across the face. Abject despair settled in upon his narrow features, as Lady Mourningwood lifted her chin.

"I will spare the Honourable Mr Robert Murray, as you have asked," the faerie lady declared to Winnie. "You and the rest of the village shall join my mortal garden."

Lady Mourningwood rose up from her throne, taking her full and dreadful height. Her shadow writhed towards Winnie, as Oliver's hackles rose and his one yellow eye narrowed. But the faerie lady gestured at him—and suddenly, there was a small black tomcat standing next to Winnie, rather than a growling beast.

Oliver's voice rose in a tiny hiss, regardless, as black roots crawled out from the earth to wind around him and climb their way up Winnie's legs, holding them both fast.

Lady Mourningwood closed the last long step between

them, reaching out to close her long fingers around Winnie's chin. "Perhaps Lady Hollowvale will visit your tree someday, and thank you for your efforts," she mused.

The perfume on Winnie's neck heated suddenly, as though someone had set fire to it, and she gasped. Winnie tried to jerk herself free, but Lady Mourningwood maintained her iron grip. The scent of bay berry curled up through the air, as Clarimonde's magic struggled against Lady Mourningwood's overwhelming power. Dimly, Winnie found herself impressed that it had held so long against a faerie of her stature.

Winnie's eyes caught upon Mr Quincy, a few steps behind Lady Mourningwood—standing by and watching helplessly, as he had promised all along. Winnie's silver knife still glinted in his hand. She gritted her teeth and sucked in a breath. "At least... give back my knife, Mr Quincy," she rasped. They both knew that it would not help her—but it would comfort her to have it, nonetheless.

The butler closed his eyes and slumped his shoulders. A flicker of pain crossed his features.

"I am sorry, governess," he said. "I cannot give it back to you, this time."

The silver knife flashed—and suddenly, the scent of blood grew sharper and more overwhelming, as crimson dribbled from his hand to the forest floor. Mr Quincy's rotten magic twisted on the air with a familiar taste as his blood crept swiftly along the leaves, withering roots and devouring all life where it passed.

The rot reached Lady Mourningwood's feet—and then, it crawled up her tattered gown and into her pale skin, flaking it away in terrible, bloody patches. The faerie dropped Winnie with a sudden cry, now clutching at her face as her black eyes mouldered and ugly tears trickled from their sockets. The skeletal branches of her crown wilted, crumbling away into a putrid dust, as her jaw fell open in a gaping scream.

Lady Mourningwood fell to rotten pieces on the ground as Mr Quincy stared down at her, clutching at his bloody hand.

His index finger had been cleanly cut away.

Winnie's mouth worked soundlessly for a moment, as the roots around her legs withered and the perfume on her skin abruptly cooled. Before her thoughts could catch up to her body, she was stumbling forward to take his hand. Somehow, despite everything which had happened, she could only manage one awful observation. "You did this to yourself," she whispered in horror. "It will not heal, Mr Quincy."

The butler grimaced, and dropped her silver knife to the ground. "It is my own fault," he muttered, in a shaky voice. "If I had let you take the splinter earlier, then it would not have come to this. I could not remove it otherwise. I had to take the finger." He stumbled against Winnie with a sudden oath, however—and she saw that Oliver had pounced upon his rat tail. Still tomcat sized, he now chewed at Mr Quincy's tail with lazy, casual violence.

Mr Quincy tore his tail away from the cat with a hiss, as he staunched his bleeding hand against his chest. "I still despise *you*," the butler informed the cat.

Oliver let out a high meow of amusement, as he rolled onto his back among the leaves.

Winnie cringed. At least, she thought, the cat had clearly decided that Mr Quincy was no longer a credible threat.

Mr Quincy let out a shivering breath, trying to regain himself. "I do not know what will come next," he admitted. Winnie had expected to hear fear in his voice... but there was a strange, grim certainty instead. "I do not know the current state of faerie. Perhaps a host will ride against me now. Or else, perhaps my brother will return."

Winnie pressed her forehead to his shoulder. "I did not mean to force this choice upon you," she whispered.

Mr Quincy smiled at her ruefully. "You did not force me, governess," he drawled. "You *should* have done—you were too kind. I would have regretted everything which followed. But knowing that the lady would torment you was a very different thing from *seeing* it before me." His wine-red eyes drifted to the ruined scone, a few feet away on the ground. "I hope you can forgive me for my tardiness."

Winnie turned her head to look at him with a trembling smile. "You were forgiven long ago," she assured him. "But I will not bother arguing. You are forgiven again—as many times as you require."

Mr Quincy raised his good hand to her cheek, brushing his fingers carefully along her jaw. Winnie shivered at the light touch of his fingertips. "And may I kiss you again?" he whispered softly.

Winnie swallowed hard. A flush of heat now stained at her cheeks as she met his reddish gaze. "As many times as you require," she mumbled back.

Mr Quincy leaned down to press his lips to hers. A familiar wild pleasure flooded Winnie as he did, twisting breathlessly along her nerves until it reached her toes. His arm slipped down to wind around her waist, drawing her gingerly against him. Winnie's eyes fluttered closed, and she smiled into the kiss.

"If I thought you were a tyrant, Mr Quincy," she whispered against his lips, "then I would not dare to tell you my real name. I am Winifred of Hollowvale... and I will stand next to you, whatever else comes next."

Mr Quincy drew a breath, and turned his head to press his lips against her hair. "My mother called me Arimanius Quincy," he murmured there. "Though I fear that I am now Lord Mourningwood."

Winnie sighed. "We have untangled just one knot," she said. "It is a start, at least."

CHAPTER 21

*W*innie was admittedly still wild looking when the new Lord Mourningwood led the Honourable Mr Robert Murray back to her. Blood still smeared her neck and hands in places; her black silk gown was tattered, and the silver knife on her chatelaine had dubious red fingerprints upon it. Still—when Robert saw her, he broke free of Mr Quincy's hand on his shoulder and hurried over to her side. He threw his arms around her silently, and Winnie saw that he was thin and shaking, dressed in the clothes which he had worn to church before his grandmother's death.

"It's over," Winnie told him quietly. "We are going home."

Slowly, she became aware of faint rustles among the trees and wary, alien eyes peering through the underbrush. The faeries of the Mourningwood watched on uneasily, as Mr Quincy pressed his hand back to her shoulder.

"Well, they have had their fears confirmed," he murmured quietly. "A traitor wears the crown."

Winnie shot him a sideways glance. Though no skeletal

brambles rose from Mr Quincy's brow, their long fingers stretched out from his shadow where it fell behind him.

"Perhaps they will soon be forced to build character," Winnie told him dryly.

Mr Quincy managed a grim smile at the words. "Perhaps they will," he said. "Either way... it seems that I have matters to resolve. But you should return to Witchwood Manor."

Presently, Winnie became aware that the door into the hallway had reappeared, standing on its own between two crooked trees. Though she could not see it, she felt the hearth fire warm against her back.

She frowned uncertainly at Mr Quincy. "I hope you will come see me soon," she said. "You have yet to teach me the rest of my song."

For the first time Winnie could remember, Mr Quincy's smile softened. "I will see you in the morning, Winifred," he promised.

The name tugged at some long unused heartstring within Winnie's chest. "That is one promise you will not escape," she warned him. The words came out with a shyness which surprised her, and she cleared her throat with embarrassment.

Winnie pulled reluctantly away from his hand in order to lead Robert to the door. Oliver padded along behind them, with his tail swishing among the leaves.

In the moment that they set foot past the threshold, Winnie felt the world change. For a moment, Oliver's form was just a wisp of smoke... and then, the cat had disappeared, winding his way back to his skull. Winnie turned to glance back through the door—and saw only her bedroom, now still and silent. A small bloodstain on the floor was the only remaining evidence that anything of note had happened there.

She led Robert back to his bedroom door—but she paused there and glanced down at him, considering. "There is a sliver of you here," she told him. "You will need to take it back."

Robert likely did not know what she meant by the words, but he nodded listlessly regardless. In that moment, Winnie could not have picked him out as any different from the overly obedient fetch.

The construct was still sitting on the edge of Robert's bed as she opened the door. It looked at Robert dimly, who looked back at it in brief confusion.

Winnie had only to blink; in the next moment, there was nothing on the bed but a pile of twigs and string.

The boy in front of her drew in a sudden breath, pressing a hand to his chest. "I have new memories," he said dimly. "But I was elsewhere. I don't understand."

Winnie squeezed his shoulder. "I would not think on it too intensely," she advised. "For now, I'm certain you are tired. If you will rest, I'll bring you up some food."

Robert continued staring at the twigs upon the bed. After another pause, Winnie took pity on him and brushed the pile into what remained of her skirts so that he could climb beneath the covers. Just as she was headed for the door to bring the pile outside, however, Robert spoke.

"Mr Quincy said my father killed grandmama," he whispered. "But you said that I shouldn't listen to faeries, Miss Hall."

Winnie pressed her lips together. "I fear they always speak the truth," she told him quietly. "I will tell you the entire story, Master Robert, though it is far from pleasant. You will need to know it, I expect. The danger has not fully passed." She met his eyes directly. "But I will help you meet it. I am your mentor, after all."

At this promise, Robert relaxed noticeably. He nodded at the blankets. "I'm... grateful that you came for me, Miss Hall," he said. "I will not ever forget it."

Winnie smiled at him from the doorway. "I doubt that I'll forget it, either," she said. "I am proud of having done it, Master Robert."

She turned back for the hallway and descended the stairs —and then, she walked out the front door of Witchwood Manor and into the woods beyond it.

Winnie laid the twigs and string gently beneath a willow tree near the river that ran through the forest. When she returned to the house, her slippers and her gown were muddy; she pulled them off and threw them into the hearth fire, and watched them burn with satisfaction.

LORD LONGFELL'S disappearance did not go unremarked within the household—but Cook, in particular, swore that he had been unwell when she last saw him, praying fervently within the chapel. As soon as she had turned her back, she said, the lord had walked out the front door into the Witchwood for some reason of his own.

As a result, Lord Longfell was not present for his mother's funeral. But Margaret and Winnie saw that it was respectful, nevertheless.

They laid her body out within the parlour, where those who wished could come and see her. Perhaps it was just Winnie's imagination, but as she stood before the dowager's body, she thought that the woman slept more peacefully than she had done before. Since Lord Longfell's transformation and Lady Mourningwood's death, the manor felt much emptier and less hostile, and Winnie had not dreamed at all.

"How queer," a woman's voice observed behind Winnie, as she stood before the dowager's body. It was a pleasant voice—the sort which poets probably referred to when they spoke of bell-like tones.

Winnie turned to look at the woman behind her. Tall and willowy in the extreme, she was the definition of the words 'fair maiden'. Her long black hair shone faintly in the light of the stained glass windows. Her lips were red as roses, and her cheeks held an attractive flush. She wore a long black mourning gown which glimmered with gold and silver thread; it was, Winnie thought, a century or two outdated.

"And what is it you find so queer?" Winnie asked the woman carefully.

The woman offered her a lovely smile. It was, Winnie thought, the sort of smile which made one's heart ache. "Only death," replied the woman. "I have not ever understood it. Imagine, never waking up again? How perfectly awful."

A hand came down on Winnie's shoulder, suddenly—tense and wary. Mr Quincy had arrived in his usual fashion, without warning. He wore his butler's glamour today, so that his rat tail did not show as people milled around them—but the copper scent he carried with him lingered on the air beneath the magic.

"Tertia," Mr Quincy said quietly. "I did not realise you had woken up."

Tertia turned her smile upon him, now an inch more brilliant in its intensity. "Oh, Quintus!" she sighed. "Look at you, now all grown up! And you have conquered your own realm —just as Father always said you would."

Somehow, Mr Quincy managed a smile back at her—though Winnie felt his hand tighten on her shoulder imperceptibly. "So I have," he said. "How long ago now since Secundus found you?"

Tertia pursed her blood red lips. "A few years," she admitted. "I have been in London, and in Bath, and... well, just everywhere, I suppose. There is so much to see." She sighed with pleasure. "I have my own realm too, you know. Secundus gave it to me. He has always been so generous."

"And what realm is that?" Mr Quincy asked her carefully.

Tertia laughed. "Well, I am Lady Hollowvale!" she said. "It suits me, don't you think?"

Winnie froze, suddenly unable to breathe. Mr Quincy released her quickly, reaching out to wind his arm around his sister's shoulders and direct her elsewhere in a hurry.

"I think I know the name," he said, just loud enough for Winnie to overhear him. "But what has happened to the previous Lady Hollowvale?"

"I did not think to ask," Tertia mused idly. "But I believe her husband sleeps beneath the earth now, on the bier which once was mine. He looks so charming—sometimes I visit, just to see him. Perhaps I'll paint his picture, someday soon."

The two of them drifted away across the room, as Winnie clenched her hand around her silver knife.

EPILOGUE

*O*nce upon a time, a *fomórach* whom we shall know as Quintus slew the lady of the Mourningwood and took her crown.

At first, Quintus expected that a host of faeries would visit their wrath upon him—but no such faeries came. In fact, they had all shut themselves away within their realms, too terrified to face the *fomórach* which had conquered London. But Lord Cassius Secundus soon sent their sister Tertia as his messenger in order to congratulate Quintus on his new kingdom. And Quintus, who was cleverest of all his siblings, allowed them both to assume that he was their ally once again.

In the days to come, the Honourable Mr Robert Murray did not go off to Eton. Instead, he stayed at Witchwood Manor and committed himself to learning what Lord Mourningwood and the governess would teach him. In all of England, there would be no pack of knaves more vicious or more cunning than the new Lord Longfell and his mentors.

Without his index finger, Quintus could not play the

pianoforte quite so well—but as it came to pass, the lady whom we know as Winifred Hall was pleased to split his music with him, so that each of them played half of every song. And perhaps the tree which lingered at the centre of the Mourningwood still heard them and took comfort, even if it was not safe yet for Quintus's mother to emerge.

Soon, other magicians came calling to the Mourningwood in secret—to hide there, and to plan. For this time, just as Secundus had foreseen, it was mortal magicians who would be the downfall of the *fomóraig*.

AFTERWORD

I have wanted to write a proper gothic story ever since I first read *Wuthering Heights*. I won't tell you how long ago that was, because I want to pretend I'm younger than I really am.

I didn't wholly anticipate how dark *The Witchwood Knot* would become as I wrote it. But I have been dissatisfied in the last few years by the near-uniform portrayal of sexual assault survivors as meek and fearful flowers. Sexual assault is sadly common, and the natural reactions to it can be widely varied. Winnie's instinct to become a careful and manipulative "cold fish" in order to protect herself is just as reasonable as the more commonly portrayed decision made by Mr Quincy's mother, who hides away in order to protect herself. Both reactions are perfectly understandable, in their own way. And both, I think, should engender understanding.

Winnie's most important triumph in the novel comes when she finally reclaims her sexuality for herself, after many years of having had it used against her. Similarly, Mr Quincy reclaims his own autonomy. As a result, they both manage to improve other people's circumstances, in defiance of their greatest fears.

I would like everyone to know that this book was made possible almost entirely by my husband, Nicholas Atwater, who kept me from losing my calm while I wrote through a funeral, a horrible travel mishap, and several miserable bureaucratic rabbit holes. In addition to his unwavering emotional support, he also added richly to the novel's atmosphere and descriptions in a way that I doubt I could have managed on my own. Truly, he is the single most incredible person in my life.

I must also thank my single most loyal alpha and beta reader, Laura Elizabeth, along with my marvellous historical nitpicker, Tamlin Thomas, who answered my questions several times with instant pictures from the textbooks sitting next to his desk and suggested an entire list of strange Victorian death rituals. Extra thanks to author Charlotte E English for catching the occasional Canadian turn of phrase and making sure that Lady Longfell wasn't accidentally Catholic!

Lastly, I would like to thank all of my readers for coming this far with me. This book was genuinely difficult to write at times, and I am truly grateful to everyone who trusted me enough to continue reading until the very last page.

THE ATWATER SCANDAL SHEETS

SCANDAL AND MAYHEM!

Searching for more faerie tales?

Join the Atwater Scandal Sheets to read a second epilogue for
The Witchwood Knot, as well as neat historical facts and several
exclusive novellas.

Subscribers to the Scandal Sheets stay in the know! Get access
to chapter previews of the next book before it goes live!

ABOUT THE AUTHOR

Olivia Atwater writes whimsical historical fantasy with a hint of satire. She lives in Montreal, Quebec with her fantastic, prose-inspiring husband and her two cats. When she told her second-grade history teacher that she wanted to work with history someday, she is fairly certain this isn't what either party had in mind. She has been, at various times, a historical re-enactor, a professional witch at a metaphysical supply store, a web developer, and a vending machine repairperson.

Want more faerie tales? I send out writing updates and neat historical facts in the Atwater Scandal Sheets. Subscribers also get early access to chapters from each book!

https://oliviaatwater.com
info@oliviaatwater.com

Printed in the USA
CPSIA information can be obtained
at www.ICGtesting.com
LVHW041945151123
764036LV00019B/107